FASTI

PUBLIUS OVIDIUS NASO (43 BC–AD 17)—known to Chaucer as 'Venus clerk Ovyde' and to Touchstone in *As You Like It* as 'the most capricious poet, honest Ovid'—was born in Sulmo (modern Sulmona) in the central highlands of Italy. He came to Rome in his teens, soon after the defeat of Antony and Cleopatra and the annexation of Egypt had brought about peace and prosperity and the rule of Caesar Augustus. Giving up his original ambition to enter public life, he soon became the sophisticated city's favourite poet. His subject was sex and love and the pursuit of pleasure, and his medium was the elegiac couplet, of which his mastery was unparalleled. Between about 25 BC and the turn of the millennium he wrote *Amores* (pseudo-autobiographical adventures of the poet as lover), *Heroides* (letters from love-lorn mythological ladies) and the 'didactic' *Art of Love* and *Remedies for Love*, varying the elegiac output with a tragedy, *Medea* (now lost). Augustus disapproved of the *Art of Love*, and Ovid turned to more serious subjects, a great mythological epic (*Metamorphoses*) that went from the creation of the world down to his own times, and a myth-historical treatment of the Roman calendar in elegiacs (*Fasti*). His celebrity life did him no good: in AD 8 he was involved in a scandal, probably involving Augustus' family, and was banished to the outpost of Tomis on the Black Sea (modern Constanţa in Romania). He continued writing (*Tristia*, *Letters from Pontus*), and outlived Augustus, but there was no recall. He died in exile.

ANNE WISEMAN taught Latin in the Exeter University Department of Classics after her retirement from school teaching.

PETER WISEMAN is Emeritus Professor of Classics, University of Exeter, and a Fellow of the British Academy.

OXFORD WORLD'S CLASSICS

*For over 100 years Oxford World's Classics have brought
readers closer to the world's great literature. Now with over 700
titles—from the 4,000-year-old myths of Mesopotamia to the
twentieth century's greatest novels—the series makes available
lesser-known as well as celebrated writing.*

*The pocket-sized hardbacks of the early years contained
introductions by Virginia Woolf, T. S. Eliot, Graham Greene,
and other literary figures which enriched the experience of reading.
Today the series is recognized for its fine scholarship and
reliability in texts that span world literature, drama and poetry,
religion, philosophy, and politics. Each edition includes perceptive
commentary and essential background information to meet the
changing needs of readers.*

OXFORD WORLD'S CLASSICS

═

OVID

Fasti

═

Translated with an Introduction and Notes by
ANNE AND PETER WISEMAN

OXFORD
UNIVERSITY PRESS

OXFORD
UNIVERSITY PRESS

Great Clarendon Street, Oxford, OX2 6DP
United Kingdom

Oxford University Press is a department of the University of Oxford.
It furthers the University's objective of excellence in research, scholarship,
and education by publishing worldwide. Oxford is a registered trade mark of
Oxford University Press in the UK and in certain other countries

First published 2011 as *Ovid: Times and Reasons*
First published as an Oxford World's Classics paperback 2013

Impression: 9

British Library Cataloguing in Publication Data

Data available

ISBN 978-0-19-282411-0

Printed in Great Britain by
Clays Ltd, Elcograf S.p.A.

CONTENTS

For Barbara Levick
magistrae discipula
1957–1961

INTRODUCTION

Teacher and prophet

OVID's calendar poem, *Fasti*, advertises itself in the first couplet as a source of information:

> *Tempora cum causis Latium digesta per annum*
> *lapsaque sub terras ortaque signa canam.*

> Times and their reasons, arranged in order through the Latin year,
> and constellations sunk beneath the earth and risen, I shall sing.

It is (among other things) a didactic poem addressed to an unnamed pupil: the narrator constantly speaks to 'you' in the singular.[1] In book 1 (a special case) you may be Germanicus Caesar, but otherwise you are the reader with the book in your hand, or the listener having it read to you.

It is assumed that you have an interest in history, and can even carry out your own research: if you have time, your instructor suggests, look up the calendars of other cities (3.87). But you may not be very scholarly about it, for instance if you are influenced by such things as popular proverbs (5.489), so there is always the danger that you will get things wrong, and your ignorance will lead you astray (2.47).

You look at the night sky (e.g. 2.79); you count the days of the month (e.g. 6.726); above all, you ask for explanations (e.g. 2.284)—and the narrator is ready to instruct you. Sometimes he can tell you from his own experience (1.389, 2.27, 4.905), sometimes from what he learned at school (6.417). If he doesn't know he will find out, questioning old men and priests (2.584, 4.938, 6.222), searching through ancient chronicles (1.7, 4.11) or looking at temple inscriptions (3.844, 6.212). Not that he believes everything he is told (2.551, 4.793), and occasionally he is simply baffled (4.784, 5.2, 6.572). But mostly he is confident in his own opinion (1.620, 4.61, 6.303), and very conscious of his duty as a teacher (2.685, 3.435, 4.682).

---

[1] Since English no longer distinguishes the singular and plural forms of the second person, we have listed the relevant passages in the Index of Names: see 'addressee, sing.' and 'addressees, plu.'

So far, so intelligible. But the poem also has a quite different dimension.

The narrator describes himself as a *uates* (e.g. 1.25), and that is what the gods call him too (Janus 1.101, Mars 3.177, Juno 6.21). We have translated that word as 'bard', in the hope of conveying something of the ambiguity of the Latin. The first meaning of *uates* is 'prophet' or 'seer', one with the gift of communicating supernatural knowledge. People like Tiresias, Calchas, and Cassandra were prominent in the world of legend, and there is a fine example in this very poem—the prophetess Carmentis, mother of Evander.[2] But they were also familiar in everyday life, in the Roman Forum, chanting oracles at times of crisis, consulted not only by private individuals but sometimes even by the Senate and magistrates.[3]

Two generations before Ovid's time the Romans had begun to use the term *uates* metaphorically, to mean 'inspired poet'. That applied most characteristically to epic, where ever since Homer the poet had appealed to the Muse to sing the song through him, but poets in other genres used the term as well, including Ovid himself in his youthful *Amores*.[4] The narrator of *Fasti* reveals himself as Naso (5.377), the same Ovid, the famous love poet, but now things are different. He has undertaken a more demanding task (2.3–8, 2.125–6, 4.9–12), explaining the rituals owed to the gods, and so he makes his identity as a *uates* more than just a metaphor.

Twice he makes the point that the *uates* has privileged access to the gods (3.167–8, 6.5–8). True, not everyone believes that (6.3), and poets sometimes don't quite tell the truth (6.253), but Juno assures him that he has indeed earned that right (6.21–4). And so the narrator is able to report face-to-face interviews with several divinities: Janus in book 1, terrifying but genial; Mars in book 3, macho but ill at ease; Venus in book 4, an old friend ironically teasing; Flora in book 5, ingenuous and very fanciable; and in book 6 a trio of goddesses quarrelling among themselves.

---

[2] Seen in action at 1.503–8 and 6.537–40; *carmen* ('song') is both poetry and prophecy.

[3] Forum: Livy 25.1.8–10 (213 BC), Appian, *Civil Wars* 1.121.563 (71 BC). Oracles: Cicero, *De diuinatione* 1.18 (63 BC), Dio Cassius 41.14.4 (49 BC), 57.18.4–5 (AD 19). Consultation: Cicero, *De diuinatione* 2.149, Plutarch, *Marius* 42.4 (consul, 87 BC), Sallust, *Histories* 1.77.3M (Senate, 78 BC).

[4] Twice in the first poem of all (*Amores* 1.1.6 and 24), and frequently thereafter.

The didactic instructor and the inspired bard merge into each other. Divine and human informants are cited with an equal guarantee of personal involvement: the narrator tells you his conversation with Minerva (6.655–6) no differently from those with a Caesarian veteran at the games (4.377–84) or an old lady at the way through to New Street (6.399–400). At just a simple question (5.635, 6.213), or a perplexity not even stated (1.659–60, 6.255–6), the gods can tell him what he needs to know.

For a poet to pray to the Muses for inspiration is commonplace enough. Our narrator prays to Carmentis, the goddess of prophetic song (1.467), to the nymph Egeria (3.261), to Bacchus (3.714, 6.483), to the Great Mother (4.191), to Pales, the shepherds' goddess (4.723), to Quirinus, the deified Romulus (4.808), to Mercury (5.447, 5.663), to Vesta (6.249)—and of course to the Muses too (2.269, 2.359, 4.193, 6.798). Sometimes he confirms that the prayer was answered, information duly provided (5.450, 6.256); usually the narrative itself is sufficient evidence of authoritative guidance. But be careful: gods can disagree (5.108, 6.98), and may have their own agendas.

Subject and metre

What is it all about? *Tempora cum causis*, times and their reasons. That is a striking formulation, since chronology and causation are two of the defining characteristics of history writing. As Cicero observed, the genre of historiography demanded the 'ordering of times' and 'explanation of reasons'.[5] This is something we shall come back to, but in the meantime, are we to think of 'Times and Reasons' as the *title* of the poem?

Certainly the opening phrase of a work could be regarded as its title, as Ovid himself demonstrates in *Tristia*, book 2, where he cites Lucretius' poem as '*Aeneadum genetrix*'. But it is also in *Tristia* 2 that Ovid refers to his own poem as *Fasti*, and since that is the title given in the oldest manuscripts, we have to infer that in the end it was the calendar aspect that he wished most to emphasize.[6]

The 'times' of the poem are, he says, 'arranged in order through the Latin year' (1.1). There was no one system in the ancient world for organizing the lunar and solar cycles into months and years, and even in Latin-speaking Italy different cities had different calendars

---

[5] Cicero, *De oratore* 2.63 (*ordo temporum*), *Ad familiares* 5.12.4 (*causae explicandae*).
[6] *Tristia* 2.261 (Lucretius), 2.549.

(3.87–96, 6.59–64). The structure of Ovid's poem is the Roman calendar, in which the adjectives *fastus* and *nefastus* meant roughly 'lawful' and 'unlawful'. However, the law invoked was not that of the magistrates but that of the priests. They laid down certain days as *dies fasti*, when public business, and in particular the civil jurisdiction of the *praetor*, was permitted, and others as *dies nefasti*, when it was not. (The latter were not ill-omened, just set aside for other activities.) The original purpose of a calendar was to list the 'lawful days', so *fasti* became the Latin word for 'calendar', and that is what Ovid's title means.

All the same, the narrator is quite selective about which days he describes (only in book 6 does he seem to want an entry for each day), and the items to which he devotes most attention are the festivals and holidays of the Roman year. The longest episode is that of Ceres and Persephone (228 lines), told to illustrate the Games of Ceres in April. Then come, in descending order of length, Janus and New Year's Day (226 lines); the festival of Vesta in June (220 lines); the Games of Flora at the beginning of May (196 lines); the Games of the Great Mother in April (194 lines); the Lupercalia in February (186 lines); the festival of Anna Perenna in March (174 lines); and the Regifugium ('Flight of the King', 168 lines), where the tale of Tarquin and Lucretia forms the foundation myth of the Roman Republic.[7]

But if times and reasons—dates and explanations—are the main theme, there is also a secondary one, stated appropriately in the second line: the setting and rising of constellations. Here too the narrator is selective. Some star signs give rise to stories, others are merely mentioned—and his astronomy is less than wholly accurate, despite the authoritative sources he claims to rely on (5.601).

It is likely that the double subject announced in the opening lines is Ovid's allusion to two great paradigm poems—the *Aitia* ('Explanations') of Callimachus and the *Phainomena* ('Star Signs') of Aratus, learned Greek works of the third century BC which had an immense influence on Roman poets. Callimachus' poem is particularly important as a model for *Fasti*, both in its variety of aetiological subject matter and in its metre, the elegiac couplet.

---

[7] 4.393–620 (Ceres), 1.63–288 (Janus), 6.249–468 (Vesta), 5.183–378 (Flora), 4.179–372 (Magna Mater), 2.267–452 (Lupercalia), 3.523–696 (Anna Perenna), 2.685–852 (Regifugium).

The couplet consists of a six-foot hexameter, the metre of heroic epic, followed by a five-foot pentameter. In the very first lines of his first work, the *Amores*, Ovid defined himself as a writer in elegiacs. At this point a metrical translation is essential:

> I was all set to produce my epic of violent warfare
> In the appropriate mode, metre and matter to fit.
> Line 2 matched line 1. But this, they say, is what happened:
> Cupid craftily stole one foot away, for a joke.

The end-stopped couplet is a quite different experience from the flexible 'blank verse' of epic hexameters, and the associations of the respective metres are also different, and quite specific. Epic is weighty, and its characteristic subject matter is 'kings and battles'.[8] Elegy is 'light' or 'slender', and its characteristic subject matter is love (often lost or unhappy love, whence 'elegiac' in our sense). Callimachus, however, had extended elegy's range to include learned aetiology, explanatory stories that overlapped on to the historical territory of the grander genres.

Hellenistic authors soon applied the Callimachean formula to Rome. Plutarch mentions two Greek elegiac poets, Simylos and Boutas, who wrote on Roman history and aetiology,[9] and there may well have been others. The influence of Callimachus and his followers on Roman poets was particularly strong in the second half of the first century BC, giving rise to a brilliant school of elegiac love-poets— Gallus, Tibullus, Propertius, Ovid himself. At first they used the didactic-aetiological aspect of the genre as a minor theme, to provide variety among their explorations of the anguish of love;[10] it was a sign that the themes of love-elegy were almost played out when Propertius reversed the emphasis in his fourth book.

In Propertius' book 4, published about 15 BC, 'the Roman Callimachus' formally announced himself with an introductory poem on the antiquities of Rome. These were grand themes for the slender voice of elegy,[11] and the bard's pretensions were immediately undercut by an ironically self-deflating companion piece. But the aetiologies duly followed—on the god Vertumnus, on Tarpeia, on Palatine Apollo, on the 'Great Altar' of Hercules, on Jupiter

---

[8] Virgil, *Eclogues* 6.3 (*reges et proelia*).

[9] Plutarch, *Romulus* 17.5, 21.6: Simylos on Tarpeia, Boutas on the origin of the Lupercalia.

[10] e.g. Tibullus 2.5 (about 20 BC), Ovid, *Amores* 3.13 (probably a little later).

[11] Propertius 4.1.58–60, cf. 64 (Callimachus).

Feretrius[12]—interspersed with love themes and a couple of guest appearances by the poet's mistress Cynthia, the anti-heroine of the first three books. This late Propertian volume, with its self-conscious generic ambivalence, is the nearest thing to a forerunner of Ovid's *Fasti*.

Our narrator is another self-conscious elegist. Once he sang of love; but now his song is of 'sacred matters' (6.8), the rites and festivals of the gods, a more substantial theme. And this is the point where we must think again about that surprisingly historiographical opening phrase, 'times and reasons'.

Poetry and history

The writing of history was not, of course, confined to prose. The great epics of Rome dealt specifically with the Roman past: Ennius' *Annales* took the reader down from the age of Aeneas to the poet's own time, while Virgil's *Aeneid* was thought only to go beyond the scope of true history when the poet narrated events in heaven or the underworld.[13] The most conspicuous forerunner of Ovid's work was a poem whose author famously claimed to 'sing nothing which is not attested'.[14] Our narrator insists that his subject matter is 'dug out of ancient annals' (1.7, 4.11); he has Juno address him as the *conditor* ('composer') of the Roman year, a term particularly appropriate to history;[15] and at the very end of the surviving text he signs off in the voice of the Muse of history, Clio (6.811).

It is possible that Ovid's original purpose was to draw attention to the particularly historical nature of his poem. We cannot argue from book 1, which was heavily revised by the poet in exile for a second edition dedicated to Germanicus, but there are clear signs of it in book 2, which opens with a significant announcement:

> *nunc primum uelis, elegi, maioribus itis:*
> *exiguum, memini, nuper eratis opus...*

---

[12] Respectively, Propertius 4.2, 4.4, 4.6, 4.9–10.

[13] Servius *ad Aen.* preface (*continens uera cum fictis*).

[14] Callimachus, *Aitia* fr. 612Pf.

[15] 6.21, and *condere* at 6.24. History: e.g. Virgil, *Eclogues* 6.7; Ovid, *Tristia* 2.335–6; Valerius Maximus 1 pref.; Seneca, *Consolatio ad Polybium* 8.2; Pliny, *Nat. Hist.* 2.43, 36.106.

Now for the first time, elegiacs, you are going under more ample
sails; recently, I remember, you were a minor work.

The bigger sails could be an allusion to epic, or tragedy, or history—or
all three of them at once. The very next couplet (2.5–6) quotes the
opening poem of *Amores*, book 3, where a younger Ovid had had to
choose between love poetry in elegiacs and the grander style of
tragedy.[16] Now he has chosen to keep the elegiac metre but go for the
grander style anyway.

The narrator is faced with the consequences of that bold decision
when he comes to 5 February, and has to deal with the anniversary of
the day when the Senate and the People of Rome conferred on
Augustus the title of *pater patriae* (2.125–6):

> *quid uolui demens elegis imponere tantum*
> *ponderis? heroi res erat ista pedis.*

Insane, why did I want to impose so much weight on elegiacs? That
was a subject for the heroic metre.

It should have been a historical epic, like the one that Propertius ele-
gantly declined to attempt,[17] and with characteristic panache the nar-
rator now shows us that he can do historical epic in elegiacs perfectly
well. On 13 February (2.195–242) he unexpectedly brings in the story
of how the Fabii in 479 BC took on themselves the responsibility of
fighting the Etruscans of Veii, and were wiped out in an ambush,
almost to the last man.[18] Livy, who narrated the event in his history,
dated it to 18 July; deliberately misplaced here, it provides a tour de
force of epic mannerisms. In a narrative of just forty-eight lines
there are no fewer than three extended epic similes, a topographical
ecphrasis, a pathos-inducing apostrophe ('O noble house, where are
you rushing to?'), and finally a verbal allusion to Ennius' *Annales*
which links the story to the great Fabius who defied Hannibal.[19]

The Fabii are also unexpectedly prominent two days later in
book 2, at the Lupercalia: the narrator's second explanation of why
the Luperci run naked gives them a role as the followers of an unusu-
ally victorious Remus (2.375–7). That may have been in compliment

---

[16] *Amores* 3.1.27–8. [17] Propertius 2.1.17–46. [18] Livy 2.48.7–11.
[19] 2.209–10, 219–22, 231–3 (similes), 215 (*ecphrasis*), 225 (apostrophe), 242 (Ennius
allusion).

to Ovid's patron, the noble Paullus Fabius Maximus;[20] but it is worth remembering that the very first historian of Rome was a patrician Fabius,[21] and that some of our narrator's allusions in book 2 are directly to prose history without reference to epic.

The entry for 3 February, for instance, uses the constellation called the Dolphin to cue the story of Arion. 'What sea hasn't heard of Arion, what land doesn't know him?' (2.83)—but they know him from book 1 of Herodotus, whose narrative is brilliantly exploited. On 23 February, discussing Terminus, the god of boundaries (2.663–6), the narrator gives a wonderfully economical four-line summary of another episode from Herodotus' first book, the battle of the Argives and Spartans for the land of Thyrea.[22]

Book 2 also contrives to narrate three of the most important events in what the Romans believed to be their history: the suckling of Romulus and Remus by the she-wolf (2.381–422), the death and deification of Romulus (2.475–512), and the expulsion of the Tarquins following the rape of Lucretia (2.685–852).[23] They were stories familiar in all three of the grand genres, epic, tragedy, and history. The last and longest of them is the most tragic, no doubt because both Ovid himself and his main prose source (Livy) must have been influenced by Accius' classic play on Lucius Brutus and Lucretia; but even here the narrator gives the story a specifically historiographical dimension by repeating (2.701–10) Livy's attribution to the elder Tarquin of the secret message Periander of Corinth used in Herodotus, book 5.[24]

Ovid is a subtle writer, and one has to listen to him carefully. When we come to the days when the dead are honoured, the Parentalia from 13 to 21 February, the narrator emphasizes how little they need to be appeased. Just a few simple offerings—but then he goes on, 'not that I forbid bigger things' (2.541, *nec maiora ueto*). Why should he make a point of that? Well, the writing of history is a way of remembering the dead—'so that the deeds of men should not be forgotten', as Herodotus put it in his opening sentence—and 'bigger things' (*maiora*) in Latin poetry have an unmistakable generic overtone, as

---

[20] Ovid, *Ex Ponto* 1.2, 3.3, 3.8, 4.6.9–12; his wife was the Marcia of *Fasti* 6.802–10 (*Ex Ponto* 1.2.138).

[21] Q. Fabius Pictor, *scriptorum antiquissimus* (Livy 1.44.2).

[22] Herodotus 1.23–4 (Arion), 1.82 (Thyrea).

[23] Respectively 15 February (Lupercalia), 17 February (Quirinalia), 24 February (Regifugium).

[24] Herodotus 5.92ζ, Livy 1.54.6.

in the famous fourth *Eclogue* of Virgil.[25] It sounds as if our poet is justifying the presence of historical themes in his February book, culminating in the great tragic history of Lucretia.

At the very end of book 2 the narrator promises a change of direction: 'from here let my boat sail in different waters'. The next book deals with the month of Mars, who might be thought to require just this sort of weighty treatment. But no: the narrator urges him to lay aside his helmet and spear (3.1–2), and begins with a story of Mars finding something to do without his armour (3.8)—that is, impregnating Silvia the Vestal with Romulus and Remus. When the god himself takes over the narrative to explain the festival of married women on the first day of his month, he has indeed taken his helmet off, and he draws attention to his unusually peaceful subject matter (3.171–4).

Playing games like this brings its own hazards. When the narrator asks Venus for her favour at the beginning of book 4, she pretends to be offended (4.3): what about those 'bigger things', she says, those weighty themes of yours? Even though a grander goddess, Juno herself, expresses approval in book 6—'you have dared to tell great things in tiny measures' (6.22)—he still knows that he must hold his horses (6.586). To get the narrative bit between his teeth would be to outrun his genre.

Poet and princeps

There was a particular reason for sensitivity in this matter, and it can be summed up in one word: Augustus. The puritanical and patriotic 'restored Republic' of the Augustan principate was always an uneasy climate for the love-elegists, with their rejection of all duties except devotion to a mistress. Ovid himself, as we shall see, had deeply offended Augustus with his brilliantly cynical *Art of Love*. That poem was one of the reasons given for the poet's exile, which evidently put an end to *Fasti* at the halfway point; though Ovid claimed to have written all twelve books,[26] no trace of the July–December part of the poem ever appeared.

What made things worse for the Augustan elegists was the expectation that poets would celebrate the greatness of the *princeps* in suitably epic style. The classic Roman epic was Ennius' *Annales*, glorifying the

---

[25] Virgil, *Eclogues* 4.1 (*paulo maiora canamus*); Ovid does the same at *Amores* 3.1.24 (*maius opus*).

[26] *Tristia* 2.549–52.

warlike history of Rome in Homeric hexameters. No doubt Augustus would have liked an Ennius for his own time. Already in the early days of the regime Propertius had assured his patron Maecenas, Augustus' friend, that if the Fates had given him epic powers he would sing the wars and deeds of Caesar; but alas, it was beyond the slender means of his Callimachean voice.[27] Our narrator takes the same line in his introduction: 'Let others sing of Caesar's wars' (1.13). Of the five civil-war campaigns Propertius had named as possible Augustan themes, Mutina (4.627–8) and Philippi (3.705–10, 5.569–78) are mentioned in *Fasti*, and Actium (1.711) is alluded to in the item on the altar of Peace. What matters is the brevity of the treatment. Battle narrative is not for this genre.

Of course generic conventions are there to be played with, not rigidly obeyed. As we have seen, the narrator can do an epic battle when he chooses, just as he can do tragedy and farce. Ovid was always brilliantly versatile, and *Fasti* provided plenty of opportunity for testing the limits of the elegiacally possible. Two good examples come in the first book, the episodes of Aristaeus and his bees (1.363–80), and of Hercules and Cacus (1.543–84), elegant and economical reworkings of Virgilian narrative in the *Georgics* and the *Aeneid* respectively.

The posthumous publication of Virgil's *Aeneid* in 19 BC had taken off some of the pressure for a Great Augustan Epic. Here, as Propertius put it, was something greater than the *Iliad*. Virgil's epic masterpiece was an instant classic, superseding Ennius as the voice of heroic Rome, and in three great set pieces (Jupiter's prophecy, the Elysian pageant, and the shield of Aeneas) it gave Augustus the immortality he craved, establishing his rule as the destined culmination of all Roman history.

What were poets to do now? The *Aeneid* could not be ignored. It was a challenge, and facing that challenge was a test of ingenuity and independence. But it was also part of the ideology of the regime. For Ovid, already *persona* not wholly *grata*, that must have doubled the problem.

He certainly wasn't intimidated. The most conspicuous reaction to Virgil in *Fasti* is a wonderfully cheeky tour de force identifying the goddess Anna Perenna with Dido's sister Anna (3.545–656): in a sequel to *Aeneid*, book 4, the narrator takes Anna on a voyage of escape

---

[27] Propertius 2.1.17–46 (*c.*25 BC).

all too similar to Aeneas' own, shipwrecks her on Aeneas' doorstep, much to his embarrassment, and reveals the murderous jealousy of the hero's wife Lavinia in what can only be described as a bedroom farce.[28] In mocking the Virgilian hero, is he also mocking Augustus? And why does he expose the dignified Vesta, who shared the house of Augustus himself (4.949–54), to the farcical lust of Priapus (6.331–44)? Is there a hidden agenda?

Some scholars think so, but before getting carried away we should remember the theme Ovid has chosen. It is well defined in the *Cambridge Ancient History*:[29]

> The Roman calendar, with its slow progression of measured feasts and rites moving through the seasons and processionally among the temples and sacred places of the city and its neighbourhood, and recapitulating as it did so the progression of Rome's history, triumphs, deliveries and commemorations, offered a wonderful opportunity for the self-presentation of the *princeps* and his family, and for the involvement of the populace. [Julius] Caesar had done some exploration in this area, but the real harnessing of the potential of the calendars is an Augustan phenomenon. The great moments in the rise to power of Caesar's adopted son, the dates of his life and career, the significant moments in his rule and in the lives of his relatives are inserted through the calendars ... into the history of Rome.

Ovid's subject was an Augustan one, and presented as such. 'Let others sing of Caesar's wars; I sing Caesar's altars, and all the days he added to the sacred list' (1.13–14). He was playful, as always, but there is no need to think he was subversive. Thanks to Callimachus' aetiological precedent, here was a patriotic theme within the scope of elegy.

The time of two lives

To understand what lies behind *Fasti*, its conception and its non-completion, we must trace the parallel stories of the poet and the *princeps*.

Ovid tells us that he was born 'when both consuls succumbed to the same fate'.[30] That happened at Mutina in April 43 BC, during the

[28] Dido's dream–warning at 3.641 copies Hector's at *Aeneid* 2.289.

[29] Nicholas Purcell, in *The Cambridge Ancient History*, vol. 10 (2nd edn., Cambridge: CUP, 1996), 799–800.

[30] Ovid, *Tristia* 4.10.6, an autobiographical poem from exile.

young Caesar's first campaign of civil war. Augustan calendars would later mark 14 and 16 April as the anniversaries of his first victory and his first salutation as *imperator*, and the narrator of *Fasti* marks them too (4.627–8 and 675–6). The future Augustus was 19; the infant Publius Ovidius Naso not yet four weeks.

The Ovidii of Sulmo were equestrian in rank, distinguished local gentry in the Paelignian country of the central Apennines. Young Publius Naso and his brother (a year older) could hope for senatorial careers, and so were sent early to Rome to get a good education. Civil war was the constant background of their childhood, but it was over, Antony and Cleopatra dead and Egypt conquered (30 BC), by the time they came of age in their mid-teens. Ovid's brother, soon to die young, was a promising orator. Ovid himself was a precocious poet, though he tried to concentrate on rhetoric to please his father. Virgil's *Georgics* and Propertius' first book of love-elegies were the literary sensations of the time, as Rome, freed from a generation of strife and warfare, celebrated the young Caesar's triumph and began to get used to peace and the principate.

The first of the love-elegists had been Cornelius Gallus. He took up a military career; one of the senior generals in the Alexandria campaign, he was put in charge of Cleopatra's kingdom as the first prefect of Egypt. But he got above himself, and lost the confidence of Caesar Augustus, as the victor was now called. Summoned home in disgrace, Gallus committed suicide—a victim, perhaps, of the new policy of constitutional propriety with which Augustus wanted to distance himself from the warlord years of his youth. Ovid was sixteen or seventeen at the time, and already a skilled practitioner in the poetic genre Gallus had pioneered.

For ten years or so after his triumph Augustus was evolving his constitutional position—first via repeated consulships, then by a special grant of the authority of the People's tribunes—and enjoying the gratitude of a prosperous Rome freed from civil war. It was a great period in Roman poetry, with Tibullus and Propertius, the *Odes* of Horace, and the expectation of Virgil's slowly maturing masterpiece. Ovid was already part of it by the time he was twenty, the first poems in his *Amores* sequence brilliantly announcing his arrival as the new master of the love elegy.

The death in 23 BC of Augustus' son-in-law Marcellus, movingly commemorated by Virgil's Anchises in the underworld,[31] marked the beginning of a long history of dynastic politics in which Ovid was to be fatefully involved. The *princeps'* daughter Julia (his only child), widowed in her teens, was now married to Agrippa (his oldest friend), and bore him two sons; in 17 BC they were adopted by Augustus as his own sons and heirs, Gaius and Lucius Caesar. Augustus' wife, Livia, had two grown sons of her own by a previous marriage, Tiberius Claudius Nero and Nero Claudius Drusus, the elder of whom was a near-contemporary of Ovid.[32] The 'Julio-Claudians' (to use the modern term) were the Julius Caesars and the Claudius Neros, descendants respectively of Augustus and of Livia.

The adoption of Gaius and Lucius came in the year Augustus announced a New Age. The 'Secular Games' of 17 BC, for which Horace wrote the official hymn, did indeed mark a turning point. Augustus was now wholly confident of his position, and keen to improve the morality of Rome. Horace in his fourth book of *Odes*, Propertius in his fourth book of *Elegies*, both marked the change in climate with a move to more serious themes. The *Aeneid*, published after Virgil's death in 19 BC, set the tone with its emphasis on duty and self-sacrifice. But Ovid, witty and irresponsible as ever, pressed on with his *Amores*, completing the collection in five books (later edited to three).

True, he did announce his conversion to serious poetry—and delivered it too, with a tragedy, *Medea* (now lost), of which a sober critic later observed, 'It shows how great that man could have been if he had chosen to control his talents instead of indulging them.'[33] Having shown he could do it if he wanted, Ovid went straight back to love and sex and elegy with the *Heroides* and the *Art of Love*.

Meanwhile (15–8 BC), Agrippa and the 'Neros', Tiberius and Drusus, were conquering Germany and central Europe in a series of campaigns deliberately intended to continue, and outdo, the great imperialist advances of the late Republic. After all, hadn't Jupiter in the *Aeneid* promised the Romans power without limit, under a Caesar whose dominion would stretch to the ends of the earth? Perhaps

---

[31] Virgil, *Aeneid* 6.860–86.
[32] Ovid was born on 20 March 43 BC, Tiberius on 16 November 42 BC.
[33] Quintilian, *Institutio oratoria* 10.1.98.

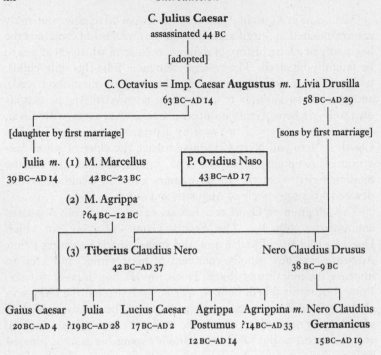

C. Julius Caesar
assassinated 44 BC

[adopted]

C. Octavius = Imp. Caesar **Augustus** *m.* Livia Drusilla
63 BC–AD 14   58 BC–AD 29

[daughter by first marriage]   [sons by first marriage]

Julia *m.* (1) M. Marcellus   P. Ovidius Naso
39 BC–AD 14   42 BC–23 BC   43 BC–AD 17

(2) M. Agrippa
?64 BC–12 BC

(3) **Tiberius** Claudius Nero   Nero Claudius Drusus
42 BC–AD 37   38 BC–9 BC

Gaius Caesar   Julia   Lucius Caesar   Agrippa   Agrippina *m.* Nero Claudius
20 BC–AD 4   ?19 BC–AD 28 17 BC–AD 2   Postumus   ?14 BC–AD 33   **Germanicus**
                                        12 BC–AD 14   15 BC–AD 19

The Julio-Claudians and Ovid

Augustus felt that the most talented poets of the new age might do worse than celebrate his wars. It didn't happen. The conquests Ovid sang were of a different kind:[34]

> Arms I have given you, men, as Vulcan gave arms to Achilles.
> > Conquer, then, just like him; that's what I've given them for.
> But when with my kind of sword you overcome Penthesilea,
> > Label the spoils you have stripped, 'Naso's tuition succeeds'.

Sophisticated Rome loved it, but Augustus was not amused.

In 12 BC Agrippa died. He and Julia had given Augustus three other grandchildren, Julia the younger, Agrippina, and a son, Agrippa Postumus, born after his father's death. The daughter of the *princeps* was still only twenty-seven, with plenty of time to have more children if she married again. There was only one possible choice as her new

---

[34] Ovid, *Ars amatoria* 2.741–4.

husband. Tiberius, happily married already, had to divorce his wife and marry Julia. The new couple disliked each other from the start, and Julia's eldest boys, aged nine and six at the time of the wedding, outranked their stepfather as the adopted sons of Augustus. Tiberius was not an easy man. He had a lot to put up with, and after five years of the marriage he had had enough. In 6 BC he retired to Rhodes, leaving Julia to her doting father—a glamorous princess in her thirties, with teenage boys who were heirs to the 'throne'.[35]

High society and the world of entertainment feed off each other. Both Julia and Ovid, in their different ways, were stars of the *beau monde*. It is not known exactly when the *Art of Love* was published, but it must have been quite close to the cataclysmic moment in 2 BC when Augustus finally understood what sort of life his daughter was leading and in fury banished her to the island of Pandataria; her lovers were executed or exiled, as if for treason. Witty, sophisticated Ovid, the playboy poet of Venus (4.7–8), was living on borrowed time.

He turned to epic. It was safer ground, and for a poet at the height of his powers (he was in his early forties) the challenge of Virgil was irresistible. During the ten years before his time ran out Ovid produced an immortal work of mythography, longer than the *Aeneid* and, in its very different way, no less great. It was evidently while he was working on the *Metamorphoses* that he started *Fasti* as well, stories of Roman myth and history dedicated to Augustus himself.[36] Again, the exact chronology of composition is uncertain, but the continued impact of external events makes the years AD 4–8 the most likely.[37]

The Julia scandal was followed by two even greater disasters for Augustus, the deaths of his heirs in AD 2 and 4. He still had three grandchildren: the younger Julia, married to a member of the old aristocracy (Lucius Aemilius Paullus); Agrippina, in her late teens in AD 4 but not yet married; and Agrippa Postumus, now sixteen. Augustus himself was 67. Of his two stepsons, the sons of Livia, Nero Drusus had died on campaign in Germany in 9 BC, and Tiberius, though back from Rhodes, was still in disgrace. But he was mature, reliable, and Augustus' only chance for a safe succession.

[35] Gaius Caesar was officially designated *princeps iuuentutis* ('Prince of Youth') in 5 BC, Lucius Caesar in 2 BC.

[36] Ovid refers to the original dedication at *Tristia* 2.551–2.

[37] Sir Ronald Syme, *History in Ovid* (Oxford: OUP, 1978), ch. 2, followed in *CAH*, vol. 10 (n. 29 above), p. 999, argued for AD 1–4, but offered no adequate reason why Ovid stopped where he did.

So Augustus adopted both Tiberius and young Agrippa Postumus; he married Agrippina to Nero Drusus' son, Germanicus (now eighteen); and he made Tiberius adopt Germanicus. Tiberius Nero was now Tiberius Caesar. He would succeed Augustus, and his own successor would be either Agrippa Postumus or Agrippina's husband Germanicus.

Tiberius immediately went off to campaign in Germany, and then in Pannonia (western Hungary) when a dangerous rebellion broke out there in AD 6. Perhaps he wouldn't come back? That would suit Agrippa Postumus and his sisters. The more Augustus aged, the more his family and their friends intrigued. It was a threat to his authority: in AD 6 Agrippa Postumus was disinherited; in AD 7 he was banished, like his mother, to an island; in AD 8 the younger Julia was banished too, and her husband disgraced. This time Ovid did not escape the fallout. He was exiled to Tomis on the Black Sea, at the very limits of Rome's empire.

It is likely that he had begun *Fasti*—worthy subject matter, dedicated to Augustus himself—at the time of Tiberius' adoption in AD 4, when he could see he was going to need all the imperial favour he could find. Presumably it was half finished when Augustus finally lost his patience.

Six years later Augustus was dead. Tiberius was now *princeps*, and the heir was Germanicus, husband of Agrippina and father of Augustus' great-grandchildren. Far away among the barbarians, Ovid began to revise *Fasti*, with a new dedication to Germanicus (1.3–26).[38] He even brought himself to honour Tiberius, though not by name (1.533, 615–16, 645–50, 707). But it was all too late. There was no recall, and Ovid died in exile in AD 17.

Dealing with the new age

Assuming that the bulk of the poem as we have it was composed in a period when relations between poet and *princeps* were, to say the least, uneasy, let us see how it deals with Augustus and his anniversaries. There is, as it happens, a convenient benchmark against which to judge it.

Substantial fragments survive of a grand annotated calendar set up in marble in the forum at Praeneste, a town not far from Rome. It was

---

[38] Part of the original dedication may survive as 2.3–18; perhaps book 2 was originally dedicated to Fabius Maximus (n. 20 above), who was now dead.

composed by Marcus Verrius Flaccus, a learned freedman chosen by Augustus as the tutor of his grandsons, and is therefore ideal first-hand evidence for the Augustan exploitation of the traditional calendar of Rome.[39] About 280 lines of the inscription are preserved (perhaps a tenth of the original total), of which about fifty-four are devoted to Augustan or Tiberian items. At a crude guess, therefore, we might say that a spokesman for the regime put its contribution to the whole history and tradition of Rome at about 20 per cent.

The narrator of *Fasti* pays proper attention to the main Augustan dates. He devotes thirty lines to the name 'Augustus' itself (1.587–616), fourteen to the dedication of the altar of Peace (1.709–22), twenty-six to the title '*pater patriae*' (2.119–44), fourteen to Augustus as *pontifex maximus* (3.415–28), fourteen to the avenging of Julius Caesar (3.697–710), and a substantial fifty-four, complete with divine epiphany, to the temple of Mars the Avenger in the Augustan Forum (5.545–98). Add to that some shorter items on the restoration of temples (2.59–66), Augustus' youthful campaigns (4.627–8, 673–6), the Palatine shrine of Vesta (4.949–54), and the Portico of Livia (6.637–48), with passing compliments at appropriate points in dealing with other matters,[40] and it becomes clear that Augustus and his preoccupations appear often enough to avoid any imputation of neglect.

But though the narrator pays proper respect to the *princeps*, he does not go over the top. A similar rough line count, including the dedication passages in the first two books, gives less than 5 per cent of the total poem to Augustan matters, a mere quarter of what Verrius Flaccus may have thought appropriate. Only once do we find the Virgilian idea of Augustus as the predestined culmination of all the history of Rome, and that is in the first book, as revised in exile. Even there, the narrator makes the point that Carmentis' prophecy could have gone on (1.529–38): there would be more Roman history *after* Augustus and Tiberius.

Polite and careful but not committed, the poet has his own perspective. Though Rome rules the world and Augustus rules Rome (4.859), his is not the only authority:[41]

[39] For Verrius, see Suetonius, *De grammaticis et rhetoribus* 17.

[40] e.g. 2.637 (Caristia), 4.39–40 (Trojan pedigree), 4.124 (Venus and Anchises), 4.859–60 (Parilia), 5.145 (Lares), 5.157–8 (Bona Dea), 6.455 (Vesta), 6.763 (Trasimene), 6.809 (Portico of Philippus).

[41] *Metamorphoses* 15.877–9, trans. A. D. Melville (Oxford: OUP, 1986).

> Wherever through the lands beneath her sway
> The might of Rome extends, my words shall be
> Upon the lips of men. If truth at all
> Is stablished by poetic prophecy,
> My fame shall live to all eternity.

The bard has as much power as the *princeps* when it comes to shaping a tradition and a mental world. Virgil was one sort of *uates*, Ovid another, and the Rome of *Fasti* is a much more complex organism than the teleological Augustan Rome of the *Aeneid*.

Times in order

Here is the history (and prehistory) of Rome according to *Fasti*, from the dawn of time to the narrator's own day:

1. *Before the Foundation*

Saturn comes to Rome	1.233–40, 5.625–8
Janus rules Rome	1.241–54
Evander and Carmentis come to Rome	1.469–542, 2.271–82, 4.65, 5.91–102, 5.643–4, 6.501–50
Hercules comes to Rome and kills Cacus	1.543–84, 4.66, 5.629–32, 5.645–60
The Trojan dynasty	4.29–36
Aeneas and Troy	4.37–8, 4.799–800, 6.419–36
Aeneas comes to Italy	4.249–54
Aeneas at Lavinium	3.601–56
The Alban dynasty	4.39–54
The youth of king Proca	6.131–68
Romulus and Remus conceived and exposed	3.9–58, 4.55–60
Romulus and Remus suckled by the she-wolf	2.383–422
Romulus and Remus as young men	2.359–80
The fall of Amulius	3.59–68

2. *The Kings*

The foundation of Rome	2.133–4, 3.69–70, 4.809–36
The death of Remus	2.143, 4.837–58, 5.151–2, 5.451–84
Romulus' asylum	2.140, 3.431–4

3. *The Republic*

In the first section, Evander and his Arcadians are much more conspicuous than Aeneas and his Trojans. In the history of the kings after Romulus, the stories are all about Numa and Servius Tullius; the Tarquins appear only in the narrative of their downfall. In the wide range of allusions to Republican history, tales of glorious conquest are conspicuous by their absence. The episodes that are treated at length show a markedly popular point of view, with Anna Perenna feeding the plebeians on the Mons Sacer (3.663); Flora gaining her temple and games by the action of the plebeian aediles against the rich (5.285); the Great Mother justifying Quinta Claudia against the disapproval of the strict old men (4.310). Here, the Virgilian story of the destiny of the Julian house is just one item among many.

So too with the gods. Apollo, so dear to Augustus and so prominent in the *Aeneid*, hardly appears at all; in *Fasti*, it is Hercules who plays the lyre to the Muses' song (6.812). Mars, of course, is present in his own month of March, but not in a very dignified role. The gods who feature in *Fasti* are Janus, Priapus, Flora, Mercury, Carna, Fortuna, Anna Perenna, Mater Matuta—old gods (6.171), gods of the People (6.781), gods at a human level (5.352), whose deeds were the subject of stage plays at the popular festivals (4.326).

The grand public themes of the imperial capital are paid their due, but what makes the poem memorable is its evocation of the easy-going pieties of a citizen community. Driven from the city by the emperor's command, Ovid left in his last pre-exile work the echo of an older, freer, less pretentious Rome.

It is a precious document, and a marvellous poem, but it has suffered in comparison with Ovid's other, more famous works. For a long time the general consensus was dismissive, as memorably expressed by Hermann Fränkel: 'Ovid's *Fasti* could never be real poetry; to versify and adorn an almanac was not a sound proposal in the first place.'[42] But all that has changed in the last thirty years. As the Bibliography shows (pp. xxxiv–xxxvii), the old prejudice has given way, and at last *Fasti* is claiming its deserved position alongside the love-elegies, the *Metamorphoses*, and the exile poetry as a work of true Ovidian brilliance. The narrator's prayers to Bacchus (3.789–90), Minerva (3.834), Venus (4.1), the Muses (5.109), Flora (5.377–8), and Vesta (6.249) have not, after all, been in vain.

[42] H. Fränkel, *Ovid: A Poet Between Two Worlds* (Berkeley: U. of California Press, 1945), 148.

A NOTE ON THE TEXT AND
TRANSLATION

THE text we have translated is the edition of E. H. Alton, D. E. W. Wormell, and E. Courtney (Bibliotheca Scriptorum Graecorum et Romanorum Teubneriana, Leipzig 1978, 3rd edn. 1988). However, at the following places we have adopted a reading different from theirs:

Line	Teubner text	Our translation	Source of our reading
1.74	*turba*	*lingua*	MSS *U G M*
1.220	*manus,*	*manus?*	Loeb edition (J. G. Frazer 1931)
1.599	*sumet*	*sumat*	MSS *A G M*
1.639	*prospiciens*	*prospicies*	MSS *U G M*
2.379	*forma*	*fama*	all MSS
3.316	*tecta*	*tela*	MSS *G M*
3.419	*quos*	*quem*	MSS *G M*
3.643	†*super ausa*†	*super arua*	MSS *G M*
3.766	†*haec erat et*†	*haec est et*	MS *G*
3.850	*deae*	*deo*	MSS *U G M*
4.627	*scilicet*	*sit licet*	MSS *I G M*
6.192	*Tectae*	*dextrae*	MSS *U G M*
6.396	*quae*	*qua*	MSS *U G*
6.424	*illi*	*illic*	MSS *G M*
6.631	*hinc*	*hic*	MSS *G M*
6.685	*Plautius*	*Claudius*	Some secondary MSS, correcting *callidus* in *U G M*
6.690	*collegi*	*collegae*	MS *M*

Line numbers of the Latin text are indicated in the margins of the translation.

Until relatively recently, *Fasti* was almost unknown to English readers. As William Massey, 'Master of a Boarding-School at Wandsworth', observed in 1757:

> Of all the Roman classics of the Augustan age, none has been so much neglected, by our English translators, as Ovid's *Fasti*; nay, this book, that is so necessary for the explaining of the greatest part of the gentile theology, and in particular the sacred usages of the Roman people, is but little known in most of our public schools. Is

it not very strange, that this most elaborate and learned of all Ovid's works, should be so little regarded, whilst his *Tristia, Epistles*, and *Metamorphoses* are in almost every school-boy's hands?

Massey began his own verse translation in the belief that he had no predecessors. 'But after I had proceeded therein as far as April, I chanced to meet with an old English translation, made by one John Gower, A.M. which was printed at Cambridge, by Roger Daniel, in the year 1640.' He didn't think much of it: 'The language and versification of that performance is such, that I could reap little or no help from it; and I flatter myself, that a comparison, made between his version and mine, would be no disadvantage to me.'[1]

In fact, neither Gower's nor Massey's translation made any impact, in stark contrast with the 1709 *Art of Love*, 'translated into English verse by several eminent hands' (i.e. Dryden, Congreve, and Nahum Tate), which was still being reprinted well into the nineteenth century. *Fasti* was translated into prose by Isaac Butt (Dublin 1833) and Henry T. Riley (London 1851), and into verse by John Taylor (Liverpool 1839, first four books only) and J. B. Rose (London 1866); Riley's translation, for Bohn's Classical Library, was the standard 'crib' for the schoolboys Massey had been so anxious about, but the others were all ephemeral. For some reason, *Fasti* never found a general English readership.

For a long time the only available translation was that in the Loeb Classical Library, by Sir James George Frazer, OM, FRS, FBA (1854–1941), author of *The Golden Bough*. It was written in six weeks in 1923, and eventually published in 1929 with a huge four-volume commentary.[2] An anthropologist, however distinguished, is not the obvious person to translate Ovid. Using Frazer to approach the wit and variety of *Fasti* is like trying to read it through frosted glass. 'They lit upon a dingle meet for joyous wassails, and there they laid them down on grassy beds...' (1.401–2). Even in 1929 that must have sounded pretty odd.

---

[1] J. Gower, *Ovids Festivalls, or Romane Calendar, translated into English verse equinumerally* (Cambridge, 1640); W. Massey, *Ovid's Fasti, or the Romans Sacred Calendar, translated into English verse* (London, 1757), quotations from pp. v, vi, vii.

[2] See Robert Ackerman, *J. G. Frazer: His Life and Work* (Cambridge: CUP, 1987), 292–4. At p. 297 Ackerman writes that 'Frazer's own decorous tendencies towards archaism and archness...are often quite suitable for a mannered writer like Ovid'—too generous a judgement, in our view.

The two modern translations of the poem, by Betty Rose Nagle (1995) and by A. J. Boyle and R. D. Woodard (2000), mark a great improvement. However, they are both in verse form, whereas we have deliberately chosen prose, for the following reasons.

The guiding principle of our work has been faithfulness to Ovid's language and manner, to enable the reader to engage with his work as directly as possible. Our aim has not been to interpret Ovid's words, but to represent them as accurately as we can. We have tried to be rigorous, and in places where we are not sure what Ovid means, we have at least done our best to render what he says.

Of course it is true that a large part of his mode of expression is the elegiac metre itself; this is, after all, a poem which insists on the significance of its own poetic form. But we are not poets, and it would have undermined our guiding principle if we had attempted to produce a version that imitated the rhythm of Latin elegiac couplets. Even the looser form of English couplets, though superficially replicating the look of the original, would require us to omit details or fudge the Latin from time to time, something we particularly want to avoid.

All translators have to decide what they are prepared to sacrifice. With what Borges describes as resigned rigour,[3] we have sacrificed the metre to gain precision: a prose translation allows us to focus on what Ovid says and how he says it. It also has the great advantage of paragraphs. In a poem of swift narrative and abrupt transitions, paragraphing helps to express the movement of the poet's thought, and offers a breathing space for the reader to savour his characteristically crisp and elliptical language.

A particular difficulty for modern readers is Ovid's elaborate allusiveness. Passages marked with an asterisk are explained in the Notes (pp. 127–48, keyed to book and line numbers of the Latin text); Latin terms left untranslated in italics are explained in the Glossary (pp. 149–50); and all proper names are explained in the Index of Names (pp. 151–85).

The translation is the work of DAW in the first instance; her draft was then worked over by TPW, and a final form was agreed by both. The Introduction and explanations are by TPW.

---

[3] Jorge Luis Borges, *The Total Library: Non–Fiction 1922–1986* (London: Allen Lane 1999), 449: his translation of Whitman's *Leaves of Grass* 'wavers between personal interpretation and a resigned rigor'.

SELECT BIBLIOGRAPHY

1. *Text, Translation, and Commentary*

Sir James George Frazer, *Publii Ovidii Nasonis Fastorum libri sex*, 5 vols. (London: Macmillan, 1929).

Franz Bömer, *P. Ovidius Naso: Die Fasten*, 2 vols. (Heidelberg: Carl Winter, 1957–8).

Robert Schilling, *Ovide: Les Fastes*, 2 vols. (Paris: Les Belles Lettres, 1992–3).

2. *Text and Commentary*

Elaine Fantham, *Ovid: Fasti Book IV* (Cambridge: CUP, 1998).

Matthew Robinson, *A Commentary on Ovid's* Fasti, *Book 2* (Oxford: OUP, 2011).

3. *Commentary*

Steven J. Green, *Ovid*, Fasti *I: A Commentary*, *Mnemosyne* Supplement vol. 251 (Leiden: Brill, 2004).

R. Joy Littlewood, *A Commentary on Ovid's* Fasti, *Book VI* (Oxford: OUP, 2006).

4. *Translation and Notes*

Sir James George Frazer, *Ovid*, vol. 5: *Fasti*, Loeb Classical Library (London: Heinemann, 1931; revised edn. by G. P. Goold, 1989).

Henri Le Bonniec, *Ovide: Les Fastes* (Paris: Les Belles Lettres, 1990).

Betty Rose Nagle, *Ovid's Fasti: Roman Holidays* (Bloomington, Ind.: Indiana UP, 1995).

A. J. Boyle and R. D. Woodard, *Ovid: Fasti*, Penguin Classics (London: Penguin Books, 2000).

5. *Some Recent Monographs and Articles (in chronological order)*

R. J. Littlewood, 'Poetic Artistry and Dynastic Politics: Ovid at the *ludi Megalenses*', *Classical Quarterly*, 31 (1981), 381–95.

Elaine Fantham, 'Sexual Comedy in Ovid's *Fasti*: Sources and Motivation', *Harvard Studies in Classical Philology*, 87 (1983), 185–216.

J. C. McKeown, '*Fabula praeposito nulla tegenda meo*: Ovid's *Fasti* and Augustan Politics', in Tony Woodman and David West (eds.), *Poetry and Politics in the Age of Augustus* (Cambridge: CUP, 1984), 169–87.

R. E. Fantham, 'Ovid, Germanicus and the Composition of the *Fasti*', *Papers of the Liverpool Latin Seminar*, 5 (1985), 243–81.

Danielle Porte, *L'Étiologie religieuse dans les* Fastes *d'Ovide* (Paris: Les Belles Lettres, 1985).

Mary Beard, 'A Complex of Times: No More Sheep on Romulus' Birthday', *Proceedings of the Cambridge Philological Society*, 33 (1987), 1–15.

Stephen Hinds, *The Metamorphosis of Persephone: Ovid and the Self-Conscious Muse* (Cambridge: CUP, 1987).

Andrew Wallace-Hadrill, 'Time for Augustus: Ovid, Augustus and the *Fasti*', in M. Whitby *et al.* (eds), *Homo Viator: Classical Essays for John Bramble* (Bristol: Bristol Classical Press, 1987), 221–30.

James Jope, 'The *Fasti*: Nationalism and Personal Involvement in Ovid's Treatment of Cybele', *Echos du Monde Classique/Classical Views*, 32 (1988), 13–22.

Byron Harries, 'Causation and the Authority of the Poet in Ovid's *Fasti*', *Classical Quarterly*, 39 (1989), 164–85.

Alessandro Barchiesi, 'Discordant Muses', *Proceedings of the Cambridge Philological Society*, 37 (1991), 1–21.

Philip Hardie, 'The Janus Episode in Ovid's *Fasti*', *Materiali e discussioni*, 26 (1991), 47–64.

Byron Harries, 'Ovid and the Fabii: *Fasti* 2.193–474', *Classical Quarterly*, 41 (1991), 150–68.

John F. Miller, *Ovid's Elegiac Festivals: Studies in the 'Fasti'* (Frankfurt: Peter Lang, 1991).

Gareth Williams, 'Vocal Variations and Narrative Complexity in Ovid's *Vestalia*: *Fasti* 6.249–468', *Ramus*, 20 (1991), 183–204.

Elaine Fantham, 'Ceres, Liber and Flora: Georgic and Anti-Georgic Elements in Ovid's *Fasti*', *Proceedings of the Cambridge Philological Society*, 38 (1992), 39–56.

D. C. Feeney, '*Si licet et fas est*: Ovid's *Fasti* and the Problem of Free Speech under the Principate', in Anton Powell (ed.), *Roman Poetry and Propaganda in the Age of Augustus* (Bristol: Bristol Classical Press, 1992), 1–25.

Nicola Mackie, 'Ovid and the Birth of Maiestas', in Anton Powell (ed.), *Roman Poetry and Propaganda in the Age of Augustus* (Bristol: Bristol Classical Press, 1992), 83–97.

Reconsidering Ovid's Fasti, Arethusa (special issue), vol. 25:1, pp. 1–180 (Baltimore: Johns Hopkins UP, 1992).

Amy Richlin, 'Reading Ovid's Rapes', in Amy Richlin (ed.), *Pornography and Representation in Greece and Rome* (Oxford: OUP, 1992), 158–79.

John Scheid, 'Myth, Cult and Reality in Ovid's *Fasti*', *Proceedings of the Cambridge Philological Society*, 38 (1992), 113–31.

S. J. Harrison, 'A Roman Hecale: Ovid *Fasti* 3.661–74', *Classical Quarterly*, 43 (1993), 455–7.

Alessandro Barchiesi, *Il poeta e il principe* (Rome: Laterza, 1994), trans. as *The Poet and the Prince: Ovid and Augustan Discourse* (Berkeley: U. of California Press, 1997).

Geraldine Herbert-Brown, *Ovid and the* Fasti: *A Historical Study* (Oxford: OUP, 1994).

Elaine Fantham, 'Recent Readings of Ovid's *Fasti*', *Classical Philology*, 90 (1995), 367–78.

Carole E. Newlands, *Playing with Time: Ovid and the* Fasti (Ithaca, NY: Cornell UP, 1995).

Elaine Fantham, 'Rewriting and Rereading the *Fasti*', *Antichthon*, 29 (1996), 42–59.

Augusto Fraschetti, 'Il *dies Cremerensis*, Ovidio e i Fabii', *Eutopia*, 5 (1996), 43–57.

Christopher Michael McDonough, 'Carna, Proca and the Strix on the Kalends of June', *Transactions of the American Philological Association*, 127 (1997), 315–34.

Katharina Volk, '*Cum carmine crescit et annus*: Ovid's *Fasti* and the Poetics of Simultaneity', *Transactions of the American Philological Association*, 127 (1997), 287–313.

T. P. Wiseman, *Roman Drama and Roman History* (Exeter: U. of Exeter Press, 1998), chs. 2, 3, 4, and 7 on Ovid.

Barbara Weiden Boyd, '*Celabitur auctor*: The Crisis of Authority and Narrative Patterning in Ovid *Fasti* 5', *Phoenix*, 54 (2000), 64–98.

Emma Gee, *Ovid, Aratus and Augustus: Astronomy in Ovid's* Fasti (Cambridge: CUP, 2000).

Molly Pasco-Pranger, '*Vates operosus*: Vatic Poetics and Antiquarianism in Ovid's *Fasti*', *Classical World*, 93: 3 (2000), 275–93.

Barbara Weiden Boyd, 'Arms and the Man: Wordplay and the Catasterism of Chiron in Ovid *Fasti* 5', *American Journal of Philology*, 122 (2001), 67–80.

Barbara Weiden Boyd (ed.), *Brill's Companion to Ovid* (Leiden: Brill, 2002).

Philip Hardie, *The Cambridge Companion to Ovid* (Cambridge: CUP, 2002).

Geraldine Herbert-Brown (ed.), *Ovid's* Fasti: *Historical Readings at its Bimillennium* (Oxford: OUP, 2002).

Niklas Holzberg, *Ovid: The Poet and His Work* (Ithaca NY: Cornell UP, 2002).

Thomas Dooley Frazel, 'Priapus' Two Rapes in Ovid's *Fasti*', *Arethusa*, 36 (2003), 61–97.

Matthew Robinson, 'Festivals, Fools and the *Fasti*', *Aevum*, 3 (2003), 609–32.

Matthew Fox, 'Stars in the *Fasti*: Ideler (1825) and Ovid's Astronomy Revisited', *American Journal of Philology*, 125 (2004), 91–133.

Stephen J. Green, 'Playing with Marble: The Monuments of the Caesars in Ovid's *Fasti*', *Classical Quarterly*, 54 (2004), 224–39.

T. P. Wiseman, *The Myths of Rome* (Exeter: U. of Exeter Press, 2004).

Paul Murgatroyd, *Mythical and Legendary Narrative in Ovid's* Fasti, *Mnemosyne* Supplement vol. 263 (Leiden: Brill, 2005).

Molly Pascoe-Pranger, *Founding the Year: Ovid's* Fasti *and the Poetics of the Roman Calendar, Mnemosyne* Supplement vol. 276 (Leiden: Brill, 2006).

Matthew Robinson, 'Ovid, the *Fasti* and the Stars', *Bulletin of the Institute of Classical Studies*, 50 (2007), 129–59.

Stephen Green, 'The Expert, the Novice, and the Exile: A Narrative Tale of Three Ovids in *Fasti*', in Genevieve Lively and Patricia Salzman-Mitchell (eds), *Latin Elegy and Narratology: Fragments of Story* (Columbus: Ohio State UP, 2008), 180–95.

T. P. Wiseman, *Unwritten Rome* (Exeter: U. of Exeter Press, 2008), chs. 6, 7, and 13 on Ovid.

Elaine Fantham, *Latin Poets and Italian Gods* (Toronto: U. of Toronto Press, 2009), chs. 3 and 4 on Ovid.

Peter E. Knox, 'Texts and Topography', *Classical Quarterly*, 59 (2009), 658–64.

Giuseppe la Bua (ed.), Vates operose dierum: *studi sui Fasti di Ovidio*, Testi e studi di cultura classica vol. 48 (Pisa: ETS, 2010).

T. P. Wiseman, 'Vesta and *Vestibulum*: An Ovidian Etymology', *Scholia*, 20 (2011), 72–9.

Further Reading in Oxford World's Classics

Catullus, *The Complete Poems*, trans. Guy Lee.

Ovid, *The Love Poems*, trans. A. D. Melville, ed. E. J. Kenney.

—— *Metamorphoses*, trans. A. D. Melville, ed. E. J. Kenney.

Propertius, *The Poems*, trans. Guy Lee, intro. R. O. A. M. Lyne.

Virgil, *Georgics*, trans. Peter Fallon, ed. Elaine Fantham.

—— *Aeneid*, trans. Frederick Ahl, intro. Elaine Fantham.

FASTI

BOOK 1

JANUARY

TIMES and their reasons, arranged in order through the Latin year, and constellations sunk beneath the earth and risen, I shall sing.

Germanicus Caesar, receive this work with tranquil countenance, and guide my timid vessel's course. Don't turn away from a modest honour; see, it is to you that this act of duty is vowed; give it your godlike blessing and support. You will rediscover rituals dug out of ancient records, and how each day has deserved to be marked out. You will find there also festivals belonging to your own house; often your father, often your grandfather will be your reading matter. The prizes they bear, adorning the painted calendars, you too will bear, with Drusus your brother.

Let others sing of Caesar's wars: we sing Caesar's altars, and all the days he added to the sacred list. Give me your blessing as I try to make my way through the praises of your family, and shake the trembling fear out of my heart. Grant me your gentleness, and you'll have given strength to my song; by your regard my talent both stands and falls.

Ready to undergo the judgement of a learned prince, my page shakes as if dispatched for the god of Claros to read. For we have experienced the eloquence of your polished speech when it has taken up arms in defence of trembling citizens on trial. We know too how great is the flow of your talent when its power has been directed to our own arts. If it is lawful and right, as a bard yourself control a bard's reins,* so that under your auspices the whole year may proceed and prosper.

When the city's founder was setting the times in order, he ordained that in his year there should be twice five months. Yes, Romulus, you were better acquainted with weapons than with stars, and conquering your neighbours was a greater concern. And yet, Caesar, there is also a logic that may have prompted him, and he does have a way to defend his mistake. The time it takes till a baby emerges from the mother's womb is what he decided was enough for a year. For the same number of months from her husband's funeral, a wife maintains the signs of mourning in her widowed home.

This, then, the care of *trabea*-wearing Quirinus saw, when he was giving rules for the year to the unlearned peoples. Mars had the first
40 month, Venus the second—she the origin of the race, he the founder's father. The third came from the old men, the fourth from the name of the young; the throng that follows was marked off by number.* But Numa overlooks neither Janus nor the ancestral shades, and placed two months before the ancient ones.

45 However, lest you be unaware of the rules of the different days, not every Light-bringer has the same function. *Nefastus* will be the day during which the three words* are unspoken; *fastus*, the day during which legal business will be allowed. And don't imagine that its rules
50 persist throughout the day: what's going to be *fastus* now was *nefastus* this morning. For as soon as the entrails have been given to the god, all utterance is permitted, and the honoured *praetor* has freedom to speak. There is also the day when it's lawful to pen the People in the enclosures;* there is also the day which returns on every ninth rotation.*

55 The worship of Juno claims the Ausonian Kalends; on the Ides a bigger white ewe-lamb falls to Jupiter; the Nones have no god to protect them. The day that follows each of them (take care not to get it wrong) will be a black one. The omen results from what happened,
60 for on those days Rome suffered grim losses when Mars withdrew his favour. These points apply throughout the whole calendar, but I shall state them only once; otherwise I should be forced to break the sequence of my subject matter.

[1 January] See, Germanicus—Janus announces a lucky year for you,
65 and is here at the start of my song. Two-headed Janus, origin of the quietly gliding year, you who alone of the gods above see your own back, be present to bless our rulers, by whose labour the fruitful earth has peace secure, the sea has peace; be present to bless your Fathers and
70 the People of Quirinus, and with your nod unbolt the shining temples.

The day dawns prosperous: be propitious all, with tongue and heart. Now good words on a good day must be spoken. Let ears be free from lawsuits, let mad disputes forthwith be absent. Malicious tongue, put off your business!

Do you see how the sky is bright with fragrant fires, how the 75
Cilician spike* crackles on the lighted braziers? The flame strikes the
gold of the temples with its own brightness, and scatters a flickering
glow on the height of the building. In spotless garments the proces-
sion goes to the Tarpeian heights, and the People itself is coloured to 80
match its festal day. And now new *fasces* go in front, new purple
gleams, new weight is felt on the bright ivory.* The bullocks, inno-
cent of toil, which Faliscan grass has fattened on its plains, offer their
necks to be struck. When Jupiter from his citadel looks out over the 85
whole earth, he has nothing to gaze on but what belongs to Rome.

Greetings, happy day, and always come back better, worthy to be
observed by a People with power over everything.

Yet what god shall I say you are, double-formed Janus? For Greece 90
has no deity equivalent to you. Reveal, at the same time, the reason
why you alone of the heavenly ones see both what is behind and what
is in front.

When I had taken up my writing-tablets and was turning these
questions over in my mind,* the house seemed brighter than it was
before. Then holy Janus, amazing in his double appearance, suddenly 95
presented his pair of faces to my eyes. I was terrified; I felt that my
hair had stood on end in fear; my heart was frozen with a sudden
chill. He held a staff in his right hand and a key in his left, and he
uttered these words to me from his front-facing mouth: 100

'Put aside your fear, industrious bard of the days. Learn what you
seek, and take in my words with your mind. The ancients—for I'm
a primitive phenomenon—used to call me Chaos.* See of how far
a time I sing the history! The bright air here and the three elements 105
that remain, fire, water, earth, used to be just one heap. When once
this mass separated, because of discord in its parts, and broke apart
and went off into new homes, flame sought the height, a nearer place
caught air, and earth and sea settled in the middle region. At that time 110
I, who had been a round mass and a bulk without form, resorted to
a shape and limbs appropriate to a god. Even now, small indication of
my once chaotic shape, what's in front and behind in me appears the
same.

'Hear the second reason for the shape you've asked about, so you 115
may know this and my function together. Whatever you see all round,
sky, sea, clouds, lands, everything is closed up and opened by my

hand. The guardianship of the vast universe rests with me alone, and
120 the right to turn the hinge is entirely mine. When it has pleased me to
send forth Peace from the tranquil houses, freely she walks on
uninterrupted ways. The whole world will be thrown into confusion
with deadly bloodshed if unbending bars do not keep wars under
restraint.

125   'I preside at the doors of heaven with the gentle Seasons:* Jupiter
himself passes to and fro through my good offices. Hence I'm called
Janus.* When the priest puts out for me Ceres' cake and spelt mixed
with salt, you'll laugh at my names; for sometimes on the sacrificer's
130 lips I'm called Patulcius, and sometimes Clusius, though the same
god. Undoubtedly that crude old time wanted to indicate my differ-
ent functions by changing my name.

'My power has been told. Now learn the reason for my shape—and
135 yet to some extent you see this as well, already. Every door has twin
fronts, this side and that, of which one looks at the People, the other
at the Lar, and just as your doorman, sitting near the entrance at the
front of the building, sees the goings-out and comings-in, so I, the
140 doorman of the court of heaven, view at the same time the Eōan and
Hesperian regions. You see Hecate's faces turning in three directions,
that she may guard the crossroads split three ways. I too, so I don't
lose time by turning my neck, am allowed to look two ways without
bodily movement.'

145   He had spoken, and had pledged by his expression that he wouldn't
be difficult with me if I wanted to question him further. I plucked up
courage. Unafraid, I offered my thanks to the god, and looking at the
ground spoke further words:

'Well now, tell me why the new year starts in the cold weather. It
150 would be better begun in the spring. That's when everything blooms,
that's when time has a new season, and the new bud swells from the
pregnant shoot, and the tree is covered with new-formed leaves, and
155 the seed's blade comes forth to the surface of the soil, and birds with
their harmonies soothe the warm air, and in the meadows the animals
frisk and frolic. That's when the suns are enticing, and the unfamiliar
swallow appears and fashions her mud work under the lofty beam.
That's when the field tolerates cultivation and is renewed by the
160 plough. By rights, this should have been called the year's newness.'

I had made my enquiry at length; not so he. Without delay he com-
pressed his words into two lines, like this:

'The winter solstice is the first day of the new sun, the last of the old. Phoebus and the year take the same starting point.'

After that, I was wondering why the first day was not free from lawsuits.

'Learn the reason,' says Janus. 'While the times were being born, I assigned them to the transaction of business, so that right from the auspices the whole year should not be inactive. For the same reason, each person does enough just to sample his skills, no more than giving evidence of his usual work.'

'Why, Janus,' I asked next, 'though I worship the power of other divinities, do I first offer incense and wine to you?'

'So that through me,' says he, 'the guardian of the threshold, you can have access to whichever gods you want.'

'But why are joyful words spoken on your Kalends? And why do we give good wishes and receive them in return?'

At that point, leaning on the staff his right hand held, 'Omens,' says the god, 'are usually inherent in beginnings. You direct your timid ears to the first word spoken, and the augur interprets the bird he has seen first. The gods' temples and ears are open, no tongue conceives prayers that fall useless, and things that are said carry weight.'

Janus had finished, and I wasn't silent long, but touched his last words with words of my own:

'What,' I said, 'is the meaning of the dates and the wrinkled figs, and the gift of shining honey in a snow-white jar?'

'The omen is the reason,' says he, 'so that that flavour may follow what ensues, and the year continue sweet on the journey it has begun.'

'I see why sweet things are given. Add the reason for giving coins, so that no part of your festival may be uncertain for me.'

He laughed. 'How wrong you are,' he said, 'about the age you live in, if you think honey is sweeter than cash in hand! Even under Saturn's reign I saw hardly anyone to whose heart profit wasn't sweet. In time the love of possessing grew, which now is at its height; by now there's scarcely any further it can go.

'Wealth is more valued now than in the years of old, the time when the People was poor, when Rome was new, when a little hut held Quirinus, offspring of Mars, and sedge from the river gave him a meagre bed. Jupiter in his cramped temple had difficulty standing upright,

and in Jupiter's right hand was a thunderbolt made of clay. With
leaves, as now with gems, they used to decorate the Capitol, and the
205 senator himself used to pasture his own sheep. There was no shame in
having taken quiet rest on straw and put hay underneath one's head.
The *praetor* used to dispense justice to the peoples having only just
put aside his plough, and a thin leaf of silver was cause for an
accusation.

'But now that the Fortune of this place* has raised her head, and
210 Rome at her highest point has touched the gods, wealth has grown too,
and the frenzied desire for wealth, and although they possess huge
amounts they seek for more. They strive to acquire in order to spend,
to acquire it again when they've spent it, and even their disasters are
215 food for their vices. Just so with those whose bellies have swollen with
dropsy, the more the fluids are drunk the more they are thirsted for.
These days the price is what's prized: your census rating* gives you
honours, gives you friendships. The poor man's out of it everywhere.

220 'And yet you ask if an omen of coins is useful, and why old bronze
delights our hands? They used to give bronze once upon a time.
Nowadays there's a better omen in gold, and the old coins, van-
quished, have yielded to the new. We too delight in golden temples,
even though we approve of the old ones; grandeur itself is fitting for
225 a god. We praise past years but enjoy our own—and yet each custom
is equally worth keeping.'

He had finished his advice. As before, I myself address again the
key-bearing god, in these calm words:

'Indeed I have learned many things. But why, on the bronze coin,
230 is one stamped image a ship and the other two-headed?'

'So that in the double image,' he said, 'you'd be able to recognize
me, if time itself hadn't worn away the old design. Next, the reason
for the ship: it was in a ship that the sickle-bearing god* came to the
235 Tuscan river, having first wandered the whole world. It was in this
land, I remember, that Saturn was received; he had been banished
from the heavenly realms by Jupiter. For a long time after that the
People kept the name "Saturnian"; the land was called Latium too
from the god in hiding.* But generous posterity shaped a ship on the
240 bronze, attesting the god's arrival as a guest.

'I myself occupied the land whose left side the all-peaceful wave of
sandy Thybris touches. Here, where now is Rome, there flourished an
unfelled forest, and so great a place was pasture for a few cattle. My

stronghold was the hill which this age commonly names after me and 245
calls Janiculum. I was the ruler at that time, when earth received gods
and divine powers mingled in the places of men.

'Not yet had mortal crime put Justice to flight (she was the last of 250
the deities to leave the earth),* and instead of fear the proper sense of
decency guided the People without force. It was no hardship to deliver
justice to the just. I had nothing to do with war; I guarded peace and
doorways, and these,' says he, showing the key, 'are the arms I carry.'

The god had closed his lips. Then I opened mine, my speech elicit- 255
ing speeches from the god:

'Since there are so many gateways, why do you stand consecrated
in just one, here where you have a temple adjoining two *fora*?'

Stroking the beard that hung down to his chest, he straight away 260
recounted the war of Oebalian Tatius*—how the fickle guard, captiv-
ated by bracelets, led the silent Sabines to the way to the top of the
Citadel.* 'From there', says he, 'there was a steep slope, just as there
is now, by which you go down through the *fora* to the valleys.

'And now he had reached the gate, from which Saturn's envious 265
daughter had removed the bars placed across. Fearing to start a fight
with so powerful a deity, I craftily brought into play a device of my
own skill. I opened the mouths of springs—a resource in which I'm
powerful—and I spurted out sudden jets of water. Before that, 270
though, I threw sulphur in the wet veins, so that boiling water would
bar Tatius' way.

'When the Sabines had been driven off, and the usefulness of my
trick perceived, the place was safe and the shape it had been was
restored to it. An altar was set up for me, next to a little shrine; with 275
its flames it burns the spelt along with the heap of cakes.'

'But why do you lie hidden in time of peace, and are opened up
when weapons are put into action?' No delay. The reason for what I'd
asked I got in return:

'So that a way back should lie open when the People has gone to
war, my door stands wide open with its bar removed. In peacetime 280
I close up the doors, so there's no way peace can leave. Under the
Caesars' divine power I shall be shut for a long time.'

He spoke, and raising his eyes that saw in opposite directions, he
looked on all there was in the whole world. There was peace, 285
Germanicus, and the Rhine, the reason for your triumph, had already
surrendered its waters to serve you.

Janus, make peace, and the ministers of peace, eternal! Grant that he who brings it about may not desert his task!

However—something I've been allowed to discover from the calendar
290 itself—on this day the Fathers dedicated two temples. The island that the river hems in with divided waters received the son of Phoebus and the nymph Coronis. Jupiter has a share: one place took them both, and the temple of the grandson is joined to that of his mighty grandfather.*

295 What stops me speaking of the stars as well, how each of them rises and sets? Let that too be a part of my promise. Fortunate souls, who first had the care to discover these things and climb to the dwellings above! One can believe that they put their heads as
300 far above human weaknesses as above human haunts. Neither Venus nor wine corrupted their lofty hearts, nor the business of the *forum* nor the labour of war. They were not tempted by petty ambition, by glory steeped in false colour, by hunger for great
305 wealth. They brought close the distant stars with the eyes of the mind, and made the heavens subject to their intellect. That is how one reaches for the sky, not making Olympus carry Ossa and Pelion's summit* touch the highest stars. With them to guide me,
310 I too will measure the sky and assign their own days to the wandering constellations.

[3 January] And so when the third night before the approaching Nones arrives, and the ground is wet and sprinkled with dew from heaven, it will be pointless to look for the arms of the eight-footed Crab: he will go headlong under the waters of the west.

315 [5 January] If the Nones are here, showers sent from black clouds will give you a sign as the Lyre rises.

[9 January] To the Nones add four days taken in a row. Janus will have to be appeased on the Agonal day. The reason for the name may
320 be the attendant with his tucked-up robe, at whose blow the victim falls in honour of the heavenly ones; having drawn the knives to stain them with warm blood, he always asks if he should go on, and doesn't go on unless he's told.*

Some people believe that the Agonal day takes its name from driving, in as much as the sheep do not come but are driven. Others think 325 that this festival was called Agnalia by the ancients, supposing that one letter has been taken from its proper place. Or was the day in question marked from the sheep's fear, because the victim is afraid of the knives it sees beforehand in the water? It is also possible that the day took a Greek name from the games that used to take place in our 330 ancestors' time. Ancient speech, too, called sheep 'agonia', and in my judgement this last reason is the true one.

Uncertain though that is, still the *rex sacrorum* is required to appease the divine powers by offering the mate of a fleecy ewe. What has fallen to the victorious right hand is called the victim; the sacrifi- 335 cial beast takes its name from conquered enemies.*

Previously, it was spelt and the sparkling grain of pure salt that had the power to win the gods over to mankind. Not yet, driven through the sea's waters, had the visiting ship brought myrrh, produced as 340 tears from its bark. The Euphrates had not sent incense, nor India spice, and the stamens of red saffron had not been discovered. The altar was content to give off smoke from Sabine herbs, and laurel was burned with no small sound. If there was anyone who could add vio- 345 lets to garlands made from meadow flowers, he was a rich man! This knife, which now opens the entrails of a stricken bull, had no work to do in sacred rites.

Ceres was the first to delight in the blood of the greedy sow, avenging her riches with the well-deserved slaughter of the guilty one. For 350 she discovered that her crops, milky with young sap at the start of spring, had been rooted up by the snout of a bristly sow.

The sow had paid the penalty; you should have been frightened by her example, billy goat, and kept away from the vine-shoot. Someone watched the goat sink his teeth into the vine, and didn't keep his 355 resentment to himself. This is what he said: 'Go on, goat, gnaw the vine! Yet there'll be something from it that can be sprinkled on your horns when you stand at the altar.' What follows bears out his words. When your enemy, Bacchus, is given up for punishment, his horns 360 are sprinkled with a pouring of wine.

Her wrongdoing did for the sow, her wrongdoing did for the she-goat too. But you, ox and peaceful sheep, what wrong have you done?

Aristaeus was weeping. He had seen that his bees, killed with their progeny, had abandoned the honeycombs they'd begun. It was hard 365

for his sea-blue mother* to console him in his grief. She added these
final words to what she'd said:

'Check your tears, my boy. Proteus will ease your losses and give you
a way to restore what has been destroyed. However, lest he deceive you
370 by changing shape, strong fetters must encumber both his hands.'

The youth makes his way to the seer. He catches the arms of the
old man of the sea relaxed in sleep, and binds them tight. That shape-
shifter uses his own art to alter his appearance; soon he turns back to
375 his own body, mastered by the bonds. Raising his dripping face with
its sea-blue beard, he said:

'Are you looking for the way to get back your bees? Slaughter
a bullock and bury the carcase in the earth. What you seek from me
the buried one will give you.'

The shepherd does what he's told. Swarms of bees boil up from
380 the rotting bullock. A thousand lives were created from one that was
ended.

Fate demands the sheep: she has wickedly cropped the shrubs that
a pious old lady used to offer to the gods of the countryside. What
safety remains, when the sheep that bear wool and the oxen that till
385 the ground lay down their lives at the altars? Persia uses a horse to
appease Hyperion, girdled with sunbeams, lest a slow victim be given
to a swift god. Because once for twin Diana it was slaughtered instead
of a virgin,* now too a hind falls instead of no virgin. I have seen the
390 Sapaeans, and those who live among your snows, Haemus, offer dogs'
entrails as a libation to the goddess of the Three Ways. A young don-
key, too, is killed for the stiff guardian of the countryside.* The reason
is certainly indecent, but all the same it suits the god.

Greece, you were celebrating the festival of ivy-berried Bacchus
which the third winter brings round at the accustomed time. The
395 gods too came together, those who honour Lyaeus and whoever wasn't
averse to a bit of fun—Pans, and young satyrs prone to Venus, and the
goddesses who haunt the rivers and the lonely countryside. Old man
Silenus had come too on his hollow-backed donkey, and the one with
400 the red member who scares the timid birds.

They found a grove that was good for a pleasant party, and stretched
out on couches strewn with grass. Liber poured the wine, everyone
had brought his own garland, a stream provided water for mixing, but
not too much.

Naiads were there, some with their hair loose and uncombed,   405
others with it artfully arranged by hand. One of them serves with
her tunic tucked up above her calves; another with her top undone
is showing her bosom; this one bares a shoulder, that one trails her
dress through the grass; no sandal-straps impede their delicate feet.   410
Over here some of them cause gentle fires in the satyrs, and others
in you, who have your temples bound with pine.* They inflame you
as well, unquenchably lustful Silenus; it's lechery that stops you
being old.

But out of all of them, red Priapus, adornment and protector of   415
gardens, was captivated by Lotis. It's her he wants, her he desires, her
alone he sighs for. He gives her clues by nodding, and pesters her
with signs. Pride dwells in the beautiful, and haughtiness goes with
good looks. She mocks him, and her face shows her disdain.   420

It was night. As wine brought on sleep, bodies were lying all over
the place, overcome by drowsiness. Furthest away on the grassy
ground, beneath a maple's branches, just as she was, exhausted by the
fun, Lotis rested. Up gets the lover, and stealthily, holding his breath,   425
he makes his silent way on the tips of his toes. Now that he's reached
the bed of the snow-white nymph, away from the rest, he takes good
care that even his breath should make no sound. And already he was
balancing his body on the grass next to her; she, however, was deep   430
asleep. Exultant, pulling the dress up from her feet, he had started to
make his way on the happy road to his desires.

Oh no! With a raucous braying, the donkey that brought Silenus
opened his mouth to sound off at just the wrong moment. Terrified,   435
up jumps the nymph, pushes Priapus off with her hands, and runs
away, rousing the whole grove.* But the god, his obscene part all too
ready, was a joke for them all by the light of the moon. The one
responsible for the noise paid for it with his life, and this is the victim   440
the god of the Hellespont likes.

You birds, the solace of the countryside, had been inviolate, a harm-
less race accustomed to the woodland; you build nests and cherish
your eggs with your feathers and from willing throats send forth
sweet music. But that's of no avail: your power of utterance is an   445
accusation, and the gods think you reveal what they have in mind.
And this charge isn't false, for as each of you is close to the gods you
give true signs, now with your flight, now with your song. The winged

race, which had for long been safe, was then at last slaughtered, and
450 the gods took pleasure in their informer's entrails.

So, partner torn from her mate, a white dove is often burned on the
altars of Idalium. And having defended the Capitol is no help to pre-
vent the goose donating its liver to your dishes, daughter of Inachus.*
455 At night for goddess Night the crested bird is slaughtered, because he
calls forth the warm day with his wakeful voice.

[10 January] Meanwhile the Dolphin rises above the sea, a bright
constellation, and thrusts his face out of ancestral waters. The next
460 day marks winter with a line drawn down the middle. What remains
will be equal to what has gone before.

[11 January] The next bride of Tithonus, leaving him behind,* will
look out on the priests' ritual for the Arcadian goddess. The same day
received you in your temple, sister of Turnus, here where the Campus
465 is visited by the Virgin water.* Where shall I look for the reasons and
custom of these rites? Who will steer my sails in the midst of the sea?
Yourself advise me, you who bear a name derived from song,* and be
favourable to my enterprise, lest your own honour be at risk.

The land that came to be before the moon, if you believe what it
470 says about itself, takes its name from great Arcas. Out of it came
Evander, who, though illustrious on both sides, was more noble
through the blood of his sacred mother. As soon as she had conceived
in her mind the heavenly fires, she would utter from truthful lips
475 chants full of god. She had said that changes loomed for herself and
her son, and much besides which in time proved to be true.

For the young man abandoned Arcadia and his Parrhasian home,
banished along with his mother, all too truthful. As he wept, his
mother said to him:
480 'This fortune of yours you must bear like a man. Check your tears,
I beg you. It was thus in your destiny: no fault of yours has caused
your banishment, but a god. You've been driven from the city because
a god has been offended. What you suffer is not due punishment for
what you've done, but the anger of divine power. It is something that
no guilt is involved in your great misfortune.
485 'As each man has his own conscience, so it conceives in his breast
both hope and fear, depending on what he has done. In any case, don't
grieve as if you were the first to have suffered such misfortunes. That

sort of storm has overwhelmed mighty men. The same thing hap-
pened to Cadmus, who long ago was driven from the shores of Tyre
and settled in exile, on Aonian soil. The same thing happened to 490
Tydeus, and to Pagasaean Jason, and others besides who would take
too long to record.

'To the brave every land is the homeland, as to fishes the sea, as to
birds the whole open space of the empty world. But fierce weather 495
doesn't rage all the year long. For you too, believe me, the time of
spring will come.'

His mind strengthened by his mother's words, Evander cuts
through the waves in his ship and reaches Hesperia. And now, advised
by the learned Carmentis, he had steered his vessel into the river and 500
was going upstream against the Tuscan waters.

She looks at the river's edge, next to which is the ford of Tarentum,
and the cottages dotted about the lonely place. Just as she was, her
hair streaming, she took her stand before the helm and sternly checked
the hand of the man who steered their way. Stretching her arms from 505
afar to the right bank, she struck the pinewood deck with a frantic
foot three times, and hardly, hardly was kept back by Evander's hand
from leaping in her haste to set foot on shore.

'Greetings,' she said, 'you gods of the place we have been seeking!
And you, a land destined to give new gods to heaven! And you, rivers
and springs which the welcoming land enjoys, and woodland 510
groves and dancing Naiads! May the sight of you be a good omen for
my son and for me, and may the foot that touches the bank be a for-
tunate one!

'Am I mistaken, or will these hills become huge walls and all other 515
lands seek justice from this land? To these hills, one day, the whole
world is promised. Who could believe the place has so much destiny?
And now Dardanian pines will touch these shores; here too a woman 520
will be the cause of a new Mars.* Dear grandson Pallas, why do you
put on deadly armour? Put it on! You'll be cut down with no lowly
avenger.

'Conquered, Troy, yet you will conquer! Overthrown, you will rise
again! That ruin of yours buries the homes of your enemies. Burn
Neptune's Pergamum, victorious flames! Are not these ashes still 525
loftier than all the world?

'Now pious Aeneas will bring the sacred things and, sacred too, his
father. Vesta, receive the gods of Ilium! The time will come when you

530 and the world have the same guardian, and your rites will be carried
out with a god himself officiating, and the protection of the homeland
will rest in Augustan hands.* It is proper that this house should hold
the reins of power.

'Then the son and grandson of a god, though he himself may
demur, will bear with godlike mind his father's burden.* And just as
535 I shall one day be consecrated at eternal altars,* so shall Julia Augusta
be a new divine power.'

As with such words she came down to our times, her prophetic
tongue stopped short in mid-utterance. Leaving his ship, the exile
540 stood on the grass of Latium—fortunate man, to have that as his
place of exile! No long time passed. New dwellings were standing,
and no one in the hills of Ausonia was greater than the Arcadian.

Look! The club-bearing hero brings there the Erythean cattle, having
545 measured out his journey the length of the world,* and while a Tegean
house offers him hospitality, the cattle roam over the broad fields
unguarded.

It was morning. Roused from sleep, the Tirynthian drover is aware
that two bulls are missing from the number. Searching, he sees no
550 traces of the silent theft. Fierce Cacus had dragged them backward
into his cave—Cacus, the terror and disgrace of the Aventine wood,
no trivial evil to neighbours and visitors alike.

The man's face was hideous, his body huge with strength to match
555 it; Mulciber was this monster's father. For a home he had a vast cave
with deep recesses, hidden away where the wild beasts themselves
could hardly find it. Skulls and limbs hang fixed above the doorway,
and the ground is foul and white with human bones.

The son of Jupiter was going away, having failed to guard part of
560 his herd, when the stolen beasts let out a hoarse bellowing noise.
'I accept the recall,' says he, and following the sound the avenger
comes through the woods to the impious cave.

The one had blocked the entrance in advance with part of the hill-
side broken off. Twice-five yoke of oxen would hardly have shifted
565 that barricade. The other heaves with his shoulders (the sky too had
rested on them), and causes the vast weight to shift and come top-
pling down. Once it was dislodged, the crash struck terror into the
heavens themselves, and the ground sank down, struck by the mas-
sive weight.

To start with, Cacus battles hand to hand, fiercely carrying on the 570
fight with rocks and tree trunks. When these get him nowhere, the
coward resorts to his father's arts and belches flames from his roaring
mouth. Every time he blows them out you might think Typhoeus is
breathing and swift lightning being hurled from Etna's fire. In goes
Alcides and brings into play his triple-knotted club, which three or 575
four times landed full in the man's face.

He falls and spews out smoke mixed with blood, and beats the
ground with his broad chest as he dies. The victor sacrifices one of
the bulls in question to you, Jupiter, summons Evander and the coun- 580
tryfolk, and sets up an altar to himself, the one called *ara maxima*,
here where part of the city takes its name from the ox.* Nor does
Evander's mother fail to tell him that a time is soon coming when the
earth will have done with Hercules as one of its own.

But the fortunate prophetess, most pleasing to the gods as she was 585
in life, so as a goddess has this day for her own in the month of
Janus.

[13 January] On the Ides in the temple of great Jupiter the chaste
priest offers to the flames the entrails of a half-male ram. Every
province was restored to our People,* and your grandfather was called 590
by the name Augustus. Read through the wax images displayed
throughout noble halls: no man has achieved so great a name.

Africa names her conqueror after herself;* another by his title
bears witness to the subjected power of Isaurians or Cretans; the
Numidians make one man proud, Messana another; yet another 595
derived his distinction from the city of Numantia. Germany gave
Drusus both death and a name; alas, how short-lived that valour was!*
If a Caesar were to look for titles from the vanquished, he would take
on as many as the nations the great world contains. 600

Some, famous for one deed, derive their titles from a stripped
torque or a raven helpful in battle.* Magnus, your name is the meas-
ure of your deeds, but the one who conquered you was greater than
a name. There's no degree of *cognomen* higher than the Fabii: that 605
house is called Maximus for its deserts. Yet it is for human distinc-
tions that all these are celebrated, whereas this man has a name allied
to Jupiter most high.

Our fathers call sacred things 'august', 'august' is what temples are
called when they have been duly consecrated by the hand of the 610

priests. Augury too is derived from this word's origin, and whatever Jupiter augments with his power. May he augment our leader's rule, may he augment his years, and may the crown of oak-leaves protect
615 your doors.* And under the gods' auspices, may the inheritor of so great a name, with the same omen as his father, undertake the burden of the world.

[15 January] When the third Titan looks back at the Ides that have passed, the rites for the Parrhasian goddess will be repeated. For previously carriages used to convey the married ladies of Ausonia
620 (I think these too took their name from Evander's mother).*
Soon the privilege is taken away, and every married lady resolves not to renew their ungrateful husbands with any offspring. To avoid giving birth, recklessly with a blind blow she forced out of her womb
625 the burden that was growing there. They say the Fathers reproached the wives for daring barbarous acts, but all the same restored to them the cancelled privilege, and they order that now two rituals be held, for boys and for girls equally, in honour of the Tegean mother.
630 It is not allowed to bring leather into that shrine, lest dead material defile the pure altars. Whoever you are, if you have a liking for ancient rituals, stand next to the one who offers the prayers: you will hear names you didn't know before. Porrima is being propitiated, and so is Postverta—either your sisters, Maenalian goddess, or the compan-
635 ions of your flight. It's thought that one of them sang what had been further back,* and the other whatever was likely to come hereafter.

[16 January] Fair goddess, the next day placed you in your snow-white temple, where lofty Moneta lifts her steps on high. Well will
640 you look out now, Concord, over the Latin throng; now hallowed hands have established you. Furius, conqueror of the Etruscan people, had vowed an ancient promise, and had paid his vow. The reason was that the crowd had taken up arms and seceded from the Fathers, and Rome herself was afraid of her own resources.
645 The new reason is a better one: under your auspices, venerated leader, Germany offers her hair unbound.* From there you have offered up the gifts of a triumphed-over nation, and built a temple for the goddess you yourself worship. This goddess your mother has
650 established, both in deeds and with an altar*—she who alone was found worthy of the couch of great Jupiter.

When these events have passed, Phoebus, you will leave Capricorn and run your course through the sign of the youth who rules water.

[23 January] When the seventh rising sun from here has plunged himself into the waves, there will now be no Lyre shining anywhere in the sky. On the night coming after this star, the fire that gleams in the 655 middle of Lion's chest will have been submerged.

Three or four times I went through the calendars that mark the dates and found no Sowing Day, when the Muse—for she understood— says this to me:

'This day is announced by proclamation. Why do you look in the 660 calendar for moveable rites? Although the day of the rite isn't fixed, the season is: it's when the seed has been sown and the land is pregnant.'

You bullocks, stand garlanded at your well-filled stall; your work will return with the warmth of spring. Let the countryman hang on 665 a post the plough that has served its time; in the cold weather the ground dreads any wound. You overseer, give the earth a rest once the sowing's finished; give the men a rest who have tilled the earth. Let the parish hold a holiday! You farmers, go the rounds of the parish, and give the parish's hearths* their yearly cakes. 670

Let Earth and Ceres, mothers of the crops, be propitiated with their own spelt, and with the entrails of a pregnant cow. Ceres and Earth maintain a joint duty: one gives the crops their origin, the other their place. Partners in the task, through whom the old ways were put 675 right and the oak acorn defeated by more beneficial food, glut the eager farmers with boundless crops, that they may reap rewards worthy of their cultivation.

Give uninterrupted growth to the tender sowings, and don't let 680 the fresh green growth be burned through chilly snows. When we sow, make the sky clear with fair winds. When the seed lies hidden, sprinkle it with water from heaven. And take care that birds don't lay waste the fields of Ceres; in armed formation bent on doing harm, they are the enemy of cultivation. You ants as well, spare the grain 685 when it's been sown; after the harvest there will be greater abundance of spoil.

In the meantime, let the standing corn grow free from flaky mildew, and let none of it be pale through the fault of the weather. Let it

690 neither wither and fail nor grow too luxuriant and perish, rank from
its own richness. Let the fields be free from darnel that harms the
eyes, and may no barren wild oats spring up in the cultivated soil.
May the land pay back with huge interest the wheat crops and the
barley and the spelt that must twice pass through fire.
695   This is what I wish for on your behalf, farmers. Wish for it your-
selves, and may each goddess bring the prayers to full effect.

Wars for a long time occupied men: the sword was handier than the
ploughshare, the ploughing bull yielded to the charger. Hoes used to
700 be idle, mattocks were turned into javelins, a helmet was made from
the weight of a rake. Thanks be to the gods and to your house! Long
now have wars been lying bound in chains beneath your feet. Let the
ox come under the plough, and the seed under the ploughed lands.
Peace nurtures Ceres. Ceres is the foster-child of Peace.

705 [27 January] But on this day, the sixth that precedes the coming
Kalends, the temple was dedicated to the gods who are Leda's sons.
For the brother gods, brothers from the race of gods* founded it near
the pools of Juturna.

[30 January] The song itself has brought me to the altar of Peace.
710 This will be the second day from the end of the month.
     Be present, Peace, your neat hair wreathed with branches from
Actium, and remain gentle in all the world. Provided enemies are
missing, let the reason for a triumph be missing too. You will be for
our leaders a glory greater than war.
715   May the soldier bear weapons only to keep weapons in check, and
may nothing but a procession be sounded by the fierce trumpet. Both
nearest and furthest, let the world dread Aeneas' descendants; may
Rome be loved by any land that feared her not enough.
     You priests, add incense to the flames at the rites of Peace, and let
720 the white victim fall, its brow well soaked. Ask the gods, who incline
towards pious prayers, that the house which guarantees her may last
long years with Peace.

But now the first part of my work is finished, and with its month my
little book finds its end.

BOOK 2

FEBRUARY

JANUS has his end. The song grows, and so does the year. As this second month progresses, so may the second book.

Now for the first time, elegiacs, you are going under more ample sails. Recently, I remember, you were a minor work. I myself used you 5 as ready assistants in love, when my early youth played with its appropriate metre. I am the same, but now I sing of sacred things and the times marked out in the calendar. Who is there who'd believe there's a way from that to this?

This is my military service; we bear what arms we can, and our right hand is not exempt from every duty. If I don't hurl javelins with 10 powerful arm, or put my weight on the back of a warrior horse, or cover my head with a helmet, or belt on a sharp sword (anyone can be handy with weapons like these)—yet, Caesar, with zealous heart I fol- 15 low up your names and advance through your titles. Be with me then, and with gentle face look on my services just a little, if you have any respite from pacifying the enemy.

Our Roman forefathers called means of purification *februa*; now too, very many indications give the word credibility. The *pontifices* ask the 20 *rex sacrorum* and the *flamen* for pieces of wool, the name for which in the language of the men of old was *februa*. The roasted spelt and salt which the lictor gets, as a means of cleansing in particular houses,* are called the same. It's the same name too for the branch which is cut from 25 a pure tree and covers with its foliage the priests' chaste brows. I have seen for myself the wife of the *flamen* asking for *februa*, and asking for *februa* she was given a stick of pine. In short, anything with which our bodies are purified had this name among our unshaven ancestors. 30

From these things the month takes its name, because the Luperci cleanse all the ground with cut hide and regard it as a purification; or else because the times are pure once the tombs have been appeased, when the Feral days have passed.

Our old people used to believe that purifications could remove all 35 sacrilege and every source of evil. Greece started the practice: she

thinks the guilty, once purified, put off their wicked deeds. Peleus
absolved Actorides, and Peleus too was himself absolved of the blood
40 of Phocus by Acastus, using Haemonian waters. When the Phasian
woman harnessed dragons and rode them through the empty air, gul-
lible Aegeus supported her with help she didn't deserve. The son of
Amphiaraus said to Naupactian Achelous, 'Cleanse my sacrilege', and
45 he cleansed it. Ah, you're too compliant, you who think grim charges
of bloodshed can be lifted with river water!

But still, so you won't go astray from not knowing the ancient
sequence, the month of Janus was formerly first as well, just as it is
now. The one that follows Janus was the last of the ancient year. You
50 too, Terminus, were the end of the sacred rites. For the month of
Janus is first because a door is first; the one that is sacred to the shades
below was last.* It's thought that later the twice-five men* linked up
times that were a long way apart.

55 [1 February] At the beginning of the month Sospita, neighbour of
the Phrygian Mother, is said to have been enhanced with new
shrines. Where are they now, the temples that were dedicated to the
goddess on those Kalends? They have fallen with the long passage
of time.

The far-sighted care of our hallowed leader has seen to it that the
60 rest of the temples should not suffer the same collapse and ruin;
under him the shrines do not feel their advancing years. It isn't enough
to bind men with his favours; he binds gods as well.

Builder of temples, holy restorer of temples, I pray the gods above
65 may have concern for you in return. May the heavenly ones grant you
the years you have granted them, and may they remain at their post to
guard your house.

At that time too the grove of neighbouring Alernus is crowded, where
the arriving Thybris makes for the waters of the sea. At Numa's sanc-
70 tuary and the Capitoline Thunderer, and on the height of Jupiter's
Citadel, a sheep is killed. Often the sky is covered with clouds and
summons up heavy rains, or the earth hides beneath a fall of snow.

[2 February] When the next Titan, about to go off into the Hesperian
waves, removes the jewelled yokes from his purple steeds, that night
75 someone, lifting his face to the stars, will say, 'Where is it today, the

Lyre that gleamed yesterday?'—and while he's looking for the Lyre he will observe that the back of the middle of the Lion too has suddenly sunk into clear waters.

[3 February] The Dolphin which just now you used to see embossed with stars will flee from your vision the following night. Either he was 80 a lucky go-between in hidden loves, or* he carried the lyre of Lesbos along with its master.

What sea hasn't heard of Arion, what land doesn't know him? It was he who used to hold still the running waters with his song.

Often the wolf chasing a lamb was held back by his voice, often the 85 lamb fleeing a greedy wolf stopped in its tracks; often hounds and hares lay down under one shade, and on a rock the doe stood next to the lioness. Without argument the chattering crow sat with the bird of Pallas,* and the dove was united with the hawk. It is said that often 90 Cynthia was astounded by your melodies, tuneful Arion, as if they were those of her brother.

The name of Arion had filled the cities of Sicily, and Auson's coast had been captured by the music of his lyre. Making his way back 95 home from there, Arion boarded a ship; he was carrying the wealth thus acquired by his art. Unlucky man, perhaps you feared the winds and waves—but the sea was safer for you than your ship. For the helmsman took his stand with a drawn sword, and the rest of the crew 100 were in the plot with weapons in hand. What are you doing with a sword? Steer the ship, sailor, it doesn't know the way! This isn't the tackle your fingers should be holding.

Arion is terrified. 'I don't beg to be spared death,' he says, 'but let me take up my lyre and play a few notes.' They give him leave, and 105 laugh at the delay. He takes a garland—such, Phoebus, as could grace your hair.

He had put on his robe, twice dyed with Tyrian purple. The string, struck by his thumb, rendered its notes, just as a swan sings in mournful strains when its white brows have been pieced with a hard arrow. 110

Straight away in his finery he leaps down into the midst of the waves; the blue stern is splashed by the smitten water. Then (too much to believe) they recall that a dolphin with its arching back placed itself beneath the unaccustomed burden. Arion, sitting and 115 holding his lyre, sings the price of his passage and soothes with his song the waters of the sea.

The gods see pious deeds. Jupiter received the dolphin among the constellations, and ordered that it should have nine stars.

[5 February] Now I could wish I had a thousand voices,* and the
120 heart, Maeonides, with which you made Achilles famous, while we sing the sacred Nones in alternating song. At this point the greatest honour is heaped upon the calendar.

My talent is inadequate. What presses me is greater than my
125 strength. This is a day I must sing with exceptional voice. Insane, why did I want to impose so much weight on elegiacs? That was a subject for the heroic metre.

Sacred father of the homeland, to you the plebeians, to you the Senate, to you we the Knights have given this name.* Yet history gave
130 it first. Late indeed did you take your true names; long since you were already father of the world. This name which Jupiter has in high heaven, you have throughout the earth. You are the father of men, he of gods.

Romulus, you will give way. This man makes your walls great by defending them; you had given them to Remus to leap across. Tatius
135 and little Cures and Caenina were aware of you; under this man's leadership both sides of the sun are Roman. You had some small area of conquered ground; whatever there is beneath high Jupiter, Caesar has. You snatch wives; this man bids them be chaste under his leadership.
140 You receive guilt in your grove;* he has repelled it. To you violence was welcome; under Caesar the laws flourish. You had the name of master; he has the name of *princeps*. Remus accuses you; he has given pardon to enemies. Your father made you a god; he made his father one.*

145 Now the Idaean boy* stands out as far as the middle of his belly, and pours streams of water mixed with nectar. Look, too—let anyone who used to shiver at Boreas be glad; a softer breeze is coming from the Zephyri.

[10 February] The fifth Light-bringer has lifted his glittering
150 radiance from the ocean waves, and it will be the time of spring's beginning. But don't be fooled. Cold spells remain for you, they remain, and as winter departs it has left great traces.

[12 February] Come the third night, you'll see at once that the Guardian of the Bear has thrust out his two feet.

Among the Hamadryads and the spear-wielding Diana, Callisto 155
was one part of the sacred chorus. Touching the goddess's bow, 'Bow
that I touch,' says she, 'be the witness of my virginity.' Cynthia praised
her, and said, 'Keep the pledge you have made, and you will be the 160
foremost of my companions.' She would have kept her pledge if she'd
not been beautiful. She was wary of mortals; she gets her guilt from
Jupiter.

Phoebe was returning, having hunted a thousand wild beasts in
the woods, and the sun was at its height or just beyond. As she reached 165
the grove—it was a grove dark with dense holm-oaks, and in the middle
was a deep spring of ice-cold water—'Virgin of Tegea,' says she, 'let's
bathe here in the wood.' Callisto blushed at the false word 'virgin'.

She had spoken to the nymphs as well, and the nymphs undress.
This one is ashamed, and gives bad signs of reluctance and delay. She 170
had taken off her tunic. Plain to see with her swollen belly, she is
betrayed by her very own evidence of the weight she carries. The god-
dess said to her, 'Lying daughter of Lycaon, leave the virgin company,
and do not defile the chaste waters.'

Ten times the moon with her horns had filled a new orb. She who 175
had been thought a virgin was a mother. Offended, Juno rages and
transforms the girl (why do that? Her breast was unwilling when she
suffered Jupiter), and when she saw on the concubine the ugly face of
a wild beast, 'Jupiter,' says she, 'this you may go to bed with!' 180

A shaggy she-bear, she wandered through the wild mountains, she
who had lately been almighty Jupiter's beloved. And now the boy con-
ceived in secret was completing thrice-five years, when his mother
encountered her son. As for her, she stood distraught as if she recog- 185
nized him; and she growled. Growls were a mother's words.

Unaware, the boy would have pierced her with his sharp spear if
the two of them had not been carried off into the dwellings above. As
constellations they glitter side by side. First is she whom we call the
Bear; the Guardian of the Bear has the appearance of one following 190
behind. Saturn's daughter still rages, and asks white-foamed Tethys
not to bathe the bear of Maenalus by letting her waters touch it.

[13 February] On the Ides the altars of rustic Faunus smoke, here
where the island breaks the divided waters.

This was the famous day* on which three hundred and thrice-two 195
Fabii fell to the weapons of Veii. One house had taken on itself the

strength and the burden of the city. That family's hands take up the weapons it has volunteered.

200   Out from the same camp go the noble soldiers, any one of whom was fit to be their leader. The nearest way is by the right-hand arch of the gate of Carmentis. Don't go through it, whoever you are; it carries an omen. Tradition tells that the three hundred Fabii went out by that way. The gate is blameless, but yet it carries the omen.

205   When at quick march they've reached the raging Cremera (it was flowing turbid with winter flood), they pitch camp on the spot. With drawn swords, with mighty Mars, they go straight through the Tyrrhenian column,* just as when lions of Libyan race rush upon
210   flocks that are scattered across wide fields. The enemy flee this way and that, and take dishonourable wounds in the back. The earth is red with Tuscan blood.

Thus again, thus often, they fall. Where no victory is given them in open fight, they prepare an ambush and hidden weapons.

215   There was a plain. The limits of the plain were shut in by hills, and by a forest fit for hiding mountain beasts. In the middle they leave a few men and scattered cattle. The rest of the crowd lies hidden, concealed in undergrowth. See! Just as a torrent, swollen by
220   rains or by snow that's turned to water, melted by warm Zephyrus, is carried over crops and over roads, and doesn't keep its waters defined by the banks' limits as it did before, so the Fabii run about widely and fill the valley, bringing down whatever they see. They have no other fear.

225   O noble house, where are you rushing to? You do wrong to trust the enemy. Guileless nobility,* beware of treacherous weapons! Courage dies by deceit. From every side the enemy spring forward into the open plain and hold every flank. What are a few brave men to
230   do against an enemy of so many thousands? What help may be left in that wretched moment?

Just as a wild boar, driven far in the woods by their barking, scatters the swift hounds with his snout like a thunderbolt, and yet soon perishes himself, so they do not die unavenged, and deal out wounds
235   and receive them in turn. One day had sent all the Fabii to war; those sent to war one day destroyed.

And yet it is believable that the gods themselves took care that the seeds of the race of Hercules should survive. For one boy of the Fabian
240   house, under-age and not yet ready to bear arms, had been left behind.

Of course—it was so that you, Maximus, might one day be born, you
who would have to save the state by delaying.*

[**14 February**] Three constellations lie placed one after the other,
the Raven, the Snake, and the Bowl in the middle between the two.
On the Ides they lie hidden; they rise the following night. I'll sing to   245
you what they are, and why the three are so close.

It happened that Phoebus was preparing a formal festival for
Jupiter. (My story won't cause a long delay.) 'Go, my own bird,' said
he, 'and so that nothing may hold up the holy rites, bring clear water   250
from living springs.' The raven lifts a gilded bowl with his hooked
feet and, rising high, flies on his mission through the air.

There was a fig-tree standing thickly covered with fruit that was
still hard. He tests it with his beak, but it wasn't ready for picking.
Forgetting his orders, he is said to have sat beneath the tree waiting   255
for the fruit to become sweet in the slow passage of time.

And now, full, he seizes a long water-snake in his black claws,
returns to his master, and tells a lying tale: 'This, that blockades living
waters, is the reason for my delay; this occupied the springs and kept   260
me from my task.'

'Are you adding lies to your fault?' says Phoebus. 'Do you dare try to
cheat the god of prophecy with words? This is your sentence: as long as
the milky fig shall cling to the tree, you will not drink cool water from
any spring.' He spoke, and as an everlasting reminder of what happened   265
long ago, Snake, bird, and Bowl glitter as joined constellations.

[**15 February**] The third dawn after the Ides beholds the Luperci
naked, and the rites of two-horned Faunus proceed. Tell me, Pierides,
what is the origin of the rites, and where were they brought from to   270
reach the homes of Latium?

The ancient Arcadians are said to have worshipped Pan, the god of
flocks; he is much in evidence on the ridges of Arcadia. Pholoe will
vouch for that; so will the waves of Stymphalus, and the Ladon run-
ning with fast waters to the sea, and the ridges of the Nonacrian for-   275
est, girt with pines, and high Tricrene and the snows of Parrhasia.
Pan was there the deity of the herd and the mares; he used to receive
offerings for the safety of the sheep.

Evander brought the gods of the woodland over with him. Here,
where now the city is, was then the site for a city. And so we worship   280

the god, and keep the rites that were brought from the Pelasgians. By ancient custom the *flamen Dialis* was present at these rites.

So why do they run, you ask? And why (it's their custom to run like that) do they take their clothes off and have their bodies naked?

285 The god himself delights in running about fast in the high mountains, and himself gives rise to sudden flight.* The god himself, naked, bids his ministers go naked; and clothes won't be quite suitable for running.

They say the Arcadians possessed their land before Jupiter was
290 born; that race existed before the moon. Their life was like that of animals, lived through no settled custom. The people were still devoid of skills, and primitive. They knew leafy boughs instead of houses, grasses instead of crops. Nectar was water drunk from their two
295 palms. No bull panted beneath the curved plough, no land was under the control of a cultivator. As yet there was no use of the horse; each man carried himself, and the sheep went with its own wool clothing its body. They survived under Jove's sky and kept their bodies naked,
300 taught to endure heavy rains and south winds. Unclothed now too, they bring a reminder of the old practice, and bear witness to the resources of ancient times.

But as to why Faunus has a particular aversion to clothes, a story is handed down full of old-fashioned fun.

305 It happened that the Tirynthian youth was travelling in attendance on his mistress.* Faunus saw them both from a lofty ridge. He saw them and got hot. 'Mountain deities,' he said, 'you've got nothing for me. This is going to be my flame.'

On went the Maeonian girl, her perfumed hair spilling over her
310 shoulders, a sight to behold with her gilded bosom. A golden parasol was keeping off the warm suns; Hercules' hands, no less, held it up for her. And now she was reaching the grove of Bacchus and the vineyards of Tmolus, and dewy Hesperus was riding his dusky steed.

315 She enters a cave, its ceiling panelled with tufa and living pumice; right at the entrance there was a babbling stream. And while the attendants prepare the banquet and the wine to drink, she dresses Alcides up in her own attire.

She gives him delicate tunics dyed in Gaetulian purple; she gives
320 him the smooth girdle which has just been round her own waist. The girdle's too small for his belly; she undoes the tunics' fastenings so he

can push his great hands through; he'd broken the bracelets not made
for those arms; his great feet were splitting the little sandal-straps.
She herself takes the heavy club and the lion spoil,* and the smaller   325
weapons stored in their quiver. That's how they enjoy the feast, that's
how they give their bodies to sleep.

They lay apart, on couches placed close to each other. Why?
Because they were preparing for the rites of the god who discovered
the vine, and when day dawned they would perform them in   330
purity.

It was midnight. What doesn't shameless passion* dare? Towards
the dewy cave comes Faunus through the shadows, and when he sees
the servants sprawled in drunken sleep he conceives the hope that the
same sleepiness affects their masters.

The reckless adulterer goes inside. He wanders this way and that.   335
He stretches out cautious hands and follows their lead. He'd come to
where he wanted, the couch where the bed had been laid. He was
going to be lucky at the first chance.

As he touched the rough bristly pelt of a tawny lion, he was terri-   340
fied and checked his hand. Astonished, he withdrew in fear, just as
often a traveller backs off agitated when he sees a snake. Then he
touches the soft coverings of the couch close by, and is deceived by
their lying impression. Up he gets and lies down on the bed closer to   345
him, and his swollen groin was harder than his horn. All the time he's
drawing up the tunic from its hem.

Rough legs were bristling with thick hair. As he tried the next stage
the Tirynthian hero suddenly shoved him off, and down he fell from   350
the top of the couch. There's a din. The Maeonian girl cries for ser-
vants and lights.

Torches are brought, and it's clear what's happened. He groans,
thrown down heavily off the high couch, and can hardly pick himself
up from the hard ground. Alcides laughs, and those who've seen him   355
lying there laugh too. The Lydian girl laughs at her lover.

Fooled by clothing, the god doesn't like clothes that cheat the eyes,
and to his own rites he summons them naked.

Add Latin reasons to the foreign ones, my Muse, and let my horse   360
run on its own dusty track.*

To horn-footed Faunus, according to custom, a she-goat had been
slaughtered and a crowd came, summoned to the meagre feast. And

while the priests prepare the entrails, skewered on spits of willow, as
365 the sun was in mid-course Romulus and his brother and the young
shepherds were offering their bodies naked to the sunshine and the
field. With crowbars and javelins and the weight of thrown stones
they were putting their arms to the test in sport.

A shepherd shouted from the height. 'Romulus! Remus!' he said.
370 'Robbers are driving the bullocks through the pathless fields.' It
would take too long to get armed. They each go off, in different direc-
tions; Remus runs into them, and the booty is recovered. When he's
returned, he takes the hissing entrails off the spits and says: 'These,
375 for certain, none but the victor shall eat.' What he's said he does, and
so do the Fabii.*

Romulus arrives there without success, and sees the tables and the
bare bones. He laughed, and grieved that the Fabii and Remus had
been able to win, and his own Quintilii not. The fame of the event
380 survives: they run without clothes, and because it turned out well its
fame is remembered.

Perhaps you may ask too why that place is 'Lupercal', or what reason
marks the day with such a name.

Silvia the Vestal, whose uncle* held the kingdom, had given birth
385 to heavenly seed. He orders the little ones to be carried off and killed
in the river. What are you doing? One of those two is going to be
Romulus! Reluctant, the servants carry out (yet they weep) their tear-
ful orders, and take the twins to a lonely spot.

The Albula, which was made Tiber by the drowning of Tiberinus
390 in its waves, happened to be swollen with winter floods. Here you
might see boats moving about where the *fora* are now, and where your
valley lies, Great Circus. When they've reached that point, for they
can't proceed any further, a couple of them say:

395 'But how alike they are! But how handsome each of them is! And
yet of the two that one has the more liveliness. If breeding is proved
by looks, and appearances aren't deceptive, I suspect some god or
other is in you. But if some god were responsible for your birth, he'd
400 be bringing you help at such a desperate time. Your mother for sure
would bring help if she didn't need help herself, she who was made a
mother and childless in a single day. Bodies born together, about to
die together, go beneath the waves together!'

He had ceased, and he laid them down from his arms. They both

cried alike. You would think they understood. The servants return to   405
their homes, their cheeks wet.

The hollow vessel they've been put in keeps them afloat on the
water. Alas, what a weight of destiny a little piece of wood has carried!
Driven towards shady woods, the vessel rests in mud as the river   410
gradually recedes.

There was a tree. Traces of it still remain, and what now is called
the Ruminal fig-tree used to be the Romulean. A miracle! There came
to the abandoned twins a she-wolf that had just given birth. Who
would believe the wild beast didn't harm the children? Not enough   415
not to harm them, she even helps them. Those whom the she-wolf
suckles the hands of a kinsman had the will to destroy.

She stood still. With her tail she caresses her tender nurslings, and
shapes their two bodies with her tongue. You would know they were
sons of Mars: they had no fear. They pull on her teats and are nour-   420
ished with a supply of milk promised not to them. She made a name
for the place, the place itself for the Luperci.* Great is the reward the
foster-mother has for the milk she gave.

What prevents the Luperci having been named from the Arcadian.
mountain? Lycaean Faunus* has temples in Arcadia.

Bride, what are you waiting for? You won't be a mother through strong   425
herbs, or prayer, or magic incantations. Submit with patience to the
blows of a right hand that fertilizes, and soon your father-in-law will
have the longed-for name of grandfather.

For that day was when by harsh chance wives rarely delivered
the pledges of their womb. This happened when Romulus was hold-   430
ing the sceptre. 'What good does it do me,' he used to cry, 'to have
carried off the Sabine women, if my act of wrong has produced not
strength but war? It would have been more useful to have done with-
out daughters-in-law!'

Beneath the Esquiline mount there was a grove, uncut in many years,   435
named after mighty Juno. When they had come here, brides and husbands
alike went down on bended knee in supplication; then suddenly the tops
of the trees trembled and shook, and through her grove the goddess spoke   440
wondrous words: 'Let the sacred he-goat enter the Italian matrons.'

The crowd was stunned, terrified at the ambiguous utterance.
There was an augur—his name has been lost in the long years—a recent
arrival, an exile from Etruscan soil. He slaughters a he-goat. Under   445

orders, the girls offered their backs to be beaten with strips cut from the hide.

The moon in her tenth course was renewing her horns, and suddenly the husband was a father, the wife a mother. Thanks to Lucina!
450 The grove gave you this name,* or it's because you, goddess, have the beginning of the light. Kindly Lucina, be merciful, I pray, to pregnant girls, and when the burden is ready take it gently from the womb.

Once the day has dawned, you should stop trusting in the winds; the
455 breeze of that season has lost trustworthiness. The blasts are not reliable, and for a six-day period the unbarred door of Aeolus' prison is open wide.

Now Aquarius has set, light with his tilted urn; Fish, be the next to receive the heavenly horses.* They say that you and your brother (for
460 you sparkle as constellations side by side) have supported two gods on your back.

Dione once was fleeing from dreadful Typhon, at the time when Jupiter took arms in defence of the sky. She came to the Euphrates, accompanied by little Cupid, and sat down at the edge of the
465 Palestinian water. Poplars and reeds held the top of the banks, and willows gave hope that they too could be concealed.

While she lay hidden, the grove rustled in the wind. Pale with fear, she believes bands of enemies are upon her. And as she held her son
470 in her arms, she says: 'Come to our aid, nymphs, and bring help for two gods.' No delay, she leapt forward, the twin fishes came up beneath her. In return for that, you see, now the stars have the name.

Hence the timid Syrians think it sacrilege to put this species on their tables, and do not defile their mouths with fish.

475 [17 February] The next day is empty, but the third is dedicated to Quirinus. He was Romulus before, and he bears this name either because a spear was called 'curis' by the ancient Sabines (the warlike god came to the stars through weaponry), or because the Quirites
480 attached their own name to their king, or because he had joined Cures to the Romans.

For after his father, powerful in arms, saw the new walls and the many wars carried through by Romulus' hand,

'Jupiter,' says he, 'the power of Rome has strength. It doesn't need
485 my offspring's services. Give the son back to his father. Though one

of the two has perished, the one I still have will stand for himself and
for Remus. "There will be one whom you will raise into the blue
heaven."* That's what you told me: let Jupiter's words be fulfilled.'

Jupiter had nodded assent. At his nod both poles were shaken, and   490
Atlas was aware of heaven's weight.

There's a place the ancients called the She-goat's Marsh. It hap-
pened, Romulus, that there you were dispensing justice to your peo-
ple. The sun vanishes. Clouds come up and blot out the sky. The
heavy rain falls down, the water streaming. On this side it thunders,   495
on that the upper air is split by bursts of lightning. Everyone flees.
The king was seeking the stars with his father's horses.

There was grief, and the Fathers were falsely accused of murder,
and perhaps that suspicion would have stuck in people's minds. But
Julius Proculus was coming from Alba Longa; the moon was shining   500
and he had no need of a torch, when the hedges suddenly shook and
trembled to his left; he took a step back, and his hair stood on end.
Handsome, larger than life, resplendent in his *trabea*, Romulus seemed
to be there in the middle of the road, and to have spoken as well: 505
'Forbid the Quirites to mourn, and let them not violate my divinity
with their tears. Let them bring incense, let the pious crowd appease
the new Quirinus, and let them cultivate my father's military arts.'

He gave his orders and vanished from sight into thin air. Proculus
calls the People together and reports the words that were ordered.   510
A temple is built for the god; the hill too has its name from him, and
fixed days bring back the paternal rites.

Learn too why the same day is called the fools' festival. There's a rea-
son for it—trivial, yes, but appropriate.

The land in ancient times did not have expert farmers. Harsh wars   515
used to wear out the able-bodied men; there was more glory in the
sword than in the curved plough. The field, neglected, produced little
for its master. But the ancients did sow spelt, and spelt they reaped,
and harvested spelt they gave as first-fruits to Ceres. Taught by ex-   520
perience, they exposed it to the flames to be roasted, and many losses
they suffered by their own mistake. For sometimes they used to sweep
up black ashes instead of spelt, and sometimes the fire caught hold of
the huts themselves.

Oven was made a goddess. Delighting in Oven, the farmers prayed   525
that she would control the heat to their crop. Now the *curio maximus*

announces Oven's festival in words prescribed by law, and he holds
the rites on no fixed day. In the *forum* many little boards hang all
530 around, and each *curia* is indicated by a specific mark. The foolish
ones among the People don't know which *curia* is theirs, but perform
the traditional rites on the very last day.

[21 February] There is honour paid also to tombs—appeasing the
paternal spirits and bringing small gifts* to the pyres erected for
535 them. Small things are what the *manes* ask for; devotion pleases them,
rather than a costly gift. Styx in the depths has no greedy gods.

A tile covered with a spread of garlands is enough, and a sprinkling
of corn and a meagre grain of salt, and Ceres softened in wine and a
540 scattering of violets. Let a clay vessel contain these, left in the middle
of the road. Not that I forbid bigger things; but even by these a ghost
can be appeased. Add prayers and appropriate words when the bra-
ziers have been set up.

This practice Aeneas, a fitting author of devotion, brought to your
545 lands, just Latinus. He used to bring the due gifts to his father's *ge-
nius*. From this the peoples learned the rituals of devotion.

But once, while they were engaged in lengthy wars with weapons
of battle, they neglected the Parental days.* It didn't go unpunished,
550 for it is said that from that omen Rome grew hot with funeral pyres
around the city.

For my part, I hardly believe it. Forefathers are said to have come
out of their graves and complained in the silent night-time, and
through the streets of the city and the broad fields they say misshapen
555 spirits howled, a phantom crowd. After that the omitted honours are
restored to the tombs, and a limit comes to both portents and
funerals.

But you unmarried girls, do nothing while these rites are taking
place. Let the pine torch* wait for days that are untainted. Though
560 your eager mother will think you ripe for marriage, don't let the bent-
back spear comb your virgin hair.* Hide your torches, Hymenaeus,
and take them away from these black fires. Mournful tombs have
torches of a different kind.

Let the gods be hidden too, the doors of their temples closed; let
the altars be without incense and the hearths stand without fire. It is
565 now that phantom spirits roam about, and bodies that have experi-
enced burial. It is now that the ghost feeds on the food put out.

But this goes no further than when there remain as many Light-bringers in the month as there are feet in my song.* They called this day Feralia because they bring due offerings. It is the last day for 570 appeasing the *manes*.

Here sits an old lady, full of years, with girls all round her. She's performing the rites of the Silent Goddess (though she herself is hardly silent!), and with three fingers she puts three pieces of incense under the threshold, where a little mouse has made a hidden way for himself. Then she fastens enchanted threads with dark lead, rolls 575 seven black beans in her mouth, and roasts on the fire the stitched-up head of a small fish which she has sealed with pitch and pierced with a bronze needle. She drops wine on it too. Whatever wine is left over she or her companions drink, but she drinks more. 'We've bound up 580 hostile tongues and unfriendly mouths,' she says as she leaves, and away the old lady goes, drunk.

At once you'll be asking me who the Silent Goddess is. Learn what I found out from the old men of former times.

Jupiter, overcome by excessive love for Juturna, put up with many things 585 that so great a god shouldn't have to endure. At one moment she'd be hiding in the woods among the hazel thickets, at another she'd be leaping down into her sisters' waters. He calls together all the nymphs who lived in Latium, and amid their dancing chorus hurls these words: 590

'Your sister spites herself, and avoids what is to her own advantage, joining limbs with the highest of the gods. Think about both our interests! For what will be my great pleasure will be your sister's great benefit. When she's fleeing, stand in her way at the edge of the bank, 595 so she doesn't plunge her body in the river water.'

He had spoken. All the nymphs of Tiber had nodded assent, and those who dwell in your chambers, goddess Ilia.

There happened to be a Naiad called Lara—but her ancient name 600 was the first syllable uttered twice, given because of her failing.* Often had Almo said to her, 'Daughter, hold your tongue,' and yet she didn't. As soon as she reached her sister Juturna's pools, 'Keep away from the banks!' she says, and repeats Jove's words. She even went to 605 Juno, and sympathizing with married ladies, 'It's the Naiad Juturna,' she says, 'that your husband loves.'

Jupiter swelled in rage. He tears out her tongue, that she used indiscreetly, and summons Mercury: 'Take her to the *manes*. That's

610 the proper place for silent ones. She'll be a nymph, but a nymph of
the infernal lake.'

Jupiter's orders are carried out. A grove received them as they
made their way. It's said that at that point she took the fancy of the
god who led her. He gets ready to use force, she pleads with her
expression instead of words, and struggles in vain to speak with her
615 silent mouth. She becomes pregnant and gives birth to twins, the
Lares who guard the crossroads and are always on watch in our city.

[22 February] Karistia is what caring kinsfolk have called the next
day, and a throng of relatives comes to the gods they share. Of course
620 it's a pleasure to turn one's face, away from tombs and relatives who
have died, directly to the living, and after the loss of so many to look
on what survives of one's own blood and reckon up degrees of
relationship.

Let those who are guiltless come. But the wicked brother, the
625 mother harsh to her own offspring, the one whose father is living too
long, the one who counts up his mother's years, the unjust mother-
in-law who hates her son's wife and gives her a hard time—let them
keep far, far away. Let the brothers descended from Tantalus stay
away, and Jason's wife, and the woman who gave toasted seeds* to the
tillers of the land, and Procne and her sister, and Tereus cruel to them
630 both, and anyone who increases his wealth through crime.

Be good, and give incense to the gods of the family; on that day in
particular, gentle Concord is said to be present. Make an offering of
food too, so that when the dish is presented it may nourish the Lares
in their tucked-up tunics, as a pledge of the respect they like.

635 And now, when damp night induces peaceful slumbers, as you are
about to pray, take a generous wine-cup in your hand and say:
'Blessings on you gods, and blessings on you, best Caesar, father of
the homeland.' The wine once poured, let the words be well-
omened.

[23 February] When the night has passed, let the god who by his
640 marker separates the fields be honoured with his customary tribute.
Terminus, whether you're a stone or a tree stump set deep in the
field, you too have divine power from of old.

Two landowners crown you from opposite sides, and bring you two
645 garlands and two cakes. An altar is set up; to this the rustic farmer's

wife herself brings, in a broken pot, fire taken from the warm hearth. The old man chops wood up small, piles the pieces skilfully, and struggles to fix branches in solid ground. Then he kindles the first flames with dry bark; his boy stands by and holds broad baskets in his hands. 650 Then, when three times he has thrown grain from these into the midst of the fire, his little daughter holds out sliced honeycombs.

Others hold cups of wine; a libation from each is poured on the flames. They look on, a company in white, and keep reverent silence.

Shared Terminus is sprinkled also with a slaughtered lamb—and 655 he doesn't complain when a sucking pig is given him. The simple neighbourhood assembles and joins in a feast, and they sing your praises, holy Terminus:

'You set the bounds of peoples, cities and vast kingdoms. Without you every field will be a source of quarrels. You have no favouritism, 660 nor are you bribed by any gold; with confidence in the law you keep safe the fields entrusted to you.

'If once upon a time you had marked out the land of Thyrea, three hundred bodies would not have been sent to death, and Othryades' 665 name would not have been read on the piled-up weapons.* O how much blood did he give for his native land!

'What about when the new Capitol was being built? Yes, of course the whole company of gods yielded to Jupiter and gave the place to him; Terminus, as the men of old tell the tale, was found in the building and stayed there, and he holds the temple along with mighty 670 Jupiter. Even now, so he may see above him nothing but the stars, the roof of the temple has a tiny opening.

'After that, Terminus, you have no freedom to be restless. Remain on station where you have been placed! Don't yield anything to the 675 neighbour who asks you to, lest you should seem to have put a mortal before Jupiter. And whether you're beaten with ploughshares or hoes, you must shout, "This field's yours, and yours is that one!".'

There is a road that takes the People into the Laurentine fields, realms once sought by the Dardanian leader. On it, Terminus, the sixth 680 milestone from the city witnesses sacrifice made to you with the entrails of a woolly sheep. Other nations have been allotted land with a fixed boundary. The city of Rome's extent is the same as the world's.

[24 February] Now I must tell of the flight of the king.* From that 685 the sixth day from the end of the month has taken its name.

The last royal authority over the Roman race was held by Tarquinius, a man unjust but powerful in warfare. Some cities he had 690 captured, others destroyed, and Gabii he had made his own by a base stratagem.

For the youngest of his three sons, obvious offspring of Superbus, comes into the midst of the enemy in the silent night. They had unsheathed their swords. 'Kill an unarmed man,' he said; 'that's what 695 my brothers would wish, and Tarquinius my father, who tore my back with a cruel flogging.' And he had endured flogging, to be able to say this.

It was moonlight. They look at the young man and sheathe their swords, and when his clothes are pulled down they see his scarred back. They even weep, and beg him to join them in guarding against 700 war. He is cunning, the men are unaware. He agrees.

Powerful by now, sending a friend he applies to his father, to ask what route he might show him to destroy Gabii.

There was a garden close by, well tended with fragrant plants, its ground divided by a stream of gently murmuring water. There 705 Tarquinius receives his son's secret despatches, and with his stick he crops the heads of the lilies. When the messenger has returned, and spoken of the lilies cut down, 'I recognize,' says the son, 'my father's orders.' No delay: the leading men of the city of Gabii are killed, and 710 the walls, stripped of their leaders, are surrendered.

Here's a monstrous sight! A snake emerges from among the altars; the fires are extinguished, it seizes the entrails. Phoebus is consulted.* The oracular response is this: 'Who first gives kisses to his mother, he shall be the victor.'

715 Each man hurried to kiss his mother, a company trusting a god they had not understood. Brutus was wise, but imitating a fool in order to be safe from your plots, terrible Superbus. Lying face-down 720 he gave his kisses to mother Earth; it was assumed he had caught his foot and fallen flat.

Meanwhile, Ardea is ringed by Roman standards, and endures a long-protracted siege.* While there's nothing happening and the enemy are afraid of joining battle, the soldiers amuse themselves in 725 the camp and while away their time. The young Tarquinius entertains his companions with feasting and drinking. From among them the king's son says:

'While Ardea is keeping us on edge in a tedious war, and doesn't let us take our weapons back to our native gods, is the marital bed really as it should be? And are we really loved in return by our wives?' 730

Each praises his own wife. Their rivalry grows with eagerness, and both tongue and heart are heated with plentiful wine. Up gets the one to whom Collatia had given a famous name.

'No need for words,'* says he, 'put your trust in facts. There's still 735 night left. Let's mount horses and make for the city!'

His words are approved, the horses are bridled. They had taken their masters all the way. The men make straight for the king's house. No guard was at the door, and look! They find the king's daughter-in-law up late, garlands draped all round her neck, with wine served neat. 740

From there, at full speed, Lucretia is their goal. Before her couch were baskets and soft wool. By a small light the maids were spinning their allotted tasks. Amongst them their mistress is saying softly:

'A cloak made by our own hands must be sent to your master as 745 soon as may be. Now, girls, hurry now! But what do you hear, for you can hear more than I can? How much of the war do they say is left? Presently, Ardea, you will be conquered and fall; shamelessly you resist your betters, you who force our menfolk to be away. 750

'May they only come back! But of course that man of mine is reckless, and rushes with drawn sword anywhere he chooses. Whenever the image of him fighting comes to me, my mind is gone and I die; an icy cold takes hold of my breast.'

She ends in tears. She let go the threads she had started and put her 755 face in her lap. That itself was proper; her tears were proper for a modest woman and her face was worthy of her spirit, and matched it.

'Put aside your fear, I have come,' says her husband. She revived, and hung, a sweet burden, from her husband's neck. 760

Meanwhile the royal youth conceives the fires of frenzy and rages, seized by blind passion. Her figure delights him, and her snowy complexion and her golden hair and the charm she had, created by no art. Her words delight him, and her voice and her uncorruptibility. The 765 smaller his hope, the more he desires.

The bird that first announces daylight had already uttered its song when the young men make their way back to camp. His stunned senses are consumed by the image of the absent woman. There's more 770 to please him as he thinks about her, and the pleasure is greater. That's how she sat, that's how she was dressed, that's how she spun the yarn, that's how her hair fell and lay about her neck. These were the looks she had, these were her words, this her complexion, this her appearance, this the charm of her face.

775   Just as after a great gale the sea-surge will grow calmer, but yet the wave swells from the wind that has been, so, although the presence of the delightful beauty was no longer there, the passion it had aroused when it was there still remained. He burns, and driven by the goads
780   of wicked desire he plans violence and fear for a bed that does not deserve it.

'The outcome is in doubt,' he said. 'We'll dare the utmost. Let her look out! Chance and god help those who dare. By daring we took Gabii too.' So saying, he belted his sword to his side and mounted his horse.

785   Collatia receives the young man through its brazen gate just as the sun is preparing to hide its face. An enemy as a guest,* he enters the privacy of Collatinus' house. He is received courteously: he was a blood relative. How much are minds mistaken! Unaware of what is
790   happening, the luckless woman prepares a meal for her own enemies.*

He had finished the meal. The right time calls for sleep. It was night, and in the whole house there were no lights.

He gets up, frees his sword from its gilded sheath, and comes,
795   chaste wife, into your chamber. And when he's mounted the bed, the king's son says: 'Lucretia, I have my sword with me, and I who speak am Tarquinius.'

Nothing from her, for she has no voice, no power to speak and no thought in all her heart. But she trembles, as sometimes a little lamb
800   that has strayed from the fold and been seized trembles as it lies under a savage wolf. What is she to do? Fight? If a woman fights she'll be overpowered. Cry out? But in his right hand the sword was there to stop that. Run away? Her breasts are forced down by the pressure of his hands—breasts then for the first time touched by the hand of a stranger.

805   An enemy as a lover, he persists, with prayers and bribery and threats; but neither with prayer nor bribery nor threats does he move her.

'It's no good,' he said. 'I'll take your life through accusations. I, the adulterer, will be false witness to adultery. I'll kill a slave, and it'll be said you were caught with him.'

Overcome by fear for her reputation, the young woman yielded. 810
Victor, why rejoice? This victory will be your ruin. Alas, how much
a single night has cost your kingdom!

And now the day had dawned. She sits with her hair loose, as
a mother does when about to go to her son's funeral pyre, and she
summons from the camp her aged father and her faithful husband. 815
Each of them came, letting nothing delay them.

And when they see the state she is in, they ask the reason for her
grief. Whose funeral is she preparing, what misfortune has struck
her? For a long time she is silent, and full of shame hides her face with
her robe. Her tears flow like a never-ending stream. Her father on one 820
side, her husband on the other comfort her tears and beg her to speak
out; they are weeping and pale with blind fear.

Three times she tried to speak, three times she stopped. She sum-
moned her courage a fourth time, but even so she did not raise her
eyes.

'Shall we owe this too to Tarquinius?' she says. 'Shall I speak it 825
aloud—myself, unhappy woman, speak aloud my own disgrace?'

What she can, she tells. The last part stayed untold. She wept, and
the cheeks of a married lady blushed. Father and husband pardon
what she has done; she was forced to do it. 'The pardon you give,' she 830
said, 'I myself refuse.'

There is no pause; she has stabbed her breast with a hidden blade,
and falls in her blood at her father's feet. Even at that moment, already
dying, she takes care not to fall unseemly; this too mattered to her as
she fell.

There they are, husband and father, lying on top of the body with 835
propriety forgotten, bemoaning the loss they share. Brutus is present,
and at last with his courage belies his name. He seizes the weapon
fixed in the half-dead body, and holding the knife that dripped with
noble blood he uttered fearless words from menacing lips: 840

'I swear to you by this brave and virtuous blood, and by your *manes*,
which for me will be a god, that Tarquinius will pay the penalty along
with his banished line. For long enough now manly courage has been
concealed.'

The woman lying there moved her sightless eyes at his words, and 845
seemed by her shaken hair to approve what he said. A wife with the
courage of a man, she is borne to her funeral and draws tears and
indignation with her. The gaping wound is exposed.

850   Brutus rouses the Quirites with a cry, and reports the king's abominable deeds. Tarquinius flees with his sons. A consul takes the judgement seat for a year. That was the final day of the rule of kings.

Am I mistaken, or has the swallow come that first announces spring,
855   unafraid that winter may turn and come back? Yet often, Procne, you'll complain that you were too hasty, and your husband Tereus will be glad of the cold you feel.

[27 February] And now two nights remain of the second month, and Mars has yoked his chariot and is urging his swift horses on. The Equirria—the truthfully given name* has persisted—are what
860   the god himself looks out at on his plain. You come by right, Gradivus: your time demands its place, and the month marked with your name is here.

We've come into harbour, the book completed with the month. From here let my boat now sail in different waters.

BOOK 3

MARCH

WARLIKE Mars, put aside for a while your shield and your spear. Be present, and release your shining hair from the helmet.

Perhaps you may do the asking: what has a poet to do with Mars? The month that's being sung has its name from you. You see yourself 5 that fierce wars are carried out by Minerva's hands; surely she has no less time to devote to the liberal arts? Follow Pallas' example, take times to put your lance aside. You'll find something to do unarmed, as well. You were unarmed on that occasion too, when the Roman priestess captured you so you might give this city great seed. 10

Silvia the Vestal (for what forbids a start being made from her?) was going to fetch water in the morning, to wash the sacred things. She had come to a sloping bank, with an easy way down. The earthenware pot is set down from the top of her hair.

Weary, she sat down on the ground, and uncovering her breast she 15 welcomed the breezes and set to rights her tousled hair. While she was sitting, the shady willows and the tuneful birds and the gentle murmur of the water brought on sleep. Soothing rest crept up on her eyes, having stealthily overpowered them, and her hand, made lan- 20 guid, falls from her chin.

Mars sees her, desires what he's seen, and takes possession of what he's desired; and with his divine power he concealed his stealthy deeds. Sleep departs. There she lies, pregnant. Of course: already the founder of the Roman city was within her flesh. She rises languid, 25 and doesn't know why she rises languid, and leaning on a tree she goes through a speech like this:

'I pray it may be propitious and fortunate, what I saw in the vision of sleep. Or was that too vivid for sleep? I was on duty at the Ilian fires,* when the woollen headband slipped from my hair and fell down 30 in front of the sacred hearth. From there, amazing to behold, two palm trees rise up together. One of them was bigger, and with its heavy branches had covered the whole world, and with its foliage had touched the highest stars. Look! My uncle* wields a blade against 35

them. I am terrified at the recollection, my heart quivers in fear.
A woodpecker, bird of Mars, and a she-wolf fight for the twin trunks.
By their doing both palm trees were safe.'

She finished speaking, and lifted the full pot with an unsteady
40 effort. She had filled it while relating what she had seen. Meanwhile,
as Remus grew and Quirinus grew, her belly was swollen with a heav-
enly weight.

There were now two signs left for the shining god before the year
45 could depart, having served out its course. Silvia becomes a mother.
The images of Vesta are said to have put their virginal hands before
their eyes. Certainly the goddess's altar shook as her priestess was
giving birth, and its flame sank in terror beneath its own ashes.

When Amulius, despiser of justice, found out about this (for as
50 victor he held the power he had seized from his brother), he orders
the twins to be drowned in the river. The water shrank from the
crime; the children are abandoned on dry land. Who does not know
that the infants grew on the milk of a wild creature, and that a wood-
pecker often brought the foundlings food?

55   Let me not fail to mention you, Larentia, nurse of so great a race,
nor your help, humble Faustulus. Your tribute will come when I tell of
the Larentalia. December, dear to the *genii*, has that festival.

The offspring of Mars had grown thrice-six years, and already
60 a new beard had come beneath their golden hair. The brothers, sons
of Ilia, used to give judgements, when they were asked for, to all the
farmers and the masters of the herds. Often they come home rejoic-
ing in the blood of robbers, and drive driven cattle back into their own
65 fields. When they have heard of their descent, the revealed father
boosts their spirits and they're ashamed to have a name among just
a few huts.

Amulius falls, run through by Romulus' sword, and the kingdom
is restored to their aged grandfather. Walls are founded, across which,
70 however small they were, it did Remus no good to have leaped. What
had recently been woods and the haunts of cattle was already a city,
when the father of the eternal city says:

'Ruler of arms, from whose blood I am believed to be born—and
75 I will give many proofs of that belief—from you we name the start of
the Roman year. The first month shall be from my father's name.'

His word is fulfilled; he calls the month from his father's name.
This act of devotion is said to have pleased the god.

Yet earlier people too worshipped Mars above all; this worship a war- 80
like crowd had given with their zealous attention.

Pallas is worshipped by the sons of Cecrops, Diana by Minoan
Crete, Vulcan by the land of Hypsipyle, Juno by Sparta and Mycenae,
descendant of Pelops, and the pine-wreathed head of Faunus by the
region of Maenalus. For Latium Mars was the one to be revered, 85
because he presides over arms; arms give the fierce race both power
and glory.

But if you happen to have time, examine non-Roman calendars: in
these too there will be a month by the name of Mars. It was the third
month for the Albans, the fifth for the Faliscans, the sixth among your 90
peoples, land of the Hernici. There is agreement between the Aricini
and the Alban times, and the high walls made by Telegonus' hand.
The Laurentes have it as the fifth, the fierce Aequicoli the tenth, the
crowd of Cures the first after three. And you, Paelignian soldier, agree 95
with your Sabine forefathers: for both these races the god is fourth.
To beat all these, at least in order, Romulus gave the first times to the
author of his blood.

The ancients did not have the same number of Kalends as now;
that year was shorter by twin months. Greece, an eloquent but uncour- 100
ageous race, had not yet handed over its vanquished arts to the vic-
tors. He who fought well knew the Roman art; he who could hurl
javelins was eloquent.

Who at that time had noticed the Hyades or the Pleiades, daugh- 105
ters of Atlas, or that there are twin poles under the sky, that there are
two Bears (one of them, Cynosura, to be tracked by the Sidonians,
the other, Helice, for the Greek ship to observe),* that the signs which
the brother travels through in a long year, the sister's horses* pass 110
through in one month? The stars ran free and unobserved through-
out the year. But yet it was agreed that they were gods.

They didn't grasp the signs gliding in the sky, but signs of their
own,* to lose which was a great offence. True, they were made of hay, 115
but hay used to have as much respect as you now see your eagles get-
ting. A long pole used to carry bundles hung on it, from which the
'manipular' soldier gets his name.* So minds that were untutored and
still lacking reason passed *lustra* that were ten months too short. 120

A year was when the moon had recovered her tenth orb. This
number was held in great honour at that time, either because that is
the number of the fingers we usually count with, or because in the

125 tenth month a woman gives birth, or because as the count increases
we get as far as ten and begin again from there on a fresh course.

Hence Romulus divided the hundred Fathers into circles of ten
each, and he instituted the ten *hastati*, and the *principes* and the *pilani*
130 had the same number of bodies, and those who were serving on horse-
back as required by law. Not only that, but he gave the same number
of divisions to the Titienses, to those they call Ramnes, and to the
Luceres. That is why he kept the accustomed numbers in the year.
This is the length of time a grieving woman mourns her husband.

135 Lest you should doubt that the Kalends of March were previously
the first, you can turn your attention to these indications. The *flamines'*
laurel, which has stayed there the whole year, is removed, and fresh
foliage is honoured. At that time the door of the *rex* is green, when
140 Phoebus' tree is in place. The same thing happens before your doors,
ancient *curia*. So Vesta too may shine, veiled in fresh leaves, the faded
laurel withdraws from the Ilian hearths. Add the fact that a new fire is
said to be made in the secret shrine, and the flame, renewed, gains
strength.

145 No small proof for me that the years of old went from this point is
the fact that in this month Anna Perenna began to be worshipped.
From this point too the magistrates of old are said to have entered
office, until the period of your war, faithless Carthaginian. Finally,
Quintilis had been the fifth month from this one, and starting from
150 there, each has its name from a number.*

The first to realize that two months were missing was Pompilius,
brought to Rome from the fields where the olives grow—either
because he'd been taught this by the man of Samos who thinks we can
be born again,* or on the advice of his own Egeria.

155 But all the same, even now the times were in error until this too
became one of Caesar's many concerns. He, a god and the founder of
so great a stock, did not believe these matters too small for his atten-
tion; he wanted to discover in advance what the heaven promised to
160 him, and not, as a god, be a stranger entering unknown homes. It is
said that with precise notation he set out the sun's delays, by which it
returns into its own signs. To three hundred and five days he added
165 ten times six, and a fifth part of a full day. This is the limit of a year;
a single day, to be compounded from the fractions, has to be added to
the *lustrum*.

[1 **March**] If bards are allowed to hear the secret advice of the gods, as rumour certainly thinks they are, tell me, Gradivus, since you are suited to men's occupations, why do married ladies keep your festivals? 170 That's what I asked, and this is what Mavors said to me after putting down his helmet (but the throwing spear was in his right hand all the same):

'Now for the first time, a god useful in arms, I am called on for the pursuits of peace, and march my way into a new camp. I don't resent 175 the undertaking. I am happy to spend time in this sector too, lest Minerva think that she alone can do it. Learn what you ask, industrious bard of the Latin days, and mark my words in your retentive heart.

'Rome, should you want to go back to the very beginning, was small. But even so, in that small Rome was the hope of this one. City 180 walls were already standing, cramped for the populations of the future but then believed too spacious for their crowd. If you ask what my son's palace was, look at the house of reed and straw.* On stubble he 185 would enjoy the gifts of peaceful sleep, and yet from that bed he reached the stars.

'Already the Roman possessed a name greater than the place, but had neither wife nor any father-in-law. Wealthy neighbours spurned poor sons-in-law, and I was hardly believed to be the author of their 190 blood. It harmed them to have lived in cattle-sheds and pastured sheep, and to hold a few acres of uncultivated soil. Birds and wild beasts too mate each with its own match, and even a snake has a female from which to procreate. Distant peoples are granted the right of intermar- 195 riage; and yet there was no woman who was willing to marry a Roman.

'I felt the pain, and I gave you, Romulus, your father's mind. "Be done with prayers," I said, "arms will give what you seek."

'He prepares a festival for Consus. Consus will tell you the rest while singing his own rites held on that day.* 200

'Cures swelled with rage, and those whom the same pain afflicted. That was the first time a father-in-law made war on sons-in-law.* And now the women who had been more or less abducted were bearing also the name of mothers, and the war between neighbours dragged on and on.

'The wives gather in the temple dedicated to Juno. Among them my 205 daughter-in-law* was bold enough to speak like this: "Women who were snatched like me, since we have this in common, no longer can we be slow to do our duty. There stand the battle lines—but choose which

²¹⁰ side we should ask the gods to favour! The weapons are held by a hus-
band here, a father there. The question is whether you'd rather be wid-
ows or orphans. I shall give you a plan which is brave and dutiful."

'She had given them the plan. They obey, and loosen their hair and
²¹⁵ cover their sorrowful bodies in mourning-clothes. Already the battle
lines had stood prepared for death by the sword, already the trumpet
was about to give the battle signal, when the abducted women come
between their fathers and their husbands, and hold in their arms their
children, pledges of love.

'When they reached the middle of the plain, their hair torn about,
²²⁰ they went down on the ground on bended knee, and the grandchil-
dren, as if they realized, with engaging cries began to stretch out their
little arms to their grandfathers. The child who could began calling
his grandfather, seen at long last. The child who hardly could was
forced to be able to.

²²⁵ 'The men's weapons and anger fall, and putting aside their swords,
fathers-in-law give their hands to sons-in-law and receive theirs in
return. They praise their daughters, and hold them, and on his shield
the grandfather carries his grandson. That was a sweeter use for
a shield.

²³⁰ 'Hence the Oebalian mothers hold it as no light duty to celebrate
the day which is first, my Kalends. Either because by daring to risk
themselves before drawn sword-points they had put an end with their
tears to the wars of Mars, or because Ilia was happily a mother by me,
mothers duly observe the rites and my day.

²³⁵ 'What of the fact that then frost-covered winter finally gives way,
and the snows perish, melted in the warming sun; that leaves shorn
by the cold return to the trees, and the bud swells moist on the tender
²⁴⁰ vine; that the fertile grass that has long lain hidden now finds secret
paths to raise itself into the breezes? Now the field is fruitful, now is
the hour for breeding cattle, now the bird prepares its shelter and
home on the branch.

'Rightly do the Latin mothers observe the fruitful times. Their
²⁴⁵ childbearing involves fighting and prayers. Add the fact that where
the Roman king kept watch,* the hill that now has the name of
Esquiline, there a public temple to Juno was set up by the young Latin
wives, if I remember, on this day.

'Why do I linger, and burden your mind with various reasons? See,
²⁵⁰ what you seek stands out before your eyes. My mother loves brides;

my mother's crowd* frequents me. This reason, so dutiful, is espe-
cially fitting for us.'

Bring flowers for the goddess; this goddess delights in flowering
plants. Wreathe your heads with the delicate flowers. Say: 'You have 255
given us the light, Lucina.' Say: 'Be present for the prayer of a woman
giving birth.' But if any woman is pregnant, let her release her hair
and pray that the goddess may gently ease her delivery.

Now, who will tell me why the *salii* carry heavenly armour of Mars 260
and sing Mamurius? Advise me, nymph, you who are busy with
Diana's grove and lake; nymph, Numa's consort, come to your own
deeds.
    In the Arician vale, encircled by a dark wood, there is a lake, hal-
lowed in ancient sanctity. Here Hippolytus lies hidden, torn apart by 265
the reins of his horses, for which reason no horses approach that
wood. Threads hang down, veiling the long hedges, and many a tablet
has been set up there for the deserving goddess. Often a woman, hav-
ing gained what she prayed for, her brow wreathed with garlands,
carries shining torches from the city. 270
    Royal power is held by those who have strong hands and runaway
feet, and each one perishes* in succession after his own example.
    A stony stream flows down, murmuring indistinctly. I have
often drunk from it, but with tiny sips. Egeria it is who supplies the 275
waters, a goddess dear to the Camenae; she was Numa's consort and
counsel.

In the beginning the Quirites were too ready to go to war. It was
decided that they should be tamed with the rule of law and the fear of
the gods. Hence laws were made, to prevent the stronger having all
power, and rituals handed down began to be scrupulously observed. 280
Savagery is stripped away, equity is more powerful than weapons, it is
a source of shame to have come to blows with a fellow-citizen, and
a person once violent is now changed, having seen the altar, and offers
wine and salted spelt on the warm hearths.
    Look! The father of the gods scatters red flames through the clouds 285
and dries up the heavens with outpourings of rain. Never before did
the hurled fires fall more thickly. The king is afraid, and terror holds
the hearts of the crowd.

'Don't be too fearful,' says the goddess to him. 'The thunderbolt
290 can be expiated, and fierce Jupiter's anger is averted. But Picus and
Faunus will be able to pass on the expiation ritual, each of them
a divinity of the Roman soil. They won't pass it on without force:
catch them and put shackles on them.' And this is how she explained
by what trick they can be caught.

295   There was a grove below the Aventine, black with the shade of
holm-oak, at the sight of which you could say: 'There's a deity in it.'
In the middle there was grass, and covered in green moss a trickle of
never-failing water dripped from a rock. Faunus and Picus used to
drink from it, usually alone.

300   To this place comes king Numa, and sacrifices a sheep to the
spring, and sets out cups full of fragrant Bacchus, and then, together
with his men, he lurks concealed in a cave. The woodland deities
come to their usual springs, and refresh their dry hearts with copious
305 wine. Rest follows wine. Numa appears from the chilly cave and puts
the sleepers' hands in tight bonds. When sleep has departed, they try
to break the shackles by struggling; as they struggle, the shackles hold
them tighter. Then Numa says:

310   'Gods of the groves, if you know that wickedness is not in my nature,
forgive what I have done, and show by what means the thunderbolt can
be expiated.' Thus Numa. Thus says Faunus, shaking his horns:

'You're asking for big things, and what it's not lawful for you to
315 learn from our instruction. Our powers have their limits. We are gods
of the countryside and masters of the high hills. Jupiter's weapons are
under his own control. You won't be able to bring him down from
heaven by yourself, but if you use our help perhaps you will.'

That's what Faunus had said. Picus' opinion is the same. 'Just take
320 the shackles off us,' says Picus. 'Jupiter will come here, drawn by
powerful art. Cloudy Styx will be the witness of my promise.'

What they do when they are released from their bonds, what incan-
tations they utter, and by what art they drag Jupiter from his high
325 seat, it is unlawful for man to know. We'll sing what we're allowed,
and what may be spoken from the pious mouth of the bard.

They draw you out from heaven, Jupiter, which is why now too
posterity worships you and calls you Elicius.* It is agreed that the
330 tops of the Aventine wood trembled, and the earth sank under the
pressure of Jupiter's weight. The king's heart trembles, the blood

leaves his whole body, and his bristling hair has stood on end. When his wits returned, he said:

'King and father of the high gods, give us sure means of expiating the thunderbolt, if with pure hands we have touched your offerings, 335 if it's a pious tongue that asks this favour too.'

He nodded assent to the prayer, but hid the truth in distant ambiguity and terrified the man with a doubtful expression.

'Cut off a head,' he said. 'We shall obey,' the king answers him: 'what must be cut is an onion dug up in my garden.' 'A man's,' he 340 added. 'You'll get the hair,' says the other. He demands a life. 'A fish's,' Numa replies.

He laughed. 'See to it,' he says, 'that with these things you expiate my weapons, O mortal not to be barred from speaking with the gods. But when Cynthius tomorrow has produced his whole orb, I shall 345 give you sure pledges of empire.'

He spoke, and with an enormous clap of thunder he is carried above the shaken sky and leaves Numa worshipping him. Joyful, Numa returns and tells the Quirites what has taken place. Belief in his 350 words comes slowly and with difficulty.

'But certainly I shall be believed,' he says, 'if the outcome follows my words. All right! Everyone present, hear what will happen tomorrow. When Cynthius has produced his whole orb from the earth, Jupiter will give us sure pledges of empire.'

They depart in doubt. The promises seem slow, and belief hangs 355 on the coming day.

The earth was soft, the morning frost was sprinkled. The People are present before their king's threshold. He appears, and has taken his seat in their midst on a throne of maple wood. Unnumbered men 360 stand round him and keep silent. Phoebus had risen with just his upper edge. Anxious minds tremble with hope and fear.

He stood up, and with his head veiled in a snow-white mantle he lifted his hands,* already well known to the gods, and thus, 'The time 365 of the promised gift is near,' he says. 'Add to your words, Jupiter, the fulfilment that was guaranteed.'

While he was speaking, the sun had already brought out its whole orb, and a heavy crash came from the vault of heaven. Thrice the god thundered in a cloudless sky, three lightning bolts he sent. Believe me 370 as I say it: I speak of marvels but they happened.* The sky from its central part began to split open. The crowd with their leader lowered their eyes.

Look! Turning gently in the light breeze, down falls a shield. The
375 shout from the People reaches the stars. He lifts the gift from the ground—having first killed a heifer which had not given her neck to be weighed down by any yoke—and he calls it *ancile*, because it is cut away on every side,* and wherever you mark it with your eyes there is no angle at all.

380 Then, remembering that the fate of empire rests on it, he embarks on a plan of much ingenuity. He orders more to be made, embossed in the same shape, so that error may meet the eyes of a would-be thief. Mamurius—and it's hard to say whether he was more scrupulous in his character or his craftsman's skill—completed that work.

385 To him generous Numa said: 'Ask a reward for what you have done. If my honesty is well known, nothing you ask will be in vain.' He had already given the *salii* a name, derived from dancing,* and weapons, and words to be sung to specific measures. Then Mamurius
390 said this: 'As wages let glory be given me, and my name sound at the end of their hymn.'

Hence the priests pay the promised reward for the ancient work, and call on Mamurius.

If any of you girls wants to marry, postpone it, even if you're both
395 going to be in a hurry; small delays have great advantages. Weapons cause fights, and fighting is alien to a married couple. When they have been stored away, the omen will be more suitable.

On these days too, the girded wife of the peak-capped *Dialis* should have her hair uncombed.

[3 March] When the third night of the month has moved its risings,
400 one of the twin Fishes will be hidden from view. For there are two: one is neighbour to the Austri, one to the Aquilones. Each one has its name from a wind.

[5 March] When Tithonus' wife begins to drop dew from her saffron
405 cheeks and brings the times of the fifth day, whether the constellation is the Guardian of the Bear or lazy Boōtes, it will sink and escape from your sight. But the Grape-gatherer will not escape: it doesn't take long to explain from where this star too draws its reason.

It is said that Bacchus on the Ismarian hills loved unshorn Ampelos, 410
son of a satyr and a nymph. He entrusted to him a vine hanging from
the leafy branches of an elm; it now takes its name from the name of
the boy.* While he was recklessly gathering bright-coloured grapes
on a branch, down he fell. He was lost, and Liber raised him to the
stars.

[6 March] When the sixth Phoebus climbs from Ocean up steep 415
Olympus, and plies the bright air with his winged horses, whoever
you are who are present in worship at the sanctuary of chaste Vesta,
wish her joy and place incense on the Ilian hearths.

To Caesar's countless titles has been added the one he preferred
to be worthy of, the honour of *pontifex*. Over the eternal fires eternal 420
Caesar's divine powers preside. You see the pledges of empire*
joined.

Gods of ancient Troy, booty most fitting for him who carried you,
under the weight of which Aeneas was safe from the foe, a priest 425
sprung from Aeneas handles kindred deities. Vesta, protect your kins-
man's head! You fires, which he tends with hallowed hand, are alive
and well. Live on unextinguished, I pray, flame and leader alike.

[7 March] There's just one note for the Nones of March: they think
the temple of Veiovis in front of the Two Groves was consecrated on 430
the Nones.

When Romulus surrounded the grove with a high stone wall,
'Whoever you are,' he says, 'take refuge here; you'll be safe.' Oh, from
how slight an origin has the Roman grown, how unenviable was the
ancient multitude!

But lest the strangeness of the name be an obstacle to you in your 435
ignorance, learn who that god is and why he is so called. He is the
young Jupiter. Look at his youthful face, then look at his hand: it
holds no thunderbolts. Thunderbolts were taken up by Jupiter only
after the Giants had dared to make an attempt on heaven; in early 440
time he was unarmed. It was with new fires that Ossa blazed, and
Pelion higher than Ossa, and Olympus firmly set in solid ground.

A she-goat too stands with him. Cretan nymphs are said to have
fed him, and she gave her milk to the infant Jupiter. Now I am called 445
to the name. 'Vegrandia' is what farmers call spelt that has not grown
properly, and the small grain they call 'vesca'. If that is the force of

the word,* why should I not suspect that the temple of Veiovis is the temple of 'not-big' Jupiter?

450 And now when the stars spangle the blue heaven, look up. You'll see the neck of the Gorgon's horse. It is believed that he leapt forth, his mane blood-spattered, from the pregnant neck of slain Medusa. For him, gliding above the clouds and beneath the stars, the sky was like
455 solid ground, his wings like feet. Already he had taken the unfamiliar bridle in his protesting mouth when his light hoof dug the Aonian waters.* Now he enjoys the sky which once he sought with wings, and shining, glitters with fifteen stars.

[8 March] Straight away in the coming night you will see the Crown
460 of Cnossos. A goddess was made through Theseus' wrongdoing.*
    Already she had well exchanged her perjured husband for Bacchus—she who gave the ungrateful man threads to be gathered up.* Rejoicing in the luck of her marriage-bed, 'Why was I weeping,' she said, 'like a country girl? It worked out well for me that he was faithless.'
465   Liber meanwhile has conquered the combed-haired Indians, and comes back wealthy from the Eōan world. Among the captive girls, whose beauty was outstanding, there was a king's daughter who was too pleasing to Bacchus. His loving wife wept, and pacing along the
470 curving shore with her hair unkempt, she uttered words like these:
    'Again! Waves, listen to the same complaints. Again! Sand, receive my tears. I used to say, I remember, "Forsworn and faithless Theseus!"
475 He's gone, now Bacchus incurs the same charge. Now too I shall cry,* "Let no woman trust a man!" My case is back in court with the name changed. If only my fate had gone where it first began, and now at the present time I no longer existed! When I was about to die on the
480 lonely sands, why did you save me, Liber? I could have given over grieving once and for all.
    'Inconstant Bacchus, less constant than the leaves that bind your brow, Bacchus, known only for my tears, have you dared to bring your harlot before my eyes, and disturb a marriage-bed so well composed?
485 Alas, where is pledged faithfulness? Where are the oaths you used to swear? Wretched me! How often am I to say these words? It was Theseus you used to blame, you yourself used to call him deceitful. By your own judgement you're sinning more shamefully yourself.

'Let no one know this. Let me be burned in silent anguish, lest it be thought I deserved to be deceived so often. Especially let me desire 490 it to be kept from Theseus, so he may not rejoice that you are a partner in his guilt.

'But, I suppose, a fair-skinned harlot is preferred to swarthy me! May my enemies have that colour. But what does this matter? By the 495 blemish itself she's more pleasing to you. What are you doing? She pollutes your embraces. Keep your faith, Bacchus, and do not put any woman before the love of your wife. It has been my custom to love a man for ever.

'The horns of a handsome bull captured my mother;* yours captured me. But this love is laudable, that one was scandalous. Let it not 500 harm me that I love. It certainly didn't harm you, Bacchus, that you yourself confessed your flames for me. And you're not performing a miracle by making me burn: you're said to have been born in fire, and snatched from fire* by your father's hand.

'I am the woman to whom you used to promise heaven. Alas, in 505 place of heaven what kind of gifts do I get?'

She had spoken. For a long time Liber had been listening to her words of complaint, as by chance he had been following behind her. He holds her in his arms and dries her tears with kisses.

'Together,' he says, 'let us seek the heights of heaven. Joined to me 510 by the marriage-bed, you will take a title joined to me, for when you are changed your name will be Libera. And I shall bring it about that there is a memorial of you and of your crown, which Vulcan gave to Venus, she to you.'

He does as he says, and transforms the nine jewels into fires. 515 Golden now it sparkles with its nine stars.

[14 March] When he who carries the rosy day in his swift chariot has raised six orbs and submerged the same number, you will watch the second Equirria on the grassy Campus, which Tiber presses at 520 the side with his curving waters. But if it happens to be occupied by the overflowing wave, let the dusty Caelian receive the horses.

[15 March] On the Ides the cheerful festival of Anna Perenna takes place not far from your banks, arriving Thybris. The common people 525 come, and scattered all over the green grass they drink and lie down each with his partner. Some rough it under the sky, a few pitch tents;

for others a leafy hut has been made from branches; some, when
530 they've set up reeds as sturdy pillars, have stretched out togas and put
them on top.

What warms them, however, is the sun and the wine, and they pray
for as many years as the cupfuls they take, and drink counting the
number. You'll find there the man who drinks up Nestor's years, and
the woman who's become a Sibyl through her wine-cups.

535 There they sing whatever they've learned from the theatres, and
they move their hands easily in time to their words, and they put
down the wine-bowl and lead rough chorus lines, and the chic girl-
friend dances with her hair undone.

When they return they're staggering, and they're a sight for the
540 crowd to behold, and the people they meet call them the blessed
ones.* The procession met me recently (it seemed to me worth
reporting): a drunk old man was being pulled along by a drunk old
lady.

Which goddess is this, though? Since that varies in common talk,
no story must be concealed in my exposition.

545 Pitiable Dido had burned with fire for Aeneas, had burned on a pyre
built for her own death. Her ashes were collected, and on the marble
of her tomb was this short verse, which she herself left as she died:*

Aeneas gave both reason for death and a sword,
550 Dido herself fell using her own hand.

Numidians immediately invade the kingdom which has no
defender, and Iarbas the Moor takes possession of the captured house.
Remembering he had been rejected, 'Just look!' he says. 'I whom she
555 spurned so often am enjoying Elissa's bedchamber!' The Tyrians
scatter and flee wherever each man's wandering takes him, as some-
times bees roam uncertain when they have lost their king.

The third threshing floor had received its harvests to be winnowed,
and the third vintage had gone into the hollow vats. Anna is driven
560 from home, and weeping, leaves her sister's walls; before that, she
gives due rites to her sister. The soft ashes drink the perfumes mixed
with tears, and receive the hair cut as an offering from her head. Three
times she said 'Farewell'; three times she took the ashes and pressed
them to her lips, and her sister seemed to be there in them.

Having found a ship and companions for her flight, she sails before 565
the wind, looking back at the walls,* the dear work of her sister.

Near barren Cosyra is the fertile island of Melite, which is lashed
by the wave of the Libyan sea. She seeks it, trusting in its king's long-
standing hospitality; her host there was king Battus, rich in wealth. 570
When he learned what had happened to each of the sisters, 'This
land,' he says, 'is yours, however small.' And yes, he would have
observed a host's duty to the end, but he was afraid of the great power
of Pygmalion.

The sun had twice reviewed his constellations and the third year 575
was passing, and a new land has to be found for exile. Her brother
comes, and seeks her with war. The king detests weapons. 'We are
unwarlike,' he says; 'flee and be safe.' She flees as ordered, and
entrusts her ship to the wind and waves. Her brother was more cruel 580
than any sea.

Near the fish-filled streams of stony Crathis there is a small terri-
tory. The people who live there call it Camere. Her course was to that
place, and she was no further away from it than nine times what
a slingshot can throw. First the sails fall, and are held suspended by 585
a doubtful breeze. 'Cleave the waters with the oars,' the seaman said.
While they prepare to haul down the sails with twisted flax, the
curved stern is beaten by swift Notus and is carried into the open sea
as its master struggles in vain, and the land they had seen flees out of 590
their sight.

The waves leap up, the sea is churned from its lowest abyss, and
the hull drinks the white waters. Skill is defeated by wind, and the
helmsman no longer holds his reins, but he too prays and begs for
help. The Phoenician exile is tossed through the swelling waves and 595
covers her wet eyes by holding her dress against them. Then for the
first time Dido was called fortunate by her sister, and so was any
woman whose body rested on dry land anywhere. The ship is brought
towards the Laurentine shore by a huge blast of wind, and perishes 600
engulfed, though all on board are thrown out.

By now dutiful Aeneas had been enriched with the kingdom and
the daughter of Latinus, and had blended the two peoples.* On the
shore that had come as a dowry, accompanied only by Achates, while
he treads barefoot a secluded path he catches sight of a wanderer and 605
cannot bring himself to believe that it is Anna. Why would she be
coming to the lands of Latium?

While Aeneas thinks this to himself, Achates cries out: 'It's Anna!'
She lifted her face at the name. Alas, what is she to do? Flee? What
610 chasms of the earth is she to seek? Before her eyes was the fate of
her unhappy sister. He understood. The Cytherean hero speaks to
her in her agitation (but he weeps, moved, Elissa, by being reminded
of you):

'Anna, I swear by this land, which you once used to hear was given
615 by a more favourable destiny,* and by the gods who came with me,
newly settled in this place, that they often reproached me for my
delay. And yet I was not afraid about her death; that fear was absent.
Alas, she was more courageous than could have been believed. Don't
620 tell me. I saw the wounds, unworthy of that body, when I dared to
approach the dwellings of Tartarus.*

'But you, whether purpose or some god has driven you to our
shores, enjoy the benefits of my kingdom. We remember that we owe
much to you, and everything to Elissa. You will be welcome in your
own name, welcome in your sister's.'

625   As he said these things she believed him (for no other hope is left),
and she described her own wanderings. And when, dressed in Tyrian
attire, she entered the house (the rest of the crowd keeps silent),
Aeneas begins:

'I have a reason of duty, Lavinia my wife, for entrusting this lady
630 to you: when I was shipwrecked I lived on her resources. She was
born in Tyre, and possessed a kingdom on the coast of Libya. I pray
that you may love her like a dear sister.'

Lavinia promises everything, buries a false wound in her silent
635 mind, and conceals her fears. Although she sees many gifts being car-
ried before her sight, still she thinks many are being sent secretly too.
She hasn't got it quite worked out what she should do. She hates like
a Fury, prepares a trap, and longs to die avenged.

It was night. Before her sister's bed Dido seemed to be standing,
640 covered in blood and with matted hair, and 'Flee!' she seemed to say.
'Don't hesitate! Flee this gloomy house!' At her word a breeze struck
the creaking door.

Up she jumps, and quickly flings herself through a low window
645 over the fields; her very fear had made her bold. Veiled in an ungirt
shift, she is carried away with her fear as a doe runs in terror after
she's heard the wolves.

Horned Numicius is believed to have snatched her away with his eager waves and hidden her in his pools. Meanwhile the lady of Sidon is sought for with loud shouting through the fields. Traces and footprints are seen. They had come to the banks; her tracks were on the banks. The river, knowing, checked his silent waters. 650

She herself seemed to speak: 'I am a nymph of the placid Numicius. Hiding in the perennial river, I am called Anna Perenna.'*

At once they feast, joyful, in the fields through which they wandered, and celebrate themselves and the day with plentiful wine. 655

There are those for whom this goddess is Luna, because she fills up the year with months. Some think she is Themis, some the Inachian cow.* You will find people, Anna, who say you're a nymph, daughter of Azan, and that you gave Jupiter his first food. 660

This story too that I'm going to relate has come to our ears, and it isn't far from what is believed to be true. The common people of old, not yet protected by any tribunes, fled, and were on the summit of the Sacred Mount.* By now too the provisions they'd taken with them, and Ceres fit for human consumption, had run out. 665

There was a certain Anna, born at Bovillae outside the city, an old lady poor but very hard working. It was she, her white hair bound up in a thin turban, who made country cakes with her trembling hand, and used to hand them out to the People in the morning, still steaming; these rations were welcome to the People. When civil peace was made they set up a statue to Perenna, because she brought them help when they were weak. 670

Now it remains for me to tell why the girls sing indecent songs; for they do get together and sing specific obscenities. 675

She had just become a goddess. Gradivus comes to Anna, takes her aside, and has this conversation with her:

'You're worshipped in my month, I've joined my times with you. A great hope of mine hangs on what you can do for me. An armed god seized with love for Minerva, an armed goddess, I'm on fire, and have been nursing this wound for a long time. Bring it about that, gods similar in inclination, we come together as one. This role suits you, obliging old lady!' 680

He had had his say. She fools the god with an empty promise, and goes on prolonging his foolish hope with doubtful delay. When he 685 presses her too often: 'We've carried out your instructions,' she says. 'She's been won over; reluctantly, she has surrendered to pleas.'

The lover believes her, and prepares a bedchamber. Anna, cover-
690 ing her face as a new bride, is escorted to it. Mars, all ready to take kisses, suddenly sees Anna! Now shame at having been fooled, now anger comes over the god. The new goddess laughs at the lover of dear Minerva, and to Venus no event was more pleasing than this.
695 That's why old jokes and indecent songs are sung, and there is delight that Anna cheated the mighty god.

I was going to pass over the swords fixed in the *princeps*, when Vesta spoke thus from her chaste hearths:
700 'Don't hesitate to recall them. He was my priest; the sacrilegious hands attacked me with their weapons. I carried the man away myself, and left a bare likeness. What fell to the sword was Caesar's shadow.'

He indeed was installed in heaven and saw the halls of Jupiter, and
705 he has a temple dedicated in the great *forum*. But all those who had defiled the head of the *pontifex*, daring sacrilege when the power of the gods forbade it, are lying dead as they deserve. Be witness, Philippi, and those whose scattered bones* make the ground white. This was the task, this the duty, this the first lesson of Caesar, to
710 avenge his father through just warfare.

[16 March] When the next dawn has refreshed the tender grass, the Scorpion will be visible in his first part.

[17 March] The third day after the Ides is the one most famed for Bacchus. Bacchus, while I sing your festival, be gracious to the bard.
715 I shall not tell of Semele, to whom Jupiter came—if he hadn't brought his thunderbolts with him you'd have been small and unarmed.* Nor shall I tell how a mother's function was fulfilled in your father's body, so that you could be born a boy at the proper time. It would take a long time to narrate Sithonian and Scythian triumphs,
720 and the conquest of your peoples, incense-bearing Indian. You too, wrongful prey of your Theban mother,* will not be spoken of, nor you, Lycurgus, driven by the Furies against your own kin.

Of course I'm happy to tell of sudden fish and Tyrrhenian
725 miracles*—but that's not the purpose of this song. The purpose of

this song is to set out the reasons why the Vine-planter calls the peoples to his own cakes.

Before your birth, Liber, the altars were without honour, and grass was found on cold hearths. They say it was you, after Ganges and all the east had been subdued, who set aside first-fruits for great Jupiter. 730 You were the first to give cinnamon and captured incense and the roasted entrails of a bull that had been led in triumph. Libations and cakes take their name from their inventor,* because they are part of what is offered on the sacred hearths.

Cakes are made for the god because he delights in sweet juices, and 735 they say that honey was discovered by Bacchus. He was on his way from sandy Hebrus, attended by the satyrs (my story contains no unwelcome frolics), and already they had come to Rhodope and flowery Pangaeum. The bronze-bearing hands of his attendants clashed. 740 Look! New winged things flock together, driven by the ringing noise; whatever sounds the bronze instruments make, the bees follow.

Liber collects them as they swarm about, shuts them up in a hollow tree, and has the reward of the discovery of honey. When the satyrs and the smooth-headed old man* had tasted the flavour, they 745 looked for the yellow combs through all the grove.

The old man hears the buzzing of the swarm in a rotted-out elm. He sees the honeycomb and pretends he hasn't. As he was sitting lazy on the back of his sagging donkey, he leads it up to the elm and the 750 hollow bark. He himself stood upright, leaning on the branchy stump, and greedily he looks for the honey stored in the trunk.

Thousands of hornets swarm, and stab their stings in his bare head and mark his snub-nosed face. He falls head-first and is kicked by the 755 donkey's hoof; he shouts to his sons and asks for help. The satyrs come running, and laugh at their parent's swelling face; he's knocked his knee, he's limping. The god himself laughs too, and shows him how to put mud on. The old man obeys instructions and smears his 760 face with dirt.

Father Liber enjoys honey, and rightly do we give to its discoverer the shining honey, poured over a warm cake.

The reason why a woman presides* is no secret: it's troupes of women he excites with his *thyrsus*. You ask why an old woman does it? This 765 stage of life is fonder of wine, and loves the pregnant vine's gifts. Why is she wreathed with ivy? Ivy is most pleasing to Bacchus. It doesn't

take long to learn why this is so too: they say that when his step-
770 mother* was searching for the boy, the nymphs of Nysa put this foli-
age in front of his cradle.

It remains for me to discover why the free toga* is given to boys
when the Light-bringer is yours, bright Bacchus. Is it that you yourself
are always seen as a boy and a youth, and your age is midway between
775 the two? Or is it that since you are Father, fathers entrust their pledges,
their sons, to your care and to your divine power? Or is it that because
you are Liber the free garment is assumed through you, and the way of
a freer life? Or is it that when the men of old worked the fields more
780 diligently, and a senator did the labour on his ancestral land, and a con-
sul took the *fasces* straight from the curved plough, and it wasn't an
offence to have rough hands, the rustic People used to come to the city
only for the games? (But that honour used to be given to the gods, not
785 to popular enthusiasm;* the discoverer of the grape used to have on his
own day the games he now shares with the torch-carrying goddess.*)
Was it, therefore, so that a crowd can honour the novice that the festival
day did not seem inappropriate for giving the toga?

Father, turn your mild head and peaceful horns this way, and give
790 my talent favourable sails.

The procession to the Argei (who they are, their own page will say)
takes place on this day, if I remember, and the one before.

The star moving down and sinking towards the Lycaonian Bear is
795 the Kite;* on that night this becomes visible. If you want to find out
what gave the bird a place in heaven, Saturn had been driven from his
kingdom by Jupiter. Angry, he stirs up the mighty Titans to arms, and
puts to the test the help that was owed by the Fates.
800   There was a bull born of mother Earth, an amazing monster, in its
hind parts a snake. At the warning of the three Parcae, violent Styx had
shut this creature up with a triple wall, in black woods. There was an
oracle that he who had given the bull's entrails to be burned by the
805 flames would be able to conquer the eternal gods. Briareus sacrifices it
with an axe made from adamant, and was even now on the point of giv-
ing the entrails to the flames. Jupiter orders the birds to snatch them;
the kite brought them to him, and came to the stars as its reward.

[19–23 March] One day intervenes, and the festival of Minerva takes
810 place which has its name from five days joined.* The first day is free

from blood, and it is not lawful to engage with the sword. The reason is that Minerva was born on that day. The second day and three more are celebrated on the smooth-swept sand; the warlike goddess is happy when swords are drawn.*

Now pray to Pallas, boys and tender girls. The one who succeeds 815 in winning Pallas' favour will be skilled. When Pallas' favour has been won, let the girls learn how to make wool soft and unload distaffs when they're full. She also teaches how to run through the standing warps with the shuttle, and with the comb she makes 820 the loose work thick.

Worship her, you who remove stains from damaged garments; worship her, whoever you are preparing bronze vats for fleeces. No one will make good straps for the sole if Pallas is unwilling, even if he's more skilful than Tychius. Even if he's better with his hands 825 when compared with ancient Epeus, if Pallas is angry he'll be maimed.

You too, who banish diseases with Phoebus' art, pay back to the goddess a few gifts from your fees. Don't spurn her, you schoolmasters, a crowd usually cheated of wealth (she brings in new pupils); nor 830 you who use the chisel and burn the panel with colours;* nor you who make stone smooth with skilful hand. She is the goddess of a thousand crafts.

Certainly she is the goddess of song: may she be present, if I deserve it, as a friend to my endeavours.

[19 March] Where the Caelian mount slopes down from its height 835 to the plain, here where the road is not level but almost level, you may see the little shrine of Minerva Capta, which the goddess began to possess on her birthday.

The reason for the name is in doubt. We call ingenious talent 'capital', and the goddess is full of talents. Or is it because, without 840 a mother, she is said to have leapt forth from the top of her father's head,* complete with her shield? Or is it because she came to us as a captive after the Faliscans had been vanquished? This is what the old writing on the statue also tells us. Or is it because she has a law 845 which orders capital punishment to be exacted for receiving things stolen from that place?

From whatever reasoning you take your title, Pallas, always hold your *aegis* in defence of our leaders.

[23 March] The last day of the five is a reminder to purify the
850 tuneful trumpets and sacrifice to the valiant god.* Now, your face
raised to the sun, you can say: 'Yesterday he trod on the fleece of
the sheep of Phrixus.'

When the seeds had been toasted by the guile of the wicked step-
mother,* the young crop had raised no foliage as it usually does.
855 Someone is sent to the tripods to bring back in a sure response what
help for the barren earth the Delphic god gives out. This person too,
corrupted along with the seed, reports that the deaths of Helle and
young Phrixus are sought by the oracle. Though the king kept on
860 refusing, the citizens and time and Ino forced him to endure the
impious orders.

Both Phrixus and his sister, their brows wrapped with ribbons,
stand together in front of the altars and bewail their shared fate. Their
mother sees them, as by chance she had floated in the air,* and beats
865 her naked breast with a frantic hand, and with clouds in attendance
leaps down into the dragon-born city* and snatches her children away
from there.

And so that they may make their escape, a ram all gleaming in gold
is given to them; it carries the two over the long straits. It is said that
the woman had been holding its horn with a weak left hand when she
870 made the name of the water from herself.* Her brother almost per-
ished with her while wanting to help her when she fell and holding
out hands that were stretched to the limit. He wept at having lost his
partner in their twin peril, unaware that she had been united with the
sea-blue god.
875   When the shore is reached, the ram becomes a star; but its golden
wool reaches the dwellings of Colchis.

[26 March] When the coming Eōs has sent ahead three Light-
bringers, you'll experience daytimes equal to those of the night.

[30 March] When four times from then the herdsman has penned
880 his well-fed kids, and four times the grass has whitened with fresh
dew, it will be time to worship Janus, and with him gentle Concord
and Roman Safety and the altar of Peace.*

[31 March] Luna governs the months. The worship of Luna on the
Aventine ridge finishes the times of this month too.

BOOK 4

APRIL

'Show favour,' I said, 'gracious mother of the twin Loves.'*

She turned her face back to the bard. 'What do you want with me?' she says. 'You were certainly singing greater things. Surely you don't have an old wound in your soft heart?'

'Goddess,' I replied, 'you know about the wound.'   5

She laughed, and immediately the sky in that part was cloudless.

'Wounded or well, have I ever abandoned your standards? You are my subject, you my work, always. In my early years I played without offence at what was proper; now a greater space is trodden by my   10
horses.* Times and their reasons, dug out of ancient records, and constellations sunk beneath the earth and risen, I sing. We have come to the fourth month, the one in which you are honoured most. Venus, you know both bard and month are yours.'

Moved, she lightly touched my brow* with Cytherean myrtle, and   15
said: 'Complete the work you have begun.'

I felt it, and suddenly the reasons for the days became clear. While it's allowed and the breezes are blowing, let the ship sail.

If any part of the calendar ought to touch you, Caesar, in April you   20
have something you should look to. This month descends to you from a great image,* and is made your own by adopted nobility.

The father, Ilia's son, saw this when he was writing the long year, and himself traced back the founders of your line. And as he gave the   25
first place in order to fierce Mars, because he was the immediate cause of his own birth, so he wanted Venus, included in his race through many generations, to have the second month's position. When searching out the origin of his own descent and the rolled-back centuries, he   30
came all the way to gods who were his kindred.

I ask you! Would he be unaware that Dardanus was the son of Electra, daughter of Atlas, and that Electra had shared Jupiter's bed? Dardanus' son was Erichthonius; from him Tros was begotten; Tros begot Assaracus, Assaracus Capys. Next was Anchises, with whom   35
Venus did not disdain to have the shared name of parent. From this

union Aeneas was conceived. His proved devotion bore through the
fires the holy things, and his father among them, on his shoulders.

40   We have come at last to Iulus' fortunate name, from where the
Julian house connects with Teucrian ancestors. Hence came Postumus,
who because he was born in the deep woods was called Silvius* among
the Latin race. And he, Latinus, is your father; Alba succeeds Latinus;
45 Epytus, Alba, is next to your titles; he gave to Capys a name derived
from Troy, and the same man became your grandfather, Calpetus.
When Tiberinus possessed his father's kingdom after him, he is said
to have drowned in the swirl of the Tuscan water.* Yet already he had
50 seen his son Agrippa and his grandson Remulus; they say thunder-
bolts were hurled at Remulus.* After these came Aventinus, from
whom the place gets its name, and the hill too; after him the kingdom
was passed to Proca, whom Numitor follows, the brother of hard
55 Amulius. Ilia and Lausus are begotten of Numitor; Lausus falls by
his uncle's sword, Ilia pleases Mars and gives birth to you, Quirinus,
joined with Remus your twin.

He always said that Venus and Mars were his parents, and he
deserved to have his words believed. And so that his coming descend-
60 ants could not be in ignorance, he gave successive times to the gods of
his birth.

But my conjecture is that Venus' month is marked in the Greek
language: the goddess was named from the foam of the sea.*

And you needn't be surprised that a thing is called by a Greek
65 name, for the Italian land was greater Greece.* Evander had come
with a fleet full of his people, Alcides had come, each of them Greek
by birth (as a guest the club-bearer pastured his herd on Aventine
grass, and the Albula was drunk by so great a god), and the Neritian
70 leader came too; the Laestrygonians stand as witnesses, and the shore
which still has Circe's name. Already Telegonus' walls were standing,
already the walls of watery Tibur, because Argive hands put them
there. Hounded by the fate of Atreus' son, Halaesus had come, from
75 whom the Faliscan land thinks it was named.* Add Antenor, who
urged peace at Troy, and Oineus' descendant, your son-in-law, Apulian
Daunus. Late from the flames of Ilium, and after Antenor, Aeneas
brought gods into our land. One of his companions was Solimus from
80 Phrygian Ida, from whom the walls of Sulmo have their name—chilly
Sulmo, my own fatherland, Germanicus. Wretched me, how far that
is from Scythian soil!

Therefore I, so far away—but check the complaints, Muse. You mustn't sing sacred themes with a mournful lyre.

Where does Envy not find its way? There are those, Venus, who want 85 to have snatched from you the honour of the month, and who begrudge it you. For because at that time the spring opens everything, and the impenetrable sharpness of cold gives way, and the teeming land lies open, they say that April is named from the open time.*

Gracious Venus claims it, having put her hand upon it. She indeed 90 regulates the whole world, most deservedly. She holds a realm inferior to no god. She gives laws to heaven, to earth and to her natal waves, and through her goings-in preserves every species. She created all the gods (it's a long task to number them), she gave the crops 95 and trees their causes, she brought together the crude hearts of human beings and taught them to be joined each with his mate.

What creates the whole race of birds, if not enticing pleasure? Nor would cattle mate in the absence of gentle love. The fierce ram uses 100 his horn to fight it out with a rival, but still holds back from hurting the brow of a loved ewe. The bull, who makes all the heathland and woodland tremble, puts off his fierceness and follows the heifer. The same force preserves whatever lives under the broad ocean, and fills 105 the waters with countless fish.

She was the first to strip man of his savage habits. From her came civilized living and clean care of oneself. It is said that a lover was the first to have sung a wakeful song, before the closed doors when a night 110 was denied him; eloquence consisted of winning over an obstinate girl, and each man was fluent for his own cause. Through her a thousand arts were set in motion, and by eagerness to please they say many things were discovered that lay hidden before. Would anyone dare to despoil 115 her of the second month's title? May that madness be far from me!

What of the fact that, though the goddess is everywhere powerful and made great by crowded temples, it is in our city that she has greater authority? Roman, for your Troy Venus bore arms, when she groaned at the spear-point's wounding of her tender hand;* with 120 a Trojan as judge she defeated two dwellers in heaven (ah, I would wish the defeated goddesses did not remember this); she was called Assaracus' daughter-in-law, so that one day, of course, great Caesar would have ancestors from Iulus.

125   Nor was any season more fitting for Venus than spring. In spring
the lands are bright, in spring the field is softened; now the grasses
break through the earth and lift their tips, now the vine-shoot drives
buds from the swelling bark. Lovely Venus deserves the lovely season,
130   and is connected, as usual, to her own Mars. In spring she tells the
curved ships to sail through the seas that gave her birth, and no longer
to have feared the threats of winter.

[1 April] You pay the goddess proper respect, matrons and young
wives of Latium, and you who don't wear headbands and the long
robe.*

135   Take off from her marble neck the golden necklaces, take off her
wealth; the goddess must be washed all over. Put back on her new-
dried neck the golden necklaces; fresh flowers, a new rose must be
given her now.

The goddess orders you too to be washed, under green myrtle, and
140   there is a sure reason why she does so. Learn it! She was naked on the
shore, drying her dripping hair. A lecherous gang of satyrs saw the
goddess. She realized, and put myrtle in the way to screen her body.
By doing so she was safe, and she bids you repeat it.

145   Now learn why you give incense to Fortuna Virilis at the place
which is wet with cold water.* That place receives all women without
their clothes, and sees every blemish of the naked body. Fortuna Virilis
150   undertakes to hide this and conceal it from men, and she does so
when asked with a little incense.

And don't be reluctant to take ground poppy in white milk, and
liquid honey squeezed from the honeycombs. When Venus was first
brought to her eager husband, this is what she drank, and from that
moment she was a wife.*

155   Appease her with words of supplication; in her control beauty and
character and good reputation stay fixed. Rome slipped from chastity
in our great-grandfathers' time; you, men of old, consulted the old
woman of Cumae. She orders a temple to be built for Venus, and it
160   was duly done; since then Venus has a name from the turning of the
heart.*

Goddess most fair, look always with a kindly face on the descend-
ants of Aeneas, and protect your young wives, so numerous.

While I speak, the Scorpion, to be feared for the tip of his raised
tail, is plunging into the green waters.

[**2 April**] When the night has passed,* and the heaven has first 165
started to grow red, and touched by the dew the birds lament, and the
traveller who has spent the night awake lays down his half-burnt
torch, and the countryman goes to his regular task, the Pleiades will
begin to relieve their father's shoulders.

They are usually said to be seven; however, they're usually six, 170
whether because six of them entered the embrace of gods (for they say
Sterope slept with Mars, Alcyone and you, lovely Celaeno, with Neptune,
Maia and Electra and Taygete with Jupiter), and the seventh, Merope, 175
married you, Sisyphus, a mortal, and regrets it and hides alone in shame
for what she did; or because Electra could not bear to watch the destruc-
tion of Troy, and put up her hand in front of her eyes.

[**4 April**] Thrice let the heaven turn on its eternal axis, thrice let 180
Titan yoke his horses and thrice release them, at once the Berecyntian
pipe will blow with its curved horn, and it will be the festival of the
Idaean Mother.

Half-men will parade and pound the hollow drums, and bronze
struck on bronze will give out ringing sounds. She herself, seated on 185
the soft necks of her attendants, will be carried, hymned with howl-
ings, through the midst of the city's streets. The stage resounds, the
games are calling. Come to watch, Quirites, and let the litigious *fora*
be empty of their Mars!

I feel like asking many questions, but I'm terrified by the noise of
the high-pitched bronze and the curved pipe whose sound makes 190
your hair stand on end. 'Goddess, give me some lady to question!'
The Cybelean saw her learned granddaughters,* and ordered them to
attend to what I wanted.

'Remember your mandate, nurslings of Helicon, and reveal why
the great goddess delights in constant noise.'

Thus I. Thus Erato (the month of Cytherea fell to her because she 195
has the name of tender love):

'This oracle was returned to Saturn: "Best of kings, you will be
thrown out of your kingdom by your son." Fearing his own offspring,
he devours them as each was born and keeps them plunged in 200
his entrails. Often did Rhea complain, so often pregnant but never
a mother, and felt pain at her own fertility.

'Jupiter was born. (Antiquity is believed as a mighty witness; avoid
disturbing accepted belief.) A rock hidden in a garment settled in the 205

heavenly gullet. Thus was the father to be tricked by the fates. Immediately steep Ida resounds with ringing noises, so the child may be safe as he wails from his infant mouth. Some pound shields with
210 stakes, some hollow helmets: this is the task the Curetes have, this the Corybantes.

'The truth lay hidden, and imitations of the ancient deed remain: the attendants of the goddess shake bronze and raucous hides. They beat cymbals for helmets, drums for shields; the pipe gives out Phrygian measures, just as it did before.'

215 She had finished. I began: 'Why does the fierce race of lions offer unaccustomed manes to her curved yoke?'

I had finished. She began: 'It is believed that wildness was tamed by her; she has borne witness to that with her chariot.'

'But why is her head burdened by a tower-bearing crown? Is it
220 because she gave towers to the first cities?' She nodded agreement.

'Where,' I said, 'does the impulse to cut their own members come from?' As I fell silent, the Pierian began to speak:

'A Phrygian boy in the woods, remarkable for his looks, Attis bound
225 the tower-bearing goddess in chaste love. She wanted him to be kept for her and guard her temples, and she said: "See to it that you want always to be a boy." He gave his promise to her orders. "If I lie," he says, "let that Venus by which I am false be my last."

'He is false, and in the nymph Sagaritis he ceases to be what he
230 was. Hence the anger of the goddess exacts punishment. She cuts down the Naiad by inflicting wounds on the tree; it dies, and the tree was the Naiad's fate. He goes mad, and believing the roof of the bedroom is falling on him, he flees, and makes for the heights of Dindymus as he runs.

235 'He shouts—now "Take the torches away!", now "Remove the whips!", and often he swears the goddesses of Palestine* are there. He even slashed his body with a sharp stone, and his long hair was dragged in filthy dust. His cry was: "I have deserved it! I pay in blood
240 the penalty I've deserved. Ah, let them perish, the parts that have ruined me! Ah, let them perish", he still kept on saying.

'He takes away the burden of his groin, and suddenly there are no signs of manhood left. This madness came to be an example, and her soft servants, tossing their hair, cut off their worthless members.'

245 With such words the reason for the queried madness was given by the eloquent voice of the Aonian Camena.*

'On this too, guide of my work, I beg you to advise me: from where was she sought when she came? Or has she always been in our city?'

'The Mother always loved Dindymus and Cybele and Ida, delight- 250
ful with springs, and the wealth of Ilium. When Aeneas was carrying Troy into the lands of Italy, the goddess almost followed the ships that bore the sacred things; but she had realized that her divine power was not yet demanded by the fates for Latium, and had stayed put in her accustomed place.

'Later, when Rome, powerful in wealth, has already seen five cen- 255
turies and raised her head in the conquest of the world, the priest examines the fateful words of Euboean song. They say what was examined was as follows:

'"The Mother is absent. Roman, I bid you seek the Mother. When she comes, she must be received by a chaste hand." 260

'The Fathers are in doubt about the riddle of the dark oracle: what parent is absent, in what place must she be sought? Paean is consulted, and "Send for the Mother of the Gods," he says. "She is to be found on the ridge of Ida."

'Leading citizens are sent. At that time Attalus held the sceptre of 265
Phrygia. He refuses the Ausonians their request. I shall sing of wonders: the earth trembled with a long, deep sound, and thus the goddess spoke from her inmost shrine:

'"I myself wished to be sought. Let there be no delay. Send me, I am willing. Rome is a worthy place for any god to go." 270

'Quaking with terror at the sound, "Depart," he said. "You will be ours: Rome is traced back to Phrygian ancestors."

'Immediately countless axes cut down pine woods, the ones the dutiful Phrygian had made use of as he fled.* A thousand hands com- 275
bine, and a hollow ship painted with burnt colours holds the Mother of the heavenly ones.

'She is carried in perfect safety through her son's waters, and comes to the long straits of Phrixus' sister and goes past wide Rhoeteum and the shores of Sigeum, and Tenedos and the ancient 280
realm of Eëtion. The Cyclades receive her, once Lesbos has been left behind, and the waves which break on the shallows of Carystus. She goes past the Icarian sea as well, where Icarus lost his fallen wings and made a name for the vast water. Then she leaves Crete to port and the 285
waters of Pelops to starboard, and makes for Venus' holy Cythera. From here she skirts the Trinacrian sea, where Brontes, Steropes, and

Acmonides habitually dip the white-hot iron,* and the seas of Africa,
290 and looks back from the port-side oars at the realms of Sardo, and
makes Ausonia.

'She had reached the mouths where Tiberinus divides himself into
the deep sea and swims in a freer range. All the Knights and the grave
Senate, with the common people mixed in, come to meet her at the
295 mouth of the Tuscan river. Equally mothers and daughters and young
wives process, and those who in virginity tend the sacred hearths.

'Men weary their willing arms as the rope is pulled tight. The
guest ship barely moves upstream against the waters. The land had
300 long been dry, drought had scorched the grasses. The keel, weighed
down, settled in the muddy shallows.

'Whoever is there to work gives more than his share of effort, and
helps strong hands with a resounding voice. She sits immovable, like
an island in mid-ocean. Thunderstruck by the portent, the men stand
and quake.

305 'Claudia Quinta traced her descent from lofty Clausus, and her face
did not fail to match her noble birth. She was chaste, yes, but had no
credit for it; malicious talk had harmed her, and she was accused on a
false charge. Her elegance was against her, and her having appeared in
310 public with her hair in different styles, and her ready tongue towards
the strict old men. Her mind knew her honour and laughed at rumour's
lies, but we're a crowd who like to believe in wrong.

'When she has stepped forward from the procession of chaste
mothers and scooped up in her hands the pure river-water, three
315 times she sprinkles her head, three times she raises her palms to
heaven (everyone who sees it thinks she is out of her mind), and bend-
ing her knee she fixes her gaze on the goddess's image. With her hair
hanging loose, she utters these words:

320 ' "Gracious one, fruitful Mother of the Gods, receive your suppli-
ant's prayers with a fixed condition. They say I am not chaste. If you
condemn me, I shall confess I have deserved it: convicted by a god-
dess as judge, I shall pay the penalty with death. But if there is no
wrongdoing, you will guarantee my life by what happens, and chaste,
you will follow chaste hands."

325 'She spoke, and with a tiny effort pulled the rope. I shall speak of
wonders, but they are attested also by the stage: the goddess is moved,
and follows her guide and in following praises her. The noise, a sign
of joy, is carried to the stars.

'They come to a bend in the river (the men of old called it "the halls of Tiber"), where it goes off to the left. Night came. They tie the 330 rope to the trunk of an oak, and when their bodies have done with food they are given to easy sleep. Daylight came. They untie the rope from the trunk of the oak, having first, however, set up a hearth and offered incense, first garlanded the ship and sacrificed a heifer, with- 335 out blemish or experience of work or mating.

'There is a place where the smooth Almo flows into the Tiber, and the smaller river loses its name in the big one. There the white-haired priest in his purple robe bathed the mistress and her sacred things in 340 the waters of Almo. Her attendants howl, and the maddening pipe is blown, and soft hands strike the bull-hides. Escorted by a great crowd, Claudia walks in front with a joyful face, believed virtuous at the very last with a goddess as witness.

'The goddess herself, seated on a wagon, was brought in by the 345 Porta Capena. The yoked oxen are sprinkled with fresh flowers. Nasica received her. Who founded her temple* has not survived; it is Augustus now, it was Metellus before.'

Here Erato stopped. There's a pause, for the rest of my questions. 'Tell me,' I say, 'why she asks for money in small offerings?' 350

'The People,' she says, 'contributed coppers, from which Metellus built the temple. The custom of giving offerings survived from that.'

I ask why people take turns going to dinners, and at that time in particular enjoy meals together by invitation.

'Because Berecyntia happily changed her home,' she said, 'they 355 catch the same omen by changing places.'

I had started to ask why in our city the Megalesia are the first games, when the goddess (for she realized), says:

'She gave birth to the gods. They deferred to their parent, and the Mother has precedence in the honour bestowed.'* 360

'So why do we call those who have castrated themselves "Galli", although Gallic soil is so far from Phrygia?'

'Between green Cybele and high Celaenae,' she says, 'a river called Gallus runs with crazy water. Who drinks from it goes mad. Go far 365 away from it, you whose care is for a healthy mind. Who drinks from it goes mad.'

'Is it not shameful to have placed a herb salad on the mistress's tables, or is there a particular reason behind it?'

'The men of old are said to have lived on pure milk,' she says, 'and
370 whatever herbs the earth produced of its own accord. White cheese is
mixed with pounded herbs, so that an ancient goddess may recognize
ancient food.'

[5 April] When the next Pallantian has shone in the sky and the stars
are gone, and Luna has unyoked her snow-white horses, the person
375 who says: 'Once, on this day, Fortuna Publica was consecrated on
Quirinus' hill,' will be right.

[6 April] It was the third day for games, I remember, and as I watch
them an elderly man in the place next to me says:
'This is the day on which Caesar on the Libyan shores crushed
380 proud-hearted Juba's treacherous arms. Caesar was my commander,
and I'm proud to have served as tribune under him. He was in com-
mand of my soldiering. This seat I acquired in military service, you in
peace, having held office among the twice-five men.'*
385 About to talk on, we are separated by a sudden shower. The swinging
Scale was moving the waters of heaven. However, before the final day can
put an end to the shows, sword-bearing Orion will have sunk in the sea.

[10 April] When the next Eōs has looked on victorious Rome, and
390 the stars in flight have given place to Phoebus, the Circus will be
crowded with the procession and the company of gods, and the first
palm will be competed for by horses swift as the wind.

[11 April] Next, the games of Ceres. There's no need to point out
the reason: the bounty and merit of the goddess are self-evident.
395 For the first mortals, bread was the green plants that the earth gave
without anyone's stimulus. Sometimes they gathered living grass
from the turf, at times their feast was a treetop with tender leaves.
Later the acorn became known; they were well off now with the acorn
400 discovered, and the hard oak held sumptuous wealth.
Having called man to better nourishment, Ceres was first to change
acorns for more beneficial food. She compelled bulls to offer their neck
to the yoke; then for the first time the upturned soil saw the sun.
405 Bronze was valued; the Chalybean ore lay hidden. Alas, it should
have been concealed for ever! Ceres delights in peace—and you
farmers, pray for perpetual peace and a leader who brings it!

You may give the goddess spelt, and the honour of leaping salt, and grains of incense on ancient hearths. And if there's no incense, kindle 410 smeared torches. Small things, be they only pure, are pleasing to good Ceres.

You attendants with your robes girt up, take your knives away from the ox! Let the ox plough, sacrifice a lazy sow. A neck that is fit for 415 a yoke should not be struck by an axe. Let it live and often work on the hard soil.

The place itself demands that I tell of the virgin's abduction. You will recognize quite a lot, but a few things you will have to be taught.

The Trinacrian land juts out with three crags into the vast sea. It got its name from the features of the place, and is a dwelling dear to 420 Ceres. She owns many cities, among which is Henna, fruitful with its cultivated soil.

Cold Arethusa had summoned the mothers of the heavenly ones, and the golden-haired goddess had come to the sacred feast. Her daughter, accompanied as she was by her usual girls, was wandering 425 barefoot through her own meadows.

At the bottom of a shady valley is a place damp with the abundant spray of water leaping down from a height. In that place there had been as many colours as nature owns, and the ground was bright, 430 painted with varied flowers. As soon as she saw it, 'Come here, companions,' she said, 'and join me in bringing back lapfuls of flowers.'

The empty booty lures the girls' minds, and in their diligence the hard work isn't noticed. One fills baskets woven from pliant 435 willow, another loads her lap, another her loosened dress. That one gathers marigolds, this one is concerned with banks of violets, that one cuts off poppy hair with her nail. These girls you attract, hyacinth; those you detain, amaranthus. Some like thyme, others wild 440 poppy and clover. Abundant roses are gathered, and there are nameless flowers too. She herself gathers delicate saffron and white lilies. In her eagerness to pluck them, little by little the distance covered is further, and it happened that no companion followed her mistress.

Her uncle* sees her, and having seen her swiftly bears her away, 445 and with dark-blue horses carries her into his kingdom.

She to be sure kept crying out, 'Oh, mother dearest, I am being borne away!', and had herself torn apart the folds of her own dress.

450 Meanwhile a way opens up for Dis, for the horses are unused to the
light of day and barely endure it.

But the chorus of equals, her attendants laden with flowers, cry,
'Persephone! Come for your presents!' When she doesn't answer
their call, they fill the mountains with their wailings and strike their
bare breasts with grieving hand.

455 Ceres (she had just come to Henna) was stunned by the lamenta-
tion. No delay. 'Woe is me!' she said. 'Daughter, where are you?'
Bereft of reason, she is swept along like the Thracian Maenads who
go, so we usually hear, with their hair streaming. Just as its mother
bellows when a calf has been snatched from the udder, and looks for
460 her offspring through every grove, so the goddess does not hold back
her groans, and is borne away running in agitation.

From your fields, Henna, she begins. From there she came upon
traces of a girl's footprint, and saw the earth pressed by a weight she
465 knew. Perhaps that would have been the last day of her wandering, if
pigs had not disturbed the tracks she found.

And now as she runs she passes Leontini and the streams of
Amenanus and your banks, grassy Acis. She passes Cyane too and the
470 springs of smooth-flowing Anapus and you, Gela, unapproachable
because of your whirlpools. She had left behind Ortygia and Megara
and Pantagias and where the sea receives the waters of Symaethus,
and the Cyclops' caves scorched by the forges set up there, and the
475 place that bears the name of the curved sickle,* and Himera and
Didyme and Acragas and Tauromenum and Mylae, joyful pasture of
consecrated cows. From here she goes to Camerina and Thapsos and
the valley of Helorus and where Eryx lies always open to Zephyrus.
And now she had encircled Pelorias and Lilybaeum, now Pachynos,
480 the first horns of her land.*

Wherever she goes she fills whole places with her pitiable com-
plaints, as when the bird bewails the loss of Itys.* By turns she cries
now 'Persephone!', now 'Daughter!', she cries, and summons up each
485 name in turn. But Persephone doesn't hear Ceres, daughter does not
hear mother, and each name dies in turn. There was one question, if
she'd seen a shepherd or a man tilling his fields: 'Has any girl passed
this way?'

Now things have one colour and all is covered in darkness; now the
490 watchful dogs have fallen silent. High Etna lies above the mouth of
huge Typhoeus, whose breathed-out fires cause the land to blaze.

There she lights twin pine trees for a lamp; from this, in the rites of Ceres now too a torch is given.

There is a cave, a rough structure of pitted pumice, a place to be 495 approached by neither man nor beast. As soon as she has come to it, she yokes harnessed serpents to her chariot and roams dry over the waters of the sea. She avoids both the Syrtes and you, Zanclaean Charybdis, and you, dogs of Nisus,* shipwrecking monsters, and the 500 wide-open Adriatic and Corinth with its two seas. Thus she comes to your harbours, land of Attica.

Here for the first time she sat down, full of grief, on the cold rock; even now the sons of Cecrops call it sad.* Many days she per- 505 sisted, motionless under the open sky, enduring the moon and the rainwater.

Every place has its own destiny. What is now called Ceres' Eleusis was the farm of an old man, Celeus. He is carrying home acorns, and berries shaken out of bramble bushes, and dry wood for hearths that 510 are going to blaze. His little daughter was driving two she-goats back from the high ground, and his young son was ill in his cradle.

'Mother,' says the girl (the goddess was moved by the name of mother), 'what are you doing in lonely places unattended?'

The old man too has stopped, though his load weighs him down, 515 and begs her to come under the shelter, however small, of his cottage. She says no. (She had taken on the likeness of an old woman and confined her hair in a turban.) As he presses her, she gives him this reply:

'May you go safe, and always a parent. My daughter has been seized from me. Alas, how much better is your lot than mine!' 520

She spoke, and like tears (for gods do not weep) a shining drop falls into her warm lap. Soft hearted, they weep just as much, the maiden and the old man; of the two of them, the righteous old man's words were these:

'So may your daughter be safe, who has been seized and whom you 525 seek; rise, and do not despise the shelter of a tiny cottage.'

To which the goddess says: 'Lead on. You have understood how to compel me.' And she raises herself from the rock and follows on the old man's heels.

Her guide explains to his companion how ill his son is, that he takes no sleep and is kept awake by his ailments. As she is about to 530 enter the little home, she gathers from the soil of the field a gently

sleep-inducing poppy. It is said that while gathering it she tasted it on her forgetful palate, and broke her long hunger without intending to.
535 Because she put aside fasting at the start of the night, the adepts of her mysteries take the sight of the stars as the time for food.

When she has crossed the threshold, she sees everything full of sorrow; for by now the child had no hope of safety. Having greeted
540 the mother (the mother is called Metanira), she deigns to touch the child's mouth with her own. His pallor goes, and they see sudden strength in his body. So great is the vigour that has come from the heavenly mouth. The whole house is joyful—that is, mother, father, and daughter: those three were the whole house.

545 Soon they set out a feast, curds dissolved in milk, apples, and golden honey in its combs. Gracious Ceres abstains, and to you, child, she gives poppies that cause sleep, to be drunk with warm milk.

550 It was midnight, and the silence of peaceful sleep. She took up Triptolemus on her lap; three times she stroked him with her hand and three spells she uttered, spells not to be repeated in mortal speech, and on the hearth she covers the body of the child with living ash, so that the fire may purge his mortal burden.

555 His mother, foolishly devoted, is roused from sleep, and out of her mind she shouts: 'What are you doing?', and snatches his limbs from the fire. To whom the goddess said:

'Though you're not wicked, you have been; because of a mother's fear my gifts are in vain. That boy of yours will indeed be mortal; but
560 he will be the first to plough and sow and reap rewards from culti-vated earth.'

She has spoken, and walks out trailing a cloud, and goes across to the serpents. Ceres is carried aloft on the winged axle.

She leaves behind unsheltered Sunion and Piraeus, safe in its
565 recess, and the coast that lies to the right side. From here she enters the Aegean, where she observes all the Cyclades, and she skirts the greedy Ionian and the Icarian seas, and through the cities of Asia she makes for the long Hellespont, and wanders aloft through a route that's varied in direction.

For at one time she looks down on incense-gathering Arabs,
570 at another on Indians; next Libya is below, next Meroe and the parched land. Now she approaches the Hesperians—the Rhine, the Rhone, the Po, and you, Thybris, destined to be the parent of powerful water.

Where am I being carried? It's a huge task to tell the lands she roamed. No place in the world is omitted by Ceres. She roams in 575 heaven too, and speaks to the constellations nearest to the icy pole, which are immune from the watery ocean:

'Parrhasian stars,* for you are able to know everything since you never go beneath the waters of the sea, show a wretched parent her daughter Persephone!'

She finished speaking. Helice gives her these words in reply: 'Night 580 is free from guilt. Consult the Sun about the maiden who's been carried off: he sees far and wide the deeds of daytime.'

The Sun is approached. 'She whom you seek,' he says, 'so you may not labour in vain, rules the third kingdom as the bride of Jupiter's brother.'

Having long lamented to herself, she thus addressed the Thunderer 585 (and very great in her look were the signs of her anguish):

'If you remember by whom Persephone was born to me, she ought to have a half of your concern. I have wandered throughout the world, and all I have discovered is the outrage of the deed. The abductor has the 590 reward of his crime. But Persephone does not deserve a brigand husband, and for me a son-in-law was not to be acquired in this way. What worse would I have suffered as a slave, if Gyges had been victorious, than I have now suffered with you holding sway in heaven? But let him get away with 595 it unpunished, I shall endure these things without seeking vengeance. Let him give her back, and mend his earlier deeds with new ones.'

Jupiter calms her, and uses love to excuse the deed.

'He is not a son-in-law we need be ashamed of,' he says. 'I am not more noble. My palace is set in heaven, another possesses the waters, 600 another the empty void. But if it happens that your heart cannot be moved, and is set to break the bonds of a marriage once joined, then let us try to do just that—if only she has remained fasting. If not, she will be the wife of an underworld husband.'

The bearer of the *caduceus* receives his orders, then puts on his 605 wings, goes to Tartarus, returns more quickly than expected, and brings a sure report of what he has seen.

'The abducted girl,' he says, 'has broken her fast with three of the grains that pomegranates conceal in their tough skin.'

No less than if she had only just been seized, her afflicted mother 610 grieved. Her recovery was difficult, and took a long time. And this is what she said:

'Heaven is not for me to live in either. Order that I too be received in the vale of Taenarus.'

And she would have done so, if Jupiter had not made an agreement
615 that the girl would be in heaven for twice three months. Then at last Ceres recovered her looks and her spirits, and put wreaths of corn-ears in her hair; a generous harvest came forth in the fallow fields, and the threshing floor could hardly hold the heaped-up riches.

White befits Ceres: put on white clothes for the Cerialia. At this
620 time the use of dark-coloured wool is avoided.

[13 April] Jupiter takes possession of April's Ides with the *cognomen* Victor. On this day temples were granted him. On this day too, if I'm not mistaken, Liberty, most appropriate for our People, first had her own hall.

625 [14 April] On the following day make for safe harbours, sailor: the wind mixed with hail will be from the west. Be that as it may, however, in hail on this day Caesar with his army struck down the weapons of Mutina.

[15 April] When the third light has dawned after Venus's Ides, make
630 a sacrifice, priests, with a *forda* cow. A *forda* cow is a cow that is carrying, and called fertile from that fact; they think the foetus too has its name from this.* Now the cattle are pregnant, and the lands also are pregnant with seed. Earth is full, and a full victim is given to her.

635 Some of them fall on Jupiter's Citadel; the *curiae* receive thrice ten cows and are wet, splashed with copious blood. But when the attend-ants have torn the calves from the flesh and consigned the cut entrails to the smoking hearths, the Virgin who is eldest burns the calves in
640 the fire, for that ash to purify the peoples on the day of Pales.

When Numa was king, the harvest was not answering to effort and the vows of the disappointed farmer were in vain. For at times the year was dry with cold Aquilones, at times the ground was lush from
645 constant rain. Ceres often deceived the master in her first shoots, and the light stalk sprouted up, infesting the soil. Cattle gave birth to unripe young before their time, and the lamb often killed the ewe by being born.

650 There stood an ancient wood, long undefiled by any axe, left sacred to the god of Maenalus. He used to give responses to the quiet mind

on silent nights. Here Numa slaughters twin ewes. The first falls for
Faunus, the second falls for gentle Sleep. Both fleeces are spread on
the hard ground.

Twice his unshorn head is sprinkled with water from the spring; 655
twice he wreathes his brow with beech-leaves. There is no act of
Venus, nor is it lawful to put flesh on tables, nor is there any ring on
his fingers. Covered with a coarse garment, he lays his body on the
fresh fleeces, having worshipped the god with words of his own. 660
Meanwhile Night comes, her peaceful brow bound with poppy, and
with her she draws dark dreams.

Here's Faunus. He presses the ewes' fleeces with his hard hoof and
from the right side of the bed utters these words:

'With the death of two cows, king, you must appease Earth. Let 665
one heifer give the two lives to the ritual.'

Rest is shaken away by terror. Numa ponders what he has seen and
repeats to himself the riddle and the blind commands. His wife, most
dear to the grove,* sets him right in his uncertainty. 'You are asked,' 670
she said, 'for the entrails of a pregnant cow.' The entrails of a preg-
nant cow are given. A more fertile year ensues, and the land and the
cattle bear fruit.

Once Cytherea ordered this day to go more quickly, and plunged
the horses down at a gallop, so that as soon as possible on the follow- 675
ing day successful wars would give the august youth the title of
command.*

[17 April] But now your fourth Light-bringer looks back on the Ides
that have passed; on this night the Hyades occupy Dōris.

[19 April] When the third light has risen after the Hyades' departure,
the Circus will have horses separated in the starting gates. So I must 680
explain the reason why vixens are let loose and have their backs on fire
with torches bound to them.

The land of Carseoli is cold and unsuitable for growing olives, but
the fields have a talent for grain crops. By this way I was making for the 685
Paeligni, the countryside where I was born—small, but always exposed
to constant waters. I entered, as usual, the house of my old friend.
Already Phoebus had unyoked the horses whose task was complete.

My friend was in the habit of telling me stories—many indeed, but
also this, by which my present work might be instructed: 690

'In this plain,' he says (and he shows me the plain), 'a thrifty countrywoman used to own a small piece of land with her sturdy husband. He used to work his own ground, whether there was need of a plough 695 or a curved sickle or a two-pronged hoe. She used now to sweep the house, which stayed upright with props, now to give eggs to a mother-hen's feathers for hatching; or she collects green mallows and white mushrooms, or makes the low hearth warm with a welcome fire; and 700 even so she keeps her arms active at the busy looms, and prepares defences against the threats of cold.

'Her son was mischievous in his first age, and had added two years to his twice five. He catches a vixen in a hollow at the edge of a willow 705 copse; she had carried off many birds from the flock. He wraps his prisoner in straw and hay and sets fire to it. She escapes from the hands that are burning her, and where she flees she sets fire to the fields clothed with harvest. The breeze gave strength to the ruinous fires.

'The deed has gone, reminders of it remain; for even now a law at 710 Carseoli forbids the naming of a specific fox.* And so that it may pay the penalty, this species burns at the Cerialia, and itself perishes in the way it destroyed the crops.'

[20 April] When the next saffron-coloured mother of Memnon 715 comes on rosy horses to see the open lands, the Sun goes away from the leader of the wool-bearing flock, who betrayed Helle. After his departure, a larger sacrificial victim is there for him.* Whether it's a cow or a bull is not simple to discover: the forepart is visible, the hindquarters hidden. But whether this sign is a bull 720 or a woman, it is against the will of Juno* that it enjoys the rewards of love.

[21 April] Night has gone, and Aurora comes up. I am asked for the Parilia; not in vain am I asked, if gracious Pales favours me. Gracious Pales, may you favour one who sings of shepherds' rites, if I honour your festival with my service.
725 Certainly I have often carried in a full hand the ashes from the calf and the beanstalks, the burned *februa*. Certainly I have leapt three times over flames set in a row, and the wet laurel has cast its sprinkled waters. The goddess is moved, and favours the work. The ship is leav-730 ing the docks; already my sails have their winds.

Go, People, seek means of fumigation from the virgin's altar. Vesta will give them, with Vesta's gift you will be pure. Those means will be the blood of a horse and the ash of a calf,* the third thing the empty stalk of a hard bean.

Shepherd, purify your well-fed sheep at first twilight. First let 735
water sprinkle the ground and twigs sweep it. Let the sheep pens be decorated with leaves and branches attached, and let a long garland cover the doors that have been adorned. Let blue smoke be created from pure sulphur, and let the sheep, touched by the smoking sul- 740
phur, bleat.

Burn male olive wood and pine and Sabine herbs, and let burned laurel crackle in the middle of the hearths. Let a basket of millet follow cakes made of millet. The rustic goddess enjoys this food especially. Add her feast and her milk pail, and when the feast has been 745
cut up, pray with warm milk to Pales who dwells in the woods. Say:

'Look after the flock and the flock's masters alike. Let wrongdoing be averted and flee from my folds. If I have pastured on sacred ground, or sat beneath a sacred tree, and my sheep have unknowingly grazed 750
from tombs; if I have entered a forbidden grove, or nymphs and the half-goat god have been frightened away by my seeing them; if my sickle has stripped a grove of a shady branch, from which a basket of leaves was given to a sick ewe, pardon my offence. 755

'Let it not be held against me that while it was hailing I sheltered my flock in a rustic shrine. Let it not harm me to have disturbed pools; forgive, nymphs, that the tread of a hoof has made your waters muddy. You, goddess, on our behalf placate the springs and the divine powers of the springs, placate the gods dispersed through every 760
grove.

'Let us not see the Dryads or the bathing places of Diana, or Faunus when he lies in the fields in the middle of the day. Drive diseases far away. Let both men and flocks be strong; let watchdogs be strong, that far-sighted pack. Let me not drive fewer back than there 765
were in the morning; let me not groan as I bring back fleeces snatched from the wolf.

'Let wicked hunger be far away. Let grass and leaves abound, and waters to wash limbs and to be drunk. Let me press udders that are full, let cheese bring me money in return, and let wicker strainers 770
give a passage to the liquid whey. May the ram be lustful, may his mate take his seed and give it back, may there be many a lamb in my

fold. May wool be produced that will not harm any girls, soft and fit for hands however delicate.

775   'Let the things I pray for come to pass, and let us for the coming year make great cakes for Pales, mistress of shepherds.'

With these words the goddess must be appeased. Say these words four times turned to the east, and wash your hands in living water. Then, having set up a vessel as if it were a mixing-bowl, you can drink
780   snow-white milk and red must, and soon with nimble feet fling your vigorous limbs over burning heaps of crackling straw.

The custom has been described. The origin of the custom remains for me to deal with. Multitude makes me uncertain, and holds back our undertaking.

785   Devouring fire purges everything, and melts out the flaw from metals. Is it for this reason that it purges the sheep with the shepherd?

Or is it that, since the opposing seeds of all things are two gods in conflict, fire and water, our ancestors joined the elements and thought
790   it fitting to touch the body with fire and sprinkled water?

Or is it that, since in these is the cause of life, and these are what an exile has lost, and by these a bride becomes a wife,* they consider these the two important things? For my part I hardly believe it.

There are those who believe that Phaethon is referred to, and the excessive waters of Deucalion.

795   Some too say that when shepherds were striking rocks with rocks a spark suddenly leapt forth; though the first went out, the second was caught on straw. Does the Parilia flame have this explanation?

Or was it rather the devotion of Aeneas that created this custom, to
800   whom after his defeat fire gave a harm-free passage?

Can it, though, be nearer the truth that, when Rome was founded, the Lares were ordered to be transferred to new quarters, and that while changing homes they set fire to their rustic roofs and the cot-
805   tage about to be abandoned, and that the flock leapt through the flames and the farmers did so too? Which happens now too on your birthday, Rome.

The occasion itself gives the bard his place: the origin of the city has arrived. Be present at your deeds, great Quirinus.

810   Numitor's brother* had now paid the penalty, and all the shepherd folk were under twin leadership. They both agree to bring the coun-

trymen together and put walls in place. Which of them should put walls in place is in dispute.

'There's no need for any contest,'* said Romulus. 'There is great faith in birds: let's try the birds.' The matter is agreed.   815

In the morning one goes on to the rocks of the wooded Palatine, the other goes on to the Aventine summit. Remus sees six birds, the other twice six, in sequence. They stand by their agreement, and Romulus has control of the city.

A suitable day is chosen for marking out the walls with a plough. The festival of Pales was at hand; the work begins from then. A trench   820
is dug down to solid rock, natural produce and earth fetched from neighbouring soil are thrown into the bottom of it. The trench is filled again with earth; when full, an altar is placed over it, and the new hearth enjoys a kindled fire. Then, pressing on the plough-handle,   825
he marks out the walls with a furrow. A white cow bore the yoke with a snow-white steer. This was the king's utterance:

'Be present as I found the city, Jupiter and father Mavors and mother Vesta, and take heed, all you gods whom it is dutiful to summon. Under your auspices may this work of mine rise. Long may its   830
life be, and the power of the ruling land, and let the rising and the setting day be subject to it.'

He was praying; Jupiter gave omens with thunder on the left, and lightning bolts were sent from the leftward sky. Delighted at the   835
augury, the citizens lay foundations, and in the briefest of time the new wall existed.

Urging on this work is Celer, whom Romulus himself had called. 'Celer,' he had said, 'let this be your concern: let no one cross either the walls or the trench made with the plough. Put to death whoever   840
dares such things.'

Unaware of that, Remus began to scorn the low walls and say, 'With these will the People be safe?' No delay, he leapt across. He has dared, but Celer gets him first with a spade. Covered in blood, he hits the hard ground.

When the king has learned of this, he swallows the tears that have   845
welled up inside and keeps the wound locked in his heart. He is unwilling to weep openly, and maintains the example of bravery. 'Thus,' he says, 'may the enemy cross my walls.'

Yet he grants funeral rites. No longer does he manage to postpone his tears, and the devotion he has concealed lies open. The bier was   850 set down, and he gave the last kisses. 'Farewell, brother,' he says, 'taken away against my will.'

He anointed the limbs for burning. Faustulus and Acca, her
855 grieving hair unbound, did as he did. Then the future Quirites wept for the young man. The pyre was grieved over and the last flame put to it.

A city rises, destined to tread victorious on the lands. (Who at that time could believe this from anyone?) May you rule all things, may
860 you always be subject to great Caesar, and often have even more of this name! And whenever you stand exalted in a mastered world, may everything be lower than your shoulders!

[23 April] I have told of Pales; likewise I shall tell of the Vinalia (but there's a day in the middle between the two).

865   Celebrate the power of Venus, girls of the street; Venus is appropriate for the earnings of women who promise a lot. With an offering of incense ask for beauty and popular favour, ask for seductiveness and words that are fit for fun. And give your mistress pleasing mint along
870 with her own myrtle, and bonds of reed covered with well-arranged roses.

Now it is proper for the temple next to the Porta Collina to be thronged. It takes its name from a Sicilian hill,* and when Claudius by force of arms took Arethusian Syracuse and captured you too,
875 Eryx, in war, thanks to the song of the long-lived Sibyl,* Venus was brought across and preferred to be worshipped in the city of her own descendants.

Why then, you ask, do they call Venus' festival Vinalia, and why is that day Jupiter's?

There was war, to decide whether Turnus or Aeneas should be the
880 son-in-law of Latian Amata. Turnus begs for Etruscan help. Mezentius was famous, and fierce when arms were taken up; he was great on horseback, and even greater on foot. The Rutuli and Turnus try to win him over to their side. In reply to this the Tuscan leader speaks as follows:

885   'My valour costs me no small price. As witness I call my wounds and the weapons I've often spattered with my own blood. You who ask help, share with me a reward, and not a great one—the next new wine from your vats. There's no delay for my service: yours is to give, ours to con-
890 quer. How Aeneas would want that reward to have been denied me!'

The Rutuli had agreed. Mezentius puts on his arms; Aeneas puts on his and addresses Jupiter: 'The enemy's vintage has been vowed to the Tyrrhenian king. You, Jupiter, will get the new wine from the Latian vines.' The better vow prevails. Huge Mezentius falls, and 895 strikes the ground with his resentful breast.

Autumn had come, soiled with trodden grapes. The wine that was due is paid to Jupiter, who deserved it. From this the day is called Vinalia; Jupiter claims it, and rejoices that it is among his festivals. 900

[**25 April**] When April has six days remaining, the times of spring will be in mid-course, and you will seek in vain the ram of Helle, daughter of Athamas; the signs bring rain, and the Dog rises too.*

On this day, when I was returning from Nomentum to Rome, a crowd 905 in white came face to face with me in the middle of the road. The *flamen* was going to the grove of ancient Mildew, to offer to the flames entrails of dog and entrails of sheep. At once I went up to him, so that I shouldn't be in ignorance of the rite. Your *flamen*, Quirinus, uttered these words: 910

'Rough Mildew, spare the blades of Ceres, and let the smooth shoot quiver on the surface of the ground. May you allow the crops to grow, nourished by the stars of a favourable sky, until they are ripe for the sickles. Your power is not slight; the grain you have marked the 915 sorrowful farmer counts as lost. Neither winds nor rains have harmed Ceres so much—and she isn't pale like this when burned by the marble frost—as when Titan warms the wet stalks: that is the occasion of 920 your anger, dread goddess.

'Spare, I pray: take your scurfy hands off the harvest and do not harm the cultivated fields. Being able to do harm is enough. Embrace hard iron, not delicate crops, and first destroy what can destroy others! You will more usefully consume swords and harmful spears. 925 There's no need for them, the world is at peace.

'Now let hoes and hard mattock and curved ploughshare, wealth of the countryside, gleam. Let rust stain weapons, and let someone trying to draw a sword from the scabbard feel it held fast by long disuse. 930 But do not violate Ceres, and may the farmer always be able to pay vows to you in your absence.'

He had spoken. To the right was a towel with loose nap, and a casket of incense with a dish of wine. He offered to the hearths the 935 incense and wine, and the guts of a sheep, and the disgusting entrails (we saw) of a filthy bitch.

Then says the *flamen* to me: 'Are you asking why a strange victim is offered in the rites?' I had asked.

'Perceive the reason. There is a Dog, they say it belonged to Icarius,
940 a star at the motion of which the scorched earth is thirsty and the crop is rushed. This dog is put on the altar in place of the starry Dog, and the only reason it happens is the name.'

[28 April] When Tithonus' wife has left the brother of Phrygian Assaracus* and three times lifted her radiance in the measureless
945 world, a goddess comes wreathed with many-coloured garlands of a thousand flowers; the stage has the custom of freer fun.* The festival of Flora extends to the Kalends of May. I shall return to it then; now a grander work presses on me.

Take the day, Vesta! Vesta has been received at her kinsman's thresh-
950 old.* So the just Fathers have decreed. Phoebus has one part, a second has gone to Vesta, he himself as the third occupies what is left from them.

Stand, you Palatine laurels! May the house stand, wreathed with oak!* One house, it holds three eternal gods.

BOOK 5
MAY

Do you want to know where I think the month of May got its name from? I haven't learned the reason clearly enough. As a traveller stops and, uncertain, doesn't know which way he should go when he sees a path in every direction, so, given the possibility of assigning different 5 reasons, I don't know where I should be taken. Abundance itself is a problem.

Speak, you who frequent the springs of Aganippian Hippocrene, welcome traces of Medusa's horse!

The goddesses disagreed. First Polyhymnia began (the others are 10 silent, and take mental note of what she says):

'After Chaos, when first the three elements were given to the world and the whole creation withdrew into new forms, the earth sank down by its own weight and pulled the seas with it, but lightness carried the sky to the highest places. The sun too, with the stars, held back by no 15 gravity, and you, horses of Luna, leaped up high.

'But for a long time earth did not give precedence to sky, nor did the other stars to Phoebus. All rank was equal. Often some utterly plebeian god dared to sit on the throne you occupied, Saturn. Nor 20 did any newcomer god walk alongside* Oceanus, and Themis was often received in the last place, until Honour and seemly Reverence, with peaceful countenance, placed their bodies on the couch sanctioned by law. From them Majesty was born; these the goddess 25 counted as her parents.

'On the very day of her birth she was mighty. No delay; she took her seat on high in the midst of Olympus, golden, conspicuous in her purple robe. Shame and Fear took their seats at the same time. You could see that all the divinities had shaped their expressions on her. 30 At once respect for honours* entered their minds; there is reward for the deserving, and none of them is self-complacent.

'This state of things in heaven lasted many years, until, by the fates, the older god fell from his citadel.* Earth brought forth savage 35 offspring, enormous monsters, Giants who would dare to go into the

house of Jupiter. A thousand hands* she gave them, and snakes instead
of legs, and she says "Take up arms against the great gods!"

'They were preparing to heap up mountains to the highest stars
40 and afflict great Jupiter with war. By hurling thunderbolts from the
citadel of heaven Jupiter turns the vast weights on to those who made
them. Well defended by these weapons of the gods, Majesty endures,
45 and remains worshipped ever since that time. Since then she sits by
Jupiter, is Jupiter's most faithful guard, and provides Jupiter with
a sceptre to be feared without violence.

'She has come to earth as well. Romulus and Numa worshipped
her, and others later, each in his own time. It is she who keeps fathers
50 and mothers in dutiful respect; it is she who comes to accompany
boys and maidens; it is she who entrusts the granted *fasces* and the
ivory chair of office;* it is she who rides high in triumph with gar-
landed horses.'

Polyhymnia had finished her speech. Both Clio and Thalia, expert at
55 the curved lyre, approved what she had said. Urania takes up the
theme. They all kept silence. No voice can be heard but hers.

'Once upon a time there was great respect for a head that was grey,
and an old person's wrinkles had their own value. Young men carried
60 out the work of Mars and spirited wars, and were there at their posts
to defend their gods. That age, less in strength and unfit for bearing
arms, often brought help to the fatherland by counsel.

'Nor at that time was the Senate-house open except after ripe
65 years: the Senate bore the mellow name of age.* An older man used to
give laws to the People, and the age from which high office could be
sought was defined by fixed statutes. An older man would walk
between young men, who themselves did not resent it, and on the
inside if there was only one companion. Who would dare to say words
70 fit to blush at in the presence of an older man? Long old age conferred
the right to rebuke.* Romulus saw this, and called his chosen hearts
Fathers; to them was referred the new city's government.

'From this I have the impression that the elders gave their name
75 to May,* in consideration of their own age. And it's possible that
Numitor said, "Romulus, grant this month to the old", and the
grandson didn't resist his grandfather. June, the month following,
called from the name of the young, provides no slight proof of the
honour proposed.'

Then, her unkempt hair wreathed in ivy, first of her chorus Calliopea 80
thus began:

'Once upon a time Oceanus, who encircles the earth with his clear
waters wherever it stretches, had married the Titaness Tethys. Pleione,
daughter of this union, is joined, so the story goes, with Atlas who
carries the sky, and gives birth to the Pleiades.

'Of them, it is reported that Maia surpassed her sisters in beauty 85
and lay with supreme Jupiter. On the ridge of cypress-bearing
Cyllene, she gave birth to the one who takes his heavenly way on
winged foot. Him the Arcadians and racing Ladon and huge Maenalus
duly worship, a land believed to pre-date the moon. 90

'An exile from Arcadia, Evander had come into the fields of Latium,
and brought gods along on board. Here, where Rome now is, the
world's capital, it was trees and grass and a few sheep and an occa-
sional hut. On arrival there, "Halt!" says his prophetic mother, "for 95
that countryside will be the place of empire."

'The Nonacrian hero obeys her as both mother and prophet, and
halted as a guest on foreign soil. The rites he taught these peoples
were many indeed, but the first ones were those of two-horned Faunus 100
and the wing-footed god. Half-goat Faunus, you are worshipped by
the Luperci in their loincloths when their cut thongs purify the
crowded ways. But you, inventor of the curved lyre and friend of
thieves, presented the month with your mother's name.

'Nor is this your first act of duty: you are thought to have given the 105
lyre seven strings, the number of the Pleiads.'

She too had finished. She was praised by the voice of her supporters.
What shall I do? Every part of the group has the same score. May the
Pierides' favour be with me equally, and may none be praised more by 110
me, or less.

[1 May] Let the work start from Jupiter. Visible to me on the first
night is a star that served at Jupiter's cradle. The rainy sign of the
Olenian she-goat is rising. She has heaven as a reward for the milk she
gave.

The Naiad Amalthea, famous on Cretan Ida, is said to have hidden 115
Jupiter in the woods.* She had a she-goat, lovely mother of two kids,
a sight to behold among the flocks of Dicte, with airy horns curving
over her back and an udder such as Jupiter's nurse could have. She 120

used to give the god milk, but she broke a horn on a tree and was maimed of half her glory. The nymph picked it up, bound it with fresh greenery, and brought it, full of fruit, to the mouth of Jupiter.

125   He, when he had control of heaven and sat on his father's throne, and nothing was greater than unconquered Jupiter, made stars of his nurse and his nurse's fruitful horn, which even now has its mistress's name.*

130 To the Guardian Lares, the Kalends of May saw an altar set up and small images of the gods. Yes, Curius had vowed them, but the passage of time destroys many things: long old age harms even stone.

However, the reason for the *cognomen* attached to them had been that they stand by, making everything safe with their eyes. They also 135 stand up for us, and protect the city's walls; they are on hand, and bring help.*

But a dog made out of the same stone used to stand before their feet: what was the reason for its standing with the Lar? Each of them 140 protects the house, each is loyal also to the master. The god likes crossroads, a dog likes crossroads. Both the Lar and Diana's pack chase away thieves. The Lares stay awake at night, dogs stay awake at night.

I was looking for the two statues of the twin gods which had been 145 brought down by the strength of the years' passing. The city has a thousand Lares, and the *genius* of the leader who presented them; the streets worship three divinities each.*

Where am I being taken? The august month will give me the right to this song. Meanwhile, I must sing the Good Goddess.

There is a natural outcrop; the thing gives a name to the place; 150 they call it the Rock. It is the good part of the hill.* It was on this that Remus had taken his stand in vain, at the time when you, birds of the Palatine, gave the first signs to his brother.

There, on a gently sloping ridge, the Fathers set up the temple that 155 hates the eyes of men. It is dedicated by an heiress of the ancient name of the Crassi, whose virgin body has known no man.* Livia restored it, so that she should not fail to imitate her husband* and follow him in every respect.

[2 May] When the stars are banished and the next daughter of 160 Hyperion lifts her rosy lamp on the horses of morning, cold Argestes

will stroke the topmost ears of corn and white sails will be unfurled
from Calabrian waters. But as soon as dusky twilight brings in the
night,* no part of the whole flock of Hyades is invisible. The face of 165
Taurus glitters, shining with seven flames which the Greek sailor calls
Hyades from the rain.*

Some think they were Bacchus' nurses, some have believed them
to be the granddaughters of Tethys and old Oceanus. Atlas was not
yet standing with the burden of Olympus on his shoulders when Hyas 170
was born, conspicuous in beauty. Aethra, offspring of Oceanus, when
birth was due, bore him and the nymphs—but Hyas was born first.

While his down is fresh, he uses a scare to frighten the timid deer,
and the hare is abundant prey for him. But once his valour has devel- 175
oped with the years, he dares to get close with boars and shaggy lion-
esses. It was while seeking the lair and cubs of a lioness newly delivered
that he himself was the bloodstained prey of the Libyan beast.

His mother wept for Hyas; for Hyas his sad sisters wept, and Atlas, 180
destined to submit his neck to the sky. But each parent was outdone
by the sisters' devotion. That is what gave them heaven; their name
Hyas made.

'Be present, mother of flowers, to be honoured with fun-filled games!
Last month I had postponed your role.* You begin in April, you cross 185
over into the times of May: the one has you as it flees, the other when
it comes. Since the borders of the months are yours and fall to you,
either of them is fitting for your praises. The Circus continues into
this month, and the palm acclaimed in the theatres. Let this song too 190
go with the Circus's show.

'Teach me yourself who you are. The opinion of men is deceptive.
You will be the best authority for your own name.'

That was what I asked, and this is what the goddess replied to my
questions (while she speaks she breathes from her mouth spring
roses):

'I who am called Flora used to be Chlōris. A Greek letter of my 195
name has been corrupted in Latin speech. I used to be Chlōris, a
nymph of the happy field where once, you hear, fortunate men had
business.* What my figure was like, it's hard for me to tell you
modestly—but it found for my mother a god as a son-in-law. 200

'It was spring, I was wandering. Zephyrus caught sight of me.
I began to leave. He pursues, I flee, he was stronger.

'Boreas, having dared to carry off a prize from the house of Erechtheus,* had given full right of rape to his brother too. The vio-
205 lence, however, he made up for by giving me the name of bride, and I have no complaint in my marriage-bed.

'Spring I enjoy always, always the year is full of bloom, always the tree has leaves, the ground has fodder. I have a fruitful garden in the
210 fields that are my dowry; the breeze warms it, it's kept moist by a spring of clear water. This my husband has filled with noble flowers, and he says to me, "Goddess, have control of the flowers."

'Often I've wanted to count the colours arranged there, and not
215 been able: the profusion was too great for counting. As soon as the dewy frost has been shaken off the leaves and the varied foliage warmed by the sunbeams, the Seasons assemble with their embroi- dered robes girt up, and they gather my gifts into light baskets.
220 Straight away the Graces arrive, and weave garlands and wreaths to entwine heavenly hair.

'I was the first to scatter new seeds throughout measureless nations. Previously the earth was monochrome. I was the first to make a flower from Therapnean blood—and the lament remains, written on its
225 petal.* You too, Narcissus, unhappy because you were not both one and the other, have a name in cultivated gardens. Why should I men- tion Crocus, or Attis, or the son of Cinyras? Through me, honour rises from their wound.

'Mars too, if you don't know, was brought to birth through my skills.
230 I pray Jupiter may keep on not knowing this, as he does so far!

'When Minerva was born without a mother, holy Juno felt pain that Jupiter hadn't needed her own services. She was on her way to complain to Oceanus about what her husband had done. Weary from
235 the effort, she stopped at my door. As soon as I saw her, "Daughter of Saturn," I said, "what has brought you here?" She reveals the place she is seeking. She added the reason as well. I began to console her with friendly words.

'"My trouble," she says, "is not to be relieved by words. If Jupiter
240 has become a father neglecting to use his spouse, and holds both names alone, why should I despair of becoming a mother without a spouse and giving birth without the touch of a man, so long as I'm chaste? I shall try all the treatments in the wide world, and search the seas and the hollows of Tartarus!"

'Her voice was in full flow. I had a hesitant expression.   245

'"Nymph," she says, "you seem to have some power."

'Three times I wanted to promise help, three times my tongue was held back. Jupiter's anger was a reason for great fear.

'"Bring help, I pray," she said. "The source will be concealed." And she calls the power of the water of Styx to witness.   250

'"What you seek," I say, "a flower of mine, sent from the fields of Olenus,* will provide. It is unique to my gardens. He who gave it said 'Touch a heifer with this, even a barren one—she'll be a mother.' I did: no delay, she was a mother."

'Straight away I plucked with my thumb the clinging flower. She is   255
touched, and conceives in the touched womb.

'And now, pregnant, she enters Thrace and the left of Propontis.* She is granted her wish, and Mars was born. Remembering that he received his birth from me, "You too," he said, "must have a place in   260
Romulus' city."

'Perhaps you may think that my realm is only among delicate garlands. My divine power touches the fields as well. If the crops have flowered well, the threshing-floor will be rich. If the vines have flowered well, there will be Bacchus. If the olives have flowered well, the   265
year is most lustrous in oil and the fruits have the outcome of this season.

'If once the flower is damaged, both vetch and beans perish, and your lentils perish too, arriving Nile.

'Wines also "flower", carefully stored in great cellars, and a cloudy   270
layer covers the top of the vats. Honey is my gift: it is I who summon to the violet, clover, and grey thyme the winged ones who will provide the honey. And we do the same thing too, when in our youthful years spirits are luxuriant and bodies themselves full of vigour.'

As she was saying this I was silently admiring her. But she says: 275
'You're entitled to learn, if you have any questions.'

'Tell me, goddess,' I replied, 'what the origin is of the games.' I had scarcely finished when she answered me:

'The rest of luxury's equipment wasn't yet flourishing. The rich man had either cattle or wide land: hence the word "landed wealth",   280
hence the word for money itself.* But already each man was acquiring wealth from a forbidden source.

'The practice had developed of grazing the People's pastures. For a long time it was allowed, and there was no punishment. The popu-
285 lace kept their public land without any champion, and by now it was a sign of inertia to graze on one's own property.

'Such licence was brought to the attention of the plebeian *aediles*, the Publicii; previously men lacked the courage. The People recover
290 their property; the guilty suffered a fine. The champions were praised for their care of public business.

'Part of the fine was given to me, and the victors set up new games with great approval. With some of it they contract for a paved incline, which at the time was a steep rock and is now a useful street. They call it Publician.'

295 I had thought that the shows were held annually. She said not, and added other words to what she said:

'Honour affects us too. Delighting in festivals and altars, we heavenly ones are an ambitious lot.

'Often by sinning someone has made the gods hostile, and there
300 has been a soothing sacrifice to pay for the transgressions. Often I have seen that Jupiter, already meaning to hurl his thunderbolts, has checked his hand after a gift of incense. But if we are neglected, the offence is paid for with great punishments and our anger goes beyond the just limit.

305 'Consider the grandson of Thestius: he was on fire* with flames that weren't there; the reason is that Phoebe's altar lacked fire. Consider the descendant of Tantalus: the same goddess held back his sails;* she is a virgin, and yet twice she avenged her scorned altars. Unlucky Hippolytus, you would wish you had worshipped Dione
310 when you were being torn apart by your panic-stricken horses.

'It takes a long time to relate examples of forgetfulness that have been put right by penalties. I too was overlooked, by the Roman Fathers.

'What was I to do? By what means was I to make my resentment plain? What kind of penalties was I to exact for the slight on me? In
315 my bitterness my duty was forgotten. I watched over no fields, my fruitful garden was of no value.

'The lilies had fallen, you could see the violets drying up, and the stamens of the crimson saffron became languid. Often Zephyrus said
320 to me, "Don't destroy your own dowry." My dowry was of no value to me. The olives were flowering; the wanton winds damaged them.

The crops were flowering; the crop was harmed by hail. The vine was promising; the sky grows black from the Austri and the leaves are dashed down by sudden rain. I didn't want it to happen, and I'm not cruel in my anger, but I took no care to drive it away. 325

'The Fathers have gathered, and vow to my divinity an annual festival if the year flowers well. I nod agreement to their vow. Consul Laenas with consul Postumius* paid the games to me in full.' 330

I was trying to enquire why these games have greater sexiness and freer fun, but it occurred to me that her divine power is not strict, and the gifts the goddess brings are appropriate to pleasure.

Brows are wholly encircled with stitched garlands, and the polished table is hidden by the roses thrown on it. Drunk, the banqueter dances, his hair bound with linden bark, and uses the wine's skill without thinking. Drunk, he sings at a lovely girlfriend's hard threshold; his perfumed hair holds soft garlands. No serious business is done when the forehead is crowned. 340

The liquid drunk by those wreathed in flowers isn't water. As long as you were mixed with no grapes, Achelous, there was no pleasure in gathering the rose. Bacchus loves flowers; you can tell from Ariadne's star that a garland pleased Bacchus. 345

A lightweight stage is proper for this goddess. She isn't, believe me she isn't, to be counted among the goddesses in tragic boots. As for why a troupe of prostitutes performs these games, the reason behind it isn't hard to find. She's not one of the frowners, she's not one of those who make big claims. She wants her rites to be open to a plebeian chorus, and she advises using the beauty of youth while it's in flower. 'The thorn,' she says, 'is despised once the roses have fallen.' 350

Why is it, though, that just as white robes are given at the Cerialia, so this goddess is proper in multicoloured dress? Is it because the harvest turns white when the ears ripen, and in flowers there's every colour and show? She nodded agreement, and flowers fell at the movement of her hair, just as the thrown rose often falls on the tables. 355

360

The lights,* the reason for which was obscure to me, were still waiting, when the goddess thus removed my uncertainties:

'Either it's because the fields are lit with bright flowers that lights are thought to befit my days; or it's because neither flower nor flame is dull-coloured, and each brightness draws eyes to itself; or it's 365

because nocturnal licence suits my pleasures. The third reason comes
from the truth.'

'There's a small point besides, about which it remains for me to
370 enquire—if I may,' I said, and she said: 'You may.'

'Why, instead of Libyan lions, are unwarlike roe-deer and the anx-
ious hare trapped in nets for you?'

She replied that forests had not fallen to her share, but gardens and
fields, not to be approached by aggressive wild animals.

375 She had finished it all. She withdrew into the airy breezes. Her
fragrance stayed: you might know a goddess had been there.

That Naso's song may flower for all time, scatter, I pray, your gifts
upon my heart!

[3 May] On the less than fourth night Chiron will bring out his stars,
380 a half-man combined with the body of a tawny horse.

Pelion, a mountain of Haemonia, faces the Austri. Its summit is
green with pine, oak occupies the rest. Phillyra's son held it; in the
ancient rock stand caves which they say the righteous old man inhab-
385 ited. He is believed to have kept occupied with the lyre's measures the
hands that would one day send Hector to his death.

Alcides had come, with part of his labours accomplished; the
orders that remained for the hero were almost the last. You might
see the two fates of Troy* standing by chance together—on one
390 side was the boy descended from Aeacus, on the other the son of
Jupiter.

The hero son of Philyra receives the young man as his guest. The
one asks the reason for his coming, the other explains. In the mean-
time he takes a look at the club and the lion-spoil, and says: 'Man
395 worthy of these arms, arms worthy of the man!' Nor did Achilles'
hands keep themselves from daring to touch the hide, rough with
bristles. And while the old man is handling the shafts caked with poi-
sons, an arrow falls out and is stuck fast in his left foot.

400 Chiron groaned, and drew the metal from his body. Alcides groans
too, and the Haemonian boy.* He himself, however, mixes herbs gath-
ered from the Pagasaean hills and soothes the wound with varied
treatment. The consuming poison was overcoming the treatment,
and the disease had been taken deep in his bones and throughout his
405 body. The blood of the Lernaean hydra, mingled with the blood of the
centaur, was giving no time for remedy.

Achilles was standing drenched with tears, as if before his father; so Peleus would have had to be mourned if he were dying. Often he would mould the feeble hands with loving hands; his teacher has the 410 reward of the character he made. Often he gave kisses, and often too he said to him lying there: 'Live, I beg you, don't leave me, dear father.'

The ninth day came, when you, most righteous Chiron, had your body encircled with twice-seven stars.

The curved Lyre would like to follow him, but the way is not yet suit- 415 able. The third night will be the right time.

When we say that the Nones dawn tomorrow, in the sky the Scorpion will be visible from his middle part.

[9 May] When three times after this Hesperus has shown his lovely face, and three times the conquered stars have yielded to Phoebus, 420 there will be the ceremony of an ancient rite; the nocturnal Lemuria. It will give offerings to the silent *manes*.

The year used to be shorter: they had not as yet come to know the pious *februa*, and you, double-formed Janus, were not the leader of the months. Already, though, they used to bring their gifts to the dead 425 ashes, and a grandson would propitiate the tomb of his buried grandfather. The month was May, so called from the name of the ancestors,* which even now has a part in the ancient custom.

When now the night is at its mid-point and providing silence for sleep, and you, dog, and you, birds of all kinds, have fallen silent, the 430 man who remembers the ancient rite and is nervous of the gods gets up (his twin feet have no bindings) and makes a sign by closing his fingers with his thumb between them, so that no insubstantial shade may meet him in the silence.

When he has washed his hands clean with spring water, he turns 435 round—he first takes some black beans—and turns his face away and throws them. But as he throws he says:

'These I send. With these beans I redeem me and mine.'

Nine times he says this, and does not look back. The shade is thought to collect them and follow behind him with nobody seeing. Again 440 he touches water, and clatters Temesan bronze, and asks the shade to go out of his house. When he has said nine times, 'Go out, paternal *manes*!', he looks back, and considers the ritual properly carried out.

445   What the day is called from, what the origin is of the name, escapes
me. It must be discovered from some god. Son of the Pleiad, revered
for your powerful wand, advise me. You have often seen the palace of
the Stygian Jupiter.
        Approached in prayer, the bearer of the *caduceus* came. Hear the
450 reason for the name. The reason was learned from the god himself.

        When Romulus had laid his brother's shade in the tomb, and the
obsequies had been performed for Remus the unfortunately quick,
unhappy Faustulus and Acca, her hair unfastened, were sprinkling
with their tears the burned-up bones.

455   From there they return home sad at early twilight. They sank down
on the hard bed, just as it was. The bloody shade of Remus seemed to
stand by the bed, and in a faint murmur to speak these words:
        'See, here I am, the half and other part of your prayer. Look at
460 what I am, I who just now was such a man! Just now, if I had had the
birds that ordain kingship, I could have been the greatest among my
people. As it is, I am an empty image escaped from the flames of the
pyre. This is the form left over from that Remus!
465   'Alas, where is Mars, my father? If only you spoke the truth, and it
was he who gave us the wild beast's teats when we were exposed. This
one, whom the she-wolf saved, a citizen's reckless hand destroyed.
Oh how much gentler she was! Savage Celer, may you yield up your
470 cruel spirit through wounds, and go beneath the earth covered in
blood, as I did.
        'My brother did not want this. In him there is matching devotion;
he gave what he could, tears for my fate. Ask him through your tears,
for the sake of your fostering, to mark a day distinguished in my
honour.'

475   As he tells them, they long to embrace him and they stretch out
their arms. The slippery shade eludes their grasping hands. When the
fleeing image has taken their sleep away with it, they each report to
the king his brother's words.
        Romulus complies, and calls that day Remuria on which the
480 obsequies are performed for buried ancestors. Over a long time the
rough letter which was first in the whole name was turned into
a smooth one.* Soon too they called the spirits of the silent ones
Lemures. This was the sense of the word, that was the force of the
utterance.

However, the men of old shut the temples on those days, just as 485
now you see them closed at the time of Feralia.* The same times were
unsuitable for the marriage torches of either widow or virgin: she who
did marry didn't last long. For this reason too, if proverbs interest
you, folk say bad women marry in May. 490

All the same, these three festivals occur about the same time, but not
in succession on any intervening day.* If in the middle of them you
look for Boeotian Orion, you'll get it wrong.

I must sing the reason for that constellation. Jupiter, and his 495
brother who is king in the wide ocean, and Mercury were travelling
the roads together. It was the time when upturned ploughs are
brought back by the yoked oxen, and the lamb, head down, drinks the
milk of the well-filled ewe.

By chance an old man, Hyrieus, farmer of a narrow plot, sees them
as he was standing in front of his little cottage. And this is what he 500
said:

'The way is long, but there isn't a long time left. And my door is
open for strangers.'

He added a look to his words, and asked a second time. They go
along with his promises, and do not reveal that they are gods. They
pass under the old man's roof, soiled with black smoke. 505

The fire was small, on yesterday's log. He himself, on his knees,
brings the flames to life with his breath, and brings out battered
torches and chops them up. There are pots standing. The smaller
held beans, the other herbs, and each froths, closely covered by its lid. 510
And while they wait he gives red wine with a trembling hand.

The god of ocean receives the first cup. As soon as he drained it, he
said: 'Now let the next to drink be Jupiter.' The old man heard
'Jupiter', and went white.

When his wits have returned, he sacrifices the ox that tilled his 515
poor field and roasts it on a great fire, and the wine he had once laid
up as a boy in early years he brings out, stored in a smoky jar.

No delay; they reclined, on couches that concealed river-sedge in
linen, but were not high, even so. The table gleamed, now with the 520
feast, now with Lyaeus set there. The bowl was red earthenware, the
cups were beech.

Jupiter's words were: 'If anything occurs to you, wish for it! You'll
gain it all.' The mild old man's words were:

525   'I had a dear wife, known to me in the spring of first youth. You ask
      where she is now? The urn covers her. To her I swore an oath, having
      called you to witness my words: "You alone," I said, "will be married
      to me." I said it, and I keep my word—but in fact I have a different
530   wish. I don't want to be a husband, and I do want to be a father.'

      They had all nodded agreement. They had all stood by the hide of the
      ox. I'm ashamed to speak further. Then they covered the dripping hide by
      throwing earth on top. And now—ten months, and a boy had been born.

535   Hyrieus calls him Urion, because that's how he was conceived; the
      first letter has lost its ancient sound. He had grown immensely. Delia
      took him as her companion: he was the guard of the goddess, he was
      her escort.

540   Unthinking words move the gods' anger. 'The wild beast I can't
      overcome,' he said, 'doesn't exist!' Earth sent in a scorpion.

      Its intent was to bring its crooked barbs against the goddess mother
      of twins.* Orion stood in its way. Latona added him to the shining
      stars, and said: 'Have the reward of what you deserve.'

545   [12 May] But why do Orion and the other stars hurry to leave the
      firmament, and Night curtail her course? Why does the bright day,
      with the Light-bringer preceding it, lift its radiance more quickly
      than usual from the watery ocean? Am I mistaken, or are weapons
550   sounding? I'm not mistaken, weapons were sounding. Mars comes,
      and coming has given the signs of war.

      The Avenger himself is coming down from heaven to his own hon-
      ours and the splendid temple in the Augustan *forum*. The god is huge
      and so is the structure. In no other way did Mars deserve to dwell in
555   his own son's city. This temple is worthy of trophies won from
      Giants;* it is right that from here Gradivus sets fierce wars in motion,
      whether any villain from the Eōan world provokes us or anyone from
      the setting sun will have to be subdued.

      Powerful in arms, he surveys the gable at the height of the struc-
560   ture and approves the fact that unconquered goddesses occupy the
      highest part.* He surveys the weapons of various forms on the doors,
      and the arms of lands overcome by his soldiery. On this side he sees
      Aeneas burdened with the dear weight,* and so many ancestors of
565   nobility from Iulus; on the other he sees the son of Ilia bearing on his
      shoulders a leader's arms,* and glorious deeds inscribed beneath* the
      ordered rows of men.

He looks too at the temple adorned with an august name, and when 'Caesar' is read the structure seems greater. The young man had vowed this at the time when he took up dutiful arms.* From such 570 great deeds was a *princeps* to be initiated. Stretching out his hands, with the just army standing on one side, the conspirators on the other, he uttered the following speech:

'If my father and Vesta's priest is my authority for war, and if I am ready to avenge the divine power of each, be present, Mars, and glut 575 my sword with the blood of criminals! May your favour stand for the better cause. You will receive a temple and be called the Avenger, if I am victorious.'

He had made the vow, and returns in joy from the routed foe.

But it's not enough to have earned the *cognomen* for Mars just once. He pursues the standards held back by the Parthian's hand. It 580 was a race protected by plains and horses and arrows, made inaccessible by rivers flowing round it. The deaths of the Crassi had added spirit to it, when soldiers and standards and leader were lost together.* The Parthian was in possession of Roman standards, the glory of war, 585 and the standard-bearer of the Roman eagle was an enemy.

That shame would have remained to this day, if the resources of Ausonia were not protected by Caesar's powerful weapons. He removed the old stains and the long age's disgrace: recaptured,* the 590 standards recognized their own people.

What good to you now were the arrows fired behind you in the usual way?* What good was the terrain, what good the use of fast horses? Parthian, you're giving back the eagles, you're offering up your vanquished bows as well. Now you possess no symbols of our shame.

Duly were both a temple and a title given to the god who twice 595 avenged us, and the well-deserved honour pays the debt of the vow.

Celebrate the ritual games in the Circus, Quirites. The stage seemed not to befit the valiant god.

[13 May] You'll see all the Pleiades and the whole line of the sisters when there's one night left before the Ides. That, according to sources 600 I do not doubt, is when summer begins and the times of the mild spring come to an end.

[14 May] The day before the Ides reveals Taurus lifting his starry face. A well-known story is behind this constellation.

605　　When Jupiter, as a bull, offered his back to the Tyrian girl and
wore horns on his false brow, she held on to his mane with her right
hand, her robe with her left, and fear itself was the cause of extra
grace. The breeze fills her dress, the breeze moves her golden hair.
610　Girl of Sidon, like that you had to be the object of Jupiter's gaze!
　　　Often she drew her girlish feet up from the sea's surface, and
feared the touch of the water leaping towards her. Often the god
deliberately lowered his back into the waves, so she would cling more
tightly to his neck.
615　　They reached the shore. Jupiter was standing without any horns,
and had been changed from a bull to a god. The bull enters heaven.
As for you, girl of Sidon, Jupiter fills you and a third part of the earth
has your name.*
620　　Others have said that this constellation is the heifer of Pharos, who
was made cow from human, goddess from cow.*

　　　At that time, too, it is the custom for the virgin to throw rush effigies
of men of old* from the oak bridge. Anyone who has believed that
after ten times six years bodies were sent to their death condemns his
ancestors on a criminal charge.
625　　There's an old story that, at the time when the land was called
Saturnia, prophetic Jupiter uttered the following words:
　　　'As an offering to the old sickle-bearer,* throw two bodies of your
people to be received by the Tuscan waters.'
　　　Until the Tirynthian came into these fields, every year the grim
630　rituals were carried out in the Leucadian manner.* They say Hercules
threw straw Quirites into the water, and following his example the
bodies hurled are false.
　　　Some think that in order for young men alone to cast votes, they
flung the frail old men from the bridges.*
635　　Thybris, teach me the truth! Your banks are older than the city.
You're able to know well the origin of the ritual.

　　　Thybris raised his reed-bearing head from the middle of the channel
and parted his hoarse mouth with the following sounds:
　　　'I have seen these places as empty grassland without walls. Each
640　bank was pasture for scattered cattle, and I, whom now the nations
know and fear as Tiber, was then to be looked down on even by
livestock.

'The name of Evander the Arcadian is often mentioned to you. As a new arrival he churned my waters with his oars. Alcides came too, accompanied by a crowd of Achaeans. Albula my name was then, if I recall. 645

'The Pallantian hero receives the young man as a guest, and the punishment he owed finally comes to Cacus. The victor departs, and takes away with him the cattle, booty of Erythea. But his companions refuse to go further. A large part of them had come having abandoned Argos; in these hills they put their hope and their home. Often, however, they are touched by sweet love of their native land, and someone on his deathbed orders this small task: 650

' "Throw me into the Tiber, so that carried by Tiber's waves I may go as empty dust to the shore of Inachus." 655

'Responsibility for the grave as ordered is unwelcome to his heir. The dead man is buried, a guest in Ausonian soil. In place of the master a rush-made image is tossed to the Tiber, to seek his Greek home again through the long straits.' 660

So much he said, and went down to a dripping cave in the living rock. You light waters maintained your course.

[15 May] Be present, bright grandson of Atlas, you whom the Pleiad once bore to Jupiter in the mountains of Arcadia.

Arbiter of peace and weapons for the gods, both those above and those below, who make your way on winged feet, happy in the striking of the lyre, happy too in the glossy wrestling school, by whose teaching the tongue has learned to speak with elegance—for you on the Ides the Fathers placed the temple that looks at the Circus. Since then, this day is your festival; all those whose business is selling their merchandise offer incense and ask you to grant them profits. 665 670

There is a spring of Mercury near the Porta Capena. If you care to believe those who've tried it, it has a divine power. Hither comes a merchant, his tunic belted up, and, pure, with a fumigated jar he draws water to take away. From this a laurel is wetted, and from the wetted laurel all the items due to have new owners are sprinkled. He sprinkles his own hair too with the dripping laurel, and goes through his prayers in a voice that normally cheats: 675 680

'Wash away,' he says, 'the false oaths of the time gone by. Wash away the dishonest words of the day gone by. If I made you a witness, or falsely invoked Jupiter's divinity, useless since he wasn't going to

685 hear, or if I knowingly deceived another god or goddess, let the swift south winds carry the wicked words away.

'And on the coming day may perjuries open up for me, and the gods not care about any I utter! Just give me profits, give me joy
690 when the profit's made, and make it a pleasure to have deceived the buyer!'

Mercury laughs from on high at the man who makes such requests, remembering that he himself stole the Ortygian cattle.*

[20 May] But since my request is so much better, reveal to me, I pray, from what time Phoebus moves into Gemini.
695 'When you see that the number of the days remaining in the month matches the number of Hercules' labours,' he says.

'Tell me,' I replied, 'the reason for this constellation.' The god of the eloquent mouth explained the reason:
700 'The Tyndarid brothers—one a horseman, the other a boxer—had seized and carried off Phoebe and Phoebe's sister. Idas and his brother, each betrothed to become the son-in-law of Leucippus, go to war and claim their women back. Love urges these to seek restitution, those to refuse it. Each of them fights for the same reason.
705 'The descendants of Oebalus could have escaped their pursuers by speed, but it seemed base to win by swift flight. There's a place free of trees, open ground suitable for fighting. In that place (name, Aphidna) they had taken their stand.
710 'Castor, his breast pierced by Lynceus' sword, hit the ground with a wound he didn't see coming. Pollux is at hand to avenge him, and runs Lynceus through with his spear just where the neck joins and presses down on the shoulders. Idas began to come at him, and was barely driven back by Jupiter's fire. They say, however, that the thunderbolt failed to tear the weapon from his right hand.
715 'And now, Pollux, the lofty heaven was lying open for you when you said: "Hear my words, father. Divide between the two of us the heaven you're giving to me alone. A half will be greater than the whole gift."

'He spoke, and ransomed his brother by alternating their pos-
720 itions.* Each of them is a useful star to a ship in distress.'

[21 May] Let him who asks what the Agonia are go back to Janus; but in the calendar they have this time as well.

[22 May] On the night that follows the day, Erigone's dog emerges. The reason for the sign has been given in another place.*

[23 May] The next day is Vulcan's. They call it Tubilustria. The 725 trumpets he makes are ritually cleansed.

[24 May] Next, there is the place with four marks,* in which, read in order, there is either the custom of the sacred rites or the flight of the king.

[25 May] Nor do I pass you over, public Fortune* of a powerful People, to whom a temple was given on the following day.   730
    When Amphitrite, rich in waters, has received this day, you will see the golden bird's beak, pleasing to Jupiter.*

[26–7 May] The coming dawn will take Boötes out of sight, and on the succeeding day the star of Hyas will be there.

BOOK 6

JUNE

THIS month too has uncertain reasons for its name. I'll set them all out, and you yourself shall choose the one to please you.

I shall sing what happened, but there will be some who say I have made it up, and think that no divinities have appeared to a mortal.
5 There is a god in us, and when he stirs us we glow; this urge has the seeds of a sacred mind.* It is permitted for me in particular to have seen the faces of the gods, whether because I am a bard or because I sing sacred themes.

There is a grove, thick with trees, a place remote from every sound
10 if it were not disturbed by waters. Here I was wondering what the origin was of the month just begun, and paying attention to the name of it.

Look! I saw goddesses. They were not the ones the instructor of ploughing* had seen when he was following Ascra's sheep, nor the
15 ones the son of Priam compared in the glens of watery Ida—but all the same, there was one of those.*

There was one of those, sister of her own husband. I recognized her: she was the one who stands on Jupiter's Citadel.* I had started to shudder, and was confessing my mind in speechless pallor. That was
20 when the goddess herself took away the fear she caused. For she says:

'O bard, composer of the Roman year, who have dared to tell great things in tiny measures, you made for yourself the right to see heavenly divinity when you decided to compose the festivals in your verses.

25 'Lest you be ignorant, however, and drawn by popular error, June has its name from my name. It is something to have married Jupiter and to be Jupiter's sister. I'm not sure whether to pride myself more in brother or husband. If descent is considered, I was the first to make
30 Saturn a parent: I was allotted to Saturn first. From my father Rome was once called Saturnia. For him this land was next after heaven.* If marriage is valued, I am called the Thunderer's lady, and my temple is joined to that of Tarpeian Jupiter.*

'If a concubine could give her name to the month of May, shall this 35
honour be begrudged to me? Why then am I called queen and *princeps*
of the goddesses? Why have they given my right hand a golden scep-
tre? Will the days' lights make a month, and I be called Lucina after
them,* and not draw a name from any month? 40

'In that case I might regret that in good faith I put aside my anger
against the offspring of Electra and the house of Dardanus. The rea-
son for my anger was twofold: I resented the abduction of Ganymede,
and my beauty was defeated by the judge on Ida.*

'I might regret not supporting the citadels of Carthage, since my 45
chariot and weapons are at that place.* I might regret having sub-
jected Sparta and Argos and my own Mycenae and ancient Samos to
Latium. Add old Tatius, and the Juno-worshipping Faliscans, whom
I allowed to become subject to the Romans. 50

'But let there be no regret! No nation is dearer to me. Here may
I be worshipped, here may I occupy the temple with my own Jupiter.
Mavors himself said to me: "I entrust these walls to you. You will be
powerful in your grandson's city." Proof follows his words. On 55
a hundred altars I am worshipped, and the honour of the month is of
no less weight to me than any.

'It is not only Rome, however, that pays me this honour. Those
who live outside the city grant me the same gift. Look into the
calendars kept by Aricia of the grove,* and the Laurentine people, 60
and my own Lanuvium: there is a month of Juno there. Look into
Tibur, and the sacred walls of the goddess of Praeneste:* you will
read a time for Juno. Romulus didn't found those cities—but Rome
was my grandson's.'

Juno had finished. I looked behind me. The wife of Hercules was 65
standing there, and in her expression were signs of vigour.*

'If,' she says, 'my mother orders me to leave the whole of heaven,
I shall not stay against my mother's wishes. Now too, I am not com-
peting about the name of this time; I am coaxing, I play the role almost 70
of a petitioner, and I would prefer to have kept by prayer the subject
of my right. Perhaps you yourself may support my cause.

'My mother has taken possession of the golden Capitol in her
shared temple, and holds the high place with Jupiter, as she should.
But all of my glory comes from the origin of a month; the honour I'm 75
worried about is the only one I have. What harm has it done, Roman,

if you've given the month's title to the wife of Hercules, and posterity has remembered?

80   'This land owes me something too, in my great husband's name. It was to here he drove the captured cattle, here that Cacus, ill defended by flames and his father's gift,* stained with his blood the ground of Aventine.

'I am called to more recent matters. Romulus divided the People
85   according to years and arranged it in two parts: one is readier to give counsel, the other to fight; one age urges war, but the other wages it. That is what he decreed, and he separated the months by the same token. June is of the young, the one before it of the old.'

She spoke, and in the keenness of their rivalry they would have
90   entered a dispute, and piety would have been concealed by anger.

Concord came, the peaceful leader's divinity and his achievement, her long hair bound with Apollo's laurel. When she has told the story that Tatius and brave Quirinus came together, and their two king-
95   doms with their peoples, and that fathers-in-law and sons-in-law were received in a common home, 'June,' she says, 'has its name from their joining.'

A threefold reason has been stated. But pardon me, you goddesses; the case is not to be decided by my verdict. Go from me as equals.
100   Pergamum perished because of the one who judged beauty: two god-desses harm more than one helps.

[1 June] Carna, the first day is given to you.

This is the goddess of the hinge. By her power she opens what's closed, closes what's open. From where she has the powers given to her is a story that time has made rather obscure. But you'll be certain of it through my song.

105   Close by Tiberinus lies Alernus' ancient grove. Even now the *pon-tifices* bring sacrifices there. From there a nymph was born (men of old called her Cranaē), often pursued in vain by many suitors. Her custom was to make for country places and chase wild beasts with
110   javelins and spread knotted nets in the hollow valley. She had no quiver, but they thought her the sister of Phoebus—and Phoebus, she didn't shame you.

If some young man had spoken words of love to her, at once she
115   would give back this reply: 'This place has too much light, and with

light too much shame. If you lead the way to a more remote cave, I'll
follow.' When he falls for it and has gone ahead, she finds the bushes,
stops, and hides. There's no way she can be found.

Janus had seen her, and seized with desire for what he'd seen, had
used soft words against her who was hard. The nymph, as usual, tells 120
him to seek a more secluded cave; she follows as if accompanying him,
and deserts him as he leads the way.

Fool! Janus sees what happens behind his back. You're achieving
nothing: he looks back at your hiding place. You're achieving nothing, 125
see, I told you! For though you're hiding under a rock, he grabs you
in his arms, and having got what he wanted says:

'Let the right of the hinge be yours,* in return for lying with me.
Have this, as payment for your lost virginity.'

So saying, he gave her a thorn (it was a white one) with which she'd 130
be able to drive grim harm away from doors.

There are some greedy birds—not the ones that used to cheat of its
meals the throat of Phineus, but that's where they're descended from.
Huge heads they have, eyes that stand out, beaks designed for plun-
der, white on their wings, hooked claws. They fly at night and look for 135
children without nurses. They snatch them from their cradles and
defile their bodies. It is said that they tear with their beaks at the milk-
fed inner parts, and have their gullet full of the blood they've drunk.

Their name is *striges*, but the reason for this name* is that they have 140
a habit of screeching in the dreadful night. So—whether they are born
birds, or become so by spells, and a Marsian incantation transfigures
old women into birds—they came into the chamber of Proca.

Proca, born there five days before, was fresh prey for the birds.
They suck out the baby's breast with their greedy tongues; yet the 145
poor child wails and cries for help. Terrified by her nursling's voice,
the nurse comes running and finds his cheeks cut with hard claws.

What was she to do? His face had the colour that late leaves some-
times tend to have when early winter has damaged them. She comes 150
to Cranaē and tells her what has happened. 'Lay fear aside,' said she,
'your nursling will be safe.' She had come to the cradle. Both mother
and father were weeping. 'Stay your tears,' she says: 'I shall heal him
myself.'

Straight away, three times in a row she touches the doorposts with 155
a branch of arbutus, three times with a branch of arbutus she marks

the threshold. She sprinkles the entrance with water (and the water
contained a remedy), she holds the raw entrails from a two-month-
old sow, and she says this:

160 'Birds of night, spare the child's flesh! In place of the little one
a little victim falls.* Take, I pray, a heart for a heart, entrails for
entrails. We give you this life in place of a better one.'

When she has made the offering in this way, she puts the cut
pieces in the open air and forbids those present at the rites to look
165 back at them. And Janus' rod of white thorn is placed below, where
a little window gave light to the chamber. After that, they say the
birds didn't defile the cradle, and the colour the child had before
returned to him.

170 Do you ask why fat bacon is eaten on these Kalends, and beans are
mixed with hot spelt? She's an ancient goddess, and is nourished by
the foods that used to nourish her before. She is not extravagant, and
doesn't seek imported banquets.

For the People then, fish were still swimming unmolested and oys-
175 ters were safe in their shells. Neither the bird that rich Ionia supplies
nor the one that delights in pygmies' blood* knew Latium yet, and
the only thing pleasing about the peacock was its feathers. Nor had
the earth sent them wild beasts skilfully captured; the pig was prized,
180 and they held their festivals with a slaughtered sow. The land gave
only beans and hard spelt. Whoever eats these two mixed together on
the sixth Kalends, his bowels, they say, cannot suffer harm.

On the summit of the Citadel also, they say, Juno Moneta's temple was
185 built as a result of your vow, Camillus. Previously it had been the house
of Manlius, who once drove back Gallic arms from Jupiter of the Capitol.
Great gods, how well would he have fallen in that fight as a defender of
your throne, Jupiter on high! He lived, to die condemned on a charge of
190 tyranny.* This is the title long old age gave him.

The same day is the festival of Mars: the Porta Capena looks forth at
him outside the city, in his position next to the road on the right.* You
too, Tempestas, we acknowledge earned a shrine when the fleet was
almost overwhelmed in the waters of Corsica.*

195   These monuments of men are plain to see. If you're looking for
stars, that is the time great Jupiter's hooked bird rises.

[2 June] The next day calls out the Hyades, the horns of the brow of Taurus, and the land is drenched with heavy rain.

[3 June] When it has twice been morning, and Phoebus has doubled his risings, and the crops have twice become wet with a covering of 200 dew, on this day Bellona is said to have been consecrated in a Tuscan war;* always she assists Latium with her favour. Appius is her founder, he who, by denying peace to Pyrrhus,* saw much in his mind though he had lost his eyesight.

From the temple a short open space looks out at the upper Circus; 205 there's a small column there of no small significance. From it the custom is for a spear to be launched by hand as a herald of war, when it is decided that arms be taken up against king and peoples.

[4 June] The other part of the Circus is safe under Guardian Hercules, which task the god has from Euboean song.* The date of 210 the task is the Light-bringer before the Nones. If you're looking for an inscription, Sulla approved the work.

[5 June] I was asking whether I should assign the Nones to Sancus or to Fidius or to you, father Semo. Then Sancus says to me: 'Whichever of them you give it to, I'll have the task. I bear three names: so 215 Cures willed it.' So it was he whom the ancient Sabines presented with a temple, and they set it up on the Quirinal ridge.

[6 June] I have a daughter, and I pray she may live longer than my years. If she is safe I shall always be happy. 220

When I was wanting to give her to a son-in-law, I began to look out the times that are proper for marriage torches, and the ones that should be avoided. June after the sacred Ides was shown to me at that time as beneficial for brides, beneficial for husbands. The first part of this month was found to be inappropriate for the bridal 225 chamber. For this is what the holy wife of the *flamen Dialis* says to me:

'Until peaceful Thybris with his yellow waters has carried the sweepings from Ilian Vesta down to the sea, I am not allowed to comb down my hair with fashioned boxwood, or to have cut my nails with 230 iron, or to have touched my husband, even though he is Jupiter's priest, even though he has been given to me by an everlasting law. You

too, be in no hurry. Your daughter will marry better when fiery Vesta
gleams on a clean floor.'

235 **[7 June]** The third Phoebe after the Nones is said to remove Lycaon,
and the Bear has nothing to fear behind her. I remember that that's
when I watch games on the grass of the Campus, and that they are
called your games, smooth-flowing Thybris. It's a festival day for those
240 who pull in dripping lines and hide bronze hooks in bits of food.

[8 June] Mind too has divine power. We see the shrine of Mind that
was vowed from fear of your war, faithless Carthaginian. Carthaginian,
you had renewed the war; stunned by a consul's death,* everyone
245 dreaded the Moorish troops. Fear had driven out hope, when the
Senate undertakes vows to Mind and immediately she comes in better
form. That day on which the vows were paid to the goddess sees the
approaching Ides with six days in between.

[9 June] Vesta, be favourable. Now we open our lips in service to
250 you, if we are permitted to come to your rites.
     I was absorbed in prayer. I was conscious of a heavenly power, and
the joyful ground shone with a purple light. No, I did not see you,
goddess (farewell, lies of bards), nor should you have been seen by a
255 man. But the things I had not known, and those about which I was
kept in error, were made known to me without anyone's instruction.
     Four times ten times, they say, Rome had held the Parilia, when
the goddess guardian of the flame was received in her temple. It was
260 the work of the peaceful king;* the Sabine land has produced no more
god-fearing temperament than his.
     What you now see roofed in bronze you would then see roofed in
thatch, and the wall was woven with pliant wicker. This little place,
which contains the hall of Vesta, was then the great palace of unshorn
Numa.

265 However, the shape of the temple is said to have been before what it
now remains, and a plausible reason is to be found for the shape. Vesta
is the same as Earth: an unsleeping fire is to be found in each. Earth
and the hearth signify their own place.
270   Earth, like a ball, resting on no prop, hangs with air beneath it, so
heavy a weight. Rotation itself keeps the globe balanced, and there is

no angle at all to press on the parts of it. And since it is positioned at the centre of everything, so that it touches no side more, or less, if it were not convex it would be closer to one part, and the universe would 275 not have Earth as its central weight.

By Syracusan skill a globe is poised, suspended in enclosed air, a tiny image of the boundless sky,* and the earth is as far distant from the top as from the bottom. Its round shape causes this to 280 happen. The appearance of the temple is the same: no corner projects on it, and a dome protects it from showers of rain.

You ask why the goddess is served by virgin attendants? I shall find the proper reasons from this place too.

The story goes that Juno and Ceres were born of Ops from 285 Saturn's seed. Vesta was the third. The first two married; both are said to have given birth.* Out of the three one remained who would not tolerate a man. What is surprising if a virgin delights in a virgin attendant and admits chaste hands to her rites? 290

You must understand Vesta as nothing other than living flame; and from flame you see no bodies born. Rightly therefore she is a virgin who puts out no seed and takes no seed, and she loves companions of virginity.

Like a fool, for a long time I thought there were images of Vesta; later 295 I learned that there are none beneath her curved dome. Concealed in that temple is a fire that has never been extinguished; neither Vesta nor fire has any effigy.

Earth stands by its own force; Vesta is named from standing by force. The reason for her Greek name* may be the same. But the 300 hearth is so called from flames and because it warms everything.* Formerly, however, it was at the front of the house; from this too I think the *uestibulum* is named; as a result, in praying we first address Vesta, who occupies the first place.*

It was once the custom to sit in front of hearths on long benches, 305 and to believe that gods were present at the table. Now too, when the rites of ancient Vacuna are being held, they stand and sit in front of Vacuna's hearths. Something of ancient practice has come down into these years: a clean platter carries the food offered to Vesta. 310

See, bread hangs down from garlanded donkeys, and wreaths of flowers cover the rough millstones. Formerly it was only spelt that

farmers roasted in their ovens (even the Oven goddess has her own
315 rites); the hearth itself prepared bread placed under the ashes, and
a broken tile was set on the warm floor. And so the baker minds the
hearth and the mistress of the hearth, and the donkey that turns
the pumice millstones.

320 Should I pass over your shame or report it, ruddy Priapus? It's a little
story full of fun.

Cybele, her brow encircled by a turreted crown, invites the eternal
gods to her festival. She also invites the satyrs and nymphs, deities of
the countryside; Silenus is there, though no one had invited him.
325 It's not permitted, and it takes too long, to narrate the banquet of
the gods. The night was spent awake with much strong wine. Some
were roaming at random in the valleys of shadowy Ida, others lie
down and rest their limbs on soft grass. Some play, others are held in
330 sleep; some link arms and stamp on the green ground with rapid tri-
ple step.*

Vesta is lying down and taking peaceful rest without a care, just as
she was, her head supported on a pillow of turf. But the red guardian
of gardens stalks nymphs and goddesses alike, and takes his wander-
335 ing steps this way and that. He catches sight of Vesta too. It's not clear
whether he thought she was a nymph or knew it was Vesta, but he
himself says he didn't know.

He conceives an obscene hope. Stealthily he tries to approach and
moves on tiptoe, his heart pounding.

It happened that old Silenus had left the donkey on which he'd
340 ridden near the banks of a gently murmuring stream. The god of the
long Hellespont was just on his way to get started when the beast
brays with an ill-timed noise. Frightened by the harsh sound, the
goddess gets up; the whole crowd rushes together; he gets away
through hostile hands.

345 Lampsacus has the custom of sacrificing this animal to Priapus,*
chanting: 'We offer to the flames the tell-tale's guts, as fitting!' You,
goddess, remember, and adorn it with necklaces of bread. Work
ceases, the empty millstones have fallen silent.

The altar of Jupiter the Baker on the Thunderer's Citadel is more
350 famous for its name than for what it cost. I shall tell you what it
means.

The Capitol was being hard pressed by savage Gauls. The siege, already long, had created famine. The gods are summoned to the royal throne. 'Begin!' says Jupiter to Mars, and immediately he replies:

'You, of course, don't know what the fortune of disaster is, and this 355 grief of my heart needs the voice of complaint. But if you insist that I briefly report bad news combined with shame—Rome lies beneath an Alpine foe.

'Is this the city to which world power had been promised,* Jupiter? Is this the city you intended to put in control of the lands? Already 360 she has crushed her neighbours and the Etruscan forces. Hope was on course, but now she has been driven from her own home.*

'We have seen the old men who had held triumphs, dressed up in their embroidered robes, fallen dead through the bronze-lined halls. We have seen the pledges of Ilian Vesta being transferred from their 365 abode.* I suppose they think some gods exist. But if they should look back and see the Citadel on which you live and so many of your dwellings being pressed by the siege, they would know that there is no help left in worship of the gods, and that incense offered by an anxious 370 hand is wasted.

'And if only a space for battle would open up! Let them take up arms, and if they cannot prevail let them fall! As it is, they are cooped up on their hill without food, fearing a coward's death, and the barbarian throng hems them in.'

Then Venus and Quirinus, handsome with his augur's staff and his 375 *trabea*, and Vesta too, said much on behalf of their own Latium.

'We have a public responsibility for those walls,' replied Jupiter, 'and conquered Gaul will pay the penalty. You, Vesta, just bring it about that the crops that are failing be thought abundant, and do not 380 desert your own dwelling. Whatever unground Ceres there is, let the hollow millstone crush it, and when it has been softened by hand let the hearth harden it in the fire.'

He had given his orders, and the virgin daughter of Saturn nodded assent to her brother's commands.

It was midnight. By now toil had given the leaders sleep. Jupiter 385 rebukes them, and from his sacred mouth tells them his will:

'Get up, and from the heights of the Citadel throw into the midst of the enemy the resource you least want to throw.'

Sleep departs, and driven by the strange riddle they ask what resource it is that they do not want to give up and are being ordered 390 to. It seemed to be Ceres; they throw the gifts of Ceres, and what's thrown down on to the helmets and long shields makes a din. Hope is lost that they can be defeated through famine. The enemy is routed, and a white altar is set up for Jupiter the Baker.

395   During Vesta's festival I happened to be returning on the way by which the Nova Via is now joined to the Roman Forum. I saw a lady coming down to this place barefoot. I was astonished, speechless, and checked my step.

An old woman noticed, a neighbour of the place. She tells me to sit
400   down, then speaks to me in a quavering voice, shaking her head:

'This, where the *fora* now are, waterlogged marshes once occupied. When the waters overflowed, the channel was flooded by the river.* That "Lake Curtius", which supports dry altars, is now firm
405   ground, but was a lake before. Where the Velabra lead regular processions to the Circus, there was nothing but willows and hollow reeds. Often a reveller sings as he comes back through the waters around the city, and tosses drunken words at the boatmen. That god over there
410   had not yet got his name from turning away the river, a name that fits his various shapes.*

'Here too there was a grove thick with rushes and reeds, and a marsh not to be approached with foot covered. The pools have receded, and their own bank holds the waters in check, and now the land is dry. The custom, though, remains.'

415   She had delivered the reason. 'Farewell, excellent old lady,' I said. 'May all the rest of your life be gentle.'

The rest I learned long ago in the years of childhood, but still, I shouldn't leave it out on that account.
420   Ilus, descendant of Dardanus,* had recently built new walls. (Rich Ilus still possessed the wealth of Asia.) It is believed that a heavenly image of armed Minerva leaped down on to the hills of Ilus' city. (I was anxious to see it; I saw the temple and its site; that's still there,
425   Pallas Rome holds.) Smintheus is consulted, and unseen in his dark wood he utters these words from the mouth that does not lie:

'Secure the heavenly goddess and you will secure your city. She will take across with her the power of the place.'

Ilus secures her, and keeps her shut away at the top of the citadel,
430   and the responsibility passes to his heir Laomedon. Under Priam she

was not well secured. She herself wished it so, from the time when
her beauty was vanquished in the contest.*

Whether it was Adrastus' son-in-law,* or Ulysses, the right man
for theft, or Aeneas, they say someone carried it off. The person 435
responsible is unknown, but it's Roman property. Vesta guards it,
because in her constant light she sees everything.

Alas, how frightened the Fathers were, at the time when Vesta
caught fire and was almost overwhelmed by her own roof!* They were
blazing, holy fires with fires of crime, and flames were mingled, pious 440
with profane. The thunderstruck attendants were weeping with their
hair down; fear itself had stolen bodily strength. Into their midst flies
forth Metellus, and shouts:

'Run to the rescue! Weeping's no help. Take up the pledges of fate 445
in your virgin hands. They must be carried off by hand, not prayer.
Alas for me!' he says: 'Do you hesitate?'

He saw that they did hesitate, and had fallen to their knees in ter-
ror. He scoops up water. Lifting his hands, he said:

'You sacred things, forgive me! A man, I shall enter where a man 450
must not go. If it's a crime, let the punishment fall on me for what has
been done. By the loss of my own life let Rome be ransomed.'

He spoke, and burst in. The goddess, carried off, approved the
deed, and thanks to the service of her *pontifex* she was safe.

Now, under Caesar, you sacred flames shine well. Now the fire will 455
be, and is, on the Ilian hearths. Under his leadership no priestess will
be said to have desecrated her headdress or be buried in the living
earth. That is how an unchaste one dies, because she is put away in
what she has defiled: Earth and Vesta are the same divinity. 460

At this time Brutus acquired his *cognomen* from the Callaican foe, and
dyed with blood the soil of Spain. Sometimes, of course, sadness is
mixed with joy, lest the People enjoy the festival wholeheartedly:
Crassus at the Euphrates lost his eagles, his son, and his army, and 465
last of all was himself given to death.

'Parthian, why do you gloat?' said the goddess. 'You will send back
the standards, and there will be an avenger to punish the killing of
Crassus.'

[10 June] But as soon as the violets are taken off the long-eared
donkeys, and the rough stones grind the fruits of Ceres, the sailor 470

sitting in the stern says: 'We shall see the Dolphin, when the day has been banished and the damp night rises.'

[11 **June**] Already, Phrygian Tithonus, you complain of being abandoned by your bride, and the watchful Light-bringer comes out
475 of the Eōan waters. Go, good mothers (it's your festival, the Matralia), and offer yellow cakes to the Theban goddess.

Adjoining the bridges and the great Circus is a much-frequented open space that takes its name from the ox placed there.* There on this day they say the sceptre-bearing hands of Servius gave a sacred
480 temple to mother Matuta.

Which goddess is she? Why does she bar slave-girls from her temple's threshold (for she does) and ask for toasted cakes? Bacchus, your berry-clustered hair adorned with ivy, if that house is your own, direct the bard's song!

485 Semele had burned, through Jupiter's compliance.* Ino receives you, child, and dutifully nurses you with utmost care. Juno swelled up in rage that she should rear a child snatched from a concubine; yet he was her sister's blood. Hence Athamas is driven by the Furies
490 and a false vision,* and you, little Learchus, fall by your father's hand.

The sorrowing mother had entombed Learchus' shade and paid all due honours at the wretched funeral pyre. She too, just as she was, her hair torn in grief, leaps forward and snatches you, Melicertes, from the cradle.

495 There is a land confined in brief extent; it keeps back the sea on both sides, and one land is pounded by two waters.* Hither she comes, clutching her son in her crazy arms, and hurls him with her from a high cliff into the deep. Panope and her hundred sisters* receive them
500 unharmed, and bear them gently gliding through their realms. Not yet Leucothea, not yet the boy Palaemon, they reach the mouth of Thybris, dense with eddies.

There was a grove—it's unclear whether it should be called Semele's or Stimula's. They say Ausonian Maenads dwelt in it. Ino
505 enquires of them what was their race. She hears they are Arcadians, and that Evander holds the sceptre of the place.

The daughter of Saturn conceals her divinity, and craftily goads the Latian bacchants with false words:

'O women too credulous, wholeheartedly taken in! This stranger 510
does not come as a friend to our dancing rites. She asks in deceit, and
plans to discover the ritual of our cult. She has a pledge by which she
may pay the penalty.'

Hardly had she finished—the Thyiades fill the air with howling,
their hair streaming over their necks, and lay hands on her and fight 515
to tear the child away. Ino calls on gods she doesn't yet know:

'Gods and men of this place, come to the help of a wretched mother!'

Her cry strikes the nearby rocks of Aventine. The hero of Oeta had
driven the Iberian cows to the river bank. He hears, and roused, he 520
makes his urgent way towards the voice. At the coming of Hercules,
those who were just now preparing to use violence turned their cow-
ardly backs and fled, just like women.

'Aunt of Bacchus,' he says (for he'd recognized her), 'What are you
seeking here? Or does the deity who hounds me hound you too?'

She tells him part of it; part of it the presence of her son keeps 525
back, and she is ashamed that the Furies drove her to crime. Rumour,
swift as it is, flies through on beating wings, and your name, Ino, is
constantly on its lips.

As a guest you are said to have entered the faithful home of
Carmentis and laid aside your long hunger. It is reported that the 530
Tegean priestess gave you cakes quickly made by her own hand and
cooked on a hurried hearth. (Now too, at the Matralia festival, cakes
delight her.) Rustic attentiveness was more pleasing than art.

'Now,' she says, 'O prophetess, unseal the coming fates so far as 535
you may! Add this, I pray, to my reception as a guest.'

There's a brief pause, the prophetess puts on heaven and its pow-
ers, and in all her breast she becomes full of her god. Suddenly you
would hardly be able to recognize her, so much holier, so much greater 540
was she than before.

'I shall sing joyful news. Rejoice, Ino, you have done with your
hardships,' she said, 'and always be present, propitious, for this peo-
ple! You will be a divinity of the sea; your son too will belong to the
ocean. In your own waters take a different name. You will be called by 545
the Greeks Leucothea, by our people Matuta; all authority over ports
will be your son's, whom we will call Portunus and his own tongue
Palaemon. Go, I pray, each of you, favourable to our land.'

Ino had bowed assent. Her faith was promised. They put aside
their hardships and changed their names. He is a god, she a goddess. 550

You ask why she forbids slave-girls to approach. She hates them.
I would sing the origin of the hatred if she would allow me.

One of your serving-women, daughter of Cadmus, often used to
555 submit to your husband's embraces. Wicked Athamas loved her
secretly; it was from her he discovered that toasted seeds were being
given to the farmers.* You yourself of course deny having done it, but
rumour accepted it. This is the reason why slave-women as a group
are hated by you.

However, let not a devoted mother pray to this goddess for her own
560 offspring. She herself seemed to have been a not too fortunate parent.
You will better entrust to her someone else's child; she was more
helpful to Bacchus than to her own.

They say she said to you, Rutilius: 'Where are you hurrying to? On
565 my day, as consul, you'll fall to the Marsic foe.' The outcome matched
the words, and Tolenus' river flowed red, its waters mingled with
blood. It was the following year when Didius, killed on the same
Pallantian, redoubled the enemy's strength.

The same day is yours, Fortuna, and the founder and the place. But
570 who is that lurking with togas thrown on top of him? It's Servius; this,
to be sure, is agreed. But the reason for his lurking is disputed, and it
has me, too, doubtful in mind.

While the goddess timidly declared her secret love, and was
ashamed, as a dweller in heaven, to have slept with a mortal (for she
575 burned, swept away by a great desire for the king, and in the case
of this man alone she was not blind), she used to enter his house
by night through a little window, from which the Porta Fenestella
takes its name. Now she's ashamed, and hides the loved features under
580 a covering, and the royal face is hidden with many togas.

Or is the truth rather that after Tullius' death the common people
were bewildered at the death of their gentle leader, and there was no
limit to their grief, but his image increased it until they covered him
up by putting togas on it?

585 A third reason I must sing on a longer course. Even so, I shall drive
my horses pulled in to the inside track.*

Tullia, having achieved her marriage at the price of crime, used to
urge on her husband with these words:

'What's the good of being two of a kind, you by my sister's death, I by your brother's, if a virtuous life satisfies us? They should have 590 lived, my husband and your wife, if we were going to dare no greater deed! My father's head and my father's kingdom I make my dowry. Go on, if you're a man, and claim the rich dowry I've announced! Crime is a thing for kings. Kill your father-in-law, take his kingdom, 595 and dye our hands with my father's blood!'

Goaded by such speeches, he had taken his seat on the high throne, a private citizen. The astonished populace rushes to arms. Hence blood and slaughter, and weak old age is conquered: son-in-law Superbus holds the sceptre wrenched from his father-in-law. 600

The king himself is murdered below the Esquiline, where his palace was, and falls on the hard ground covered in blood. His daughter, intending to enter her father's house, was proceeding through the middle of the streets in her carriage, haughty and fierce. The driver 605 halted in floods of tears when he saw the body. She rails at him in words like these:

'Are you going on, or waiting for a bitter price for your loyalty? I tell you, drive your reluctant wheels over his very face!'

There is sure proof of what was done: Wicked Street is named after her, and that deed is branded with an everlasting mark. 610

Even so, after this she dared to set foot in the temple, her father's monument. I shall speak of what is wondrous indeed, but yet it happened.* There was a statue, in the likeness of Tullius, seated on a throne. It is said to have put its hand over its eyes, and a voice was 615 heard:

'Hide my face, lest it should see my daughter's abominable features.'

A robe is provided; it is covered. Fortuna forbids the robe to be moved, and this is how she spoke from her own temple:

'The day Servius first appears with face uncovered will be the first 620 day of modesty abandoned.'

Ladies, refrain from touching the forbidden robes (it's enough to utter prayers in solemn voice); and may he who was seventh king* in our city always have his head covered by a Roman cloak.

This temple had burned down,* yet that fire spared the statue: 625 Mulciber himself brought aid to his son.

For Vulcan was Tullius' father, and Ocresia of Corniculum, renowned for beauty, was his mother.* When the rites had been

630 carried out according to custom, Tanaquil ordered her to pour
wine with her on the decorated hearth. Here among the ashes was
the shape of a male organ, or it seemed to be—but no, it really was.
Ordered, the captive woman squats at the hearth. Servius, conceived
by her, has from heaven the seed of his race.

635   The god who begot him gave a sign, at the time when he touched his
head with glittering fire, and on his hair there burned a cap of flame.*

You too, Concord, Livia dedicates in a magnificent shrine, which she
herself has bestowed* on her own husband.

640   But learn, you coming age! Where the Livian portico now is, there
were the roofs of a vast house.* One house was the work of a city, and
occupied a space greater than many towns contain within their walls.
This was levelled to the ground, not for any charge of treason but
because its luxury seemed to be harmful.

645   Caesar had inherited it. He undertook the demolition of so vast a
structure and the loss of so much of his own wealth. That is how a
censor's duty is fulfilled;* that is how examples are provided, when
the punisher himself does what he warns others to do.

[12 June] There is no mark you could mention on the coming day.

650 [13 June] On the Ides a temple was given to Unconquered Jupiter,
and already I am ordered to narrate the lesser Quinquatrus. O fair-
haired Minerva, be present now for my endeavour.

'Why does the wandering piper parade all over the city?* What do
the masks, what does the long gown mean?'

655   That was my question. This is what Tritonia said, putting down
her spear (if only I can repeat the learned goddess's words!):

'In the times of your ancient forebears, great use was made of the
piper, and he was always in great honour. The pipe played in temples,
660 it played at the games, the pipe played at mournful funerals. The task
was agreeable because of the pay.

'A time then followed which would suddenly break the practice of
the pleasing art. In addition, the *aedilis* had ordered that there should
665 be only ten performers* to attend a funeral procession. Banished,
they change city and retire to Tibur. (Once upon a time, Tibur was
banishment!) The hollow pipe is missed on the stage, it is missed at
the altars; no dirge conducts the couches of the dead.

'A certain man at Tibur, worthy of any rank, had been a slave but 670
was long since free. He prepares a feast at his country place, and
invites the tuneful crowd. They gather for the merry feast.

'It was night. Eyes and minds alike were swimming with wine,
when a messenger comes with a pre-arranged story. This is what he 675
said: "What are you waiting for, break up the party! For look, here
comes the man who freed you!"* No delay—the guests stir limbs that
totter from strong wine. Their unsteady feet both stand and give way.
But the master says "Clear off!", and when they dawdled he got rid of
them by cart.

'On the cart was a broad wicker basket. The time, the movement, 680
and the wine induce sleep, and the party of drunks think they're going
back to Tibur. And now they had entered the city of Rome through the
Esquiline. In the morning the cart was in the middle of the *forum*.

'Claudius,* so as to be able to deceive the Senate about their 685
appearance and their number, orders their faces to be covered with
masks and mixes others with them; and so that women pipers may
increase this company, he orders them to be in long garments; in this
way the returners can be well concealed, lest they should happen to
be censured for coming back against his colleague's instructions.* 690
The plan was approved, and they are allowed on the Ides to wear their
new costume, and to sing words of fun to the ancient tunes.'

When she had given me this detailed explanation, I said: 'It remains
for me to learn why that day is called Quinquatrus.'

'March,' says she, 'holds a festival of mine by that name,* and this 695
group of people too is among my inventions. I was the first, having
drilled boxwood by means of spaced holes, to cause the long pipe to
produce notes. The sound was pleasing; but as the clear waters
reflected my face, I saw that my virgin cheeks had swollen out. 700

'"Art isn't worth that much to me," I said. "Farewell, my pipe!"
I threw it away, and the river-bank caught it on its turf.

'A satyr found it.* At first he's amazed, and doesn't know how to
use it. Then he realizes that when blown into it contains sound. Using
his fingers, he first releases his breath, then draws it in. And now he 705
was boastful of his skill among the nymphs. He challenges even
Phoebus. When Phoebus won, he hung: his flayed limbs came away
from their own skin.

'I, however, am the inventor and originator of this music. This is
the reason why that art observes my days.' 710

[15 June] The third night will come, and on it, Dodonian Thyone, you will stand conspicuous on the brow of Agenor's bull. This is the day, Thybris, on which you send Vesta's sweepings through your Etruscan waters to the sea.

715 [16 June] If there is any trust in winds, sailors, spread your canvas to Zephyrus. Tomorrow he will come favourable to your waters.

[17 June] But when the father of the Heliades has dipped his rays in the waves, and the clear stars encircle the twin poles, the son of Hyrieus will raise his powerful arms from the earth.

720 [18 June] On the following night the Dolphin will be visible. He indeed had once seen Volsci and Aequi put to flight on your plains, land of Algidus. Whence you, Tubertus, later rode as victor on snow-white horses, glorious in your suburban triumph.

725 [19 June] Now six days and as many again are left of the month, but to this number you must add one day.
The sun leaves the Twins, and the stars of the Crab grow red. Pallas began to be worshipped on the Aventine citadel.

[20 June] Now, Laomedon, your daughter-in-law is rising, and once
730 risen she drives the night away and the damp frost flees from the meadows. A temple is said to have been granted to Summanus, whoever he is.* That was when you, Pyrrhus, were a source of fear to the Romans.

[21 June] When Galatea has received this day too in her father's
735 waves and the land is full of tranquil rest, there rises from the earth the young man blasted by his grandfather's weapons,* and he stretches out hands that are wreathed with twin snakes.
Well known is Phaedra's passion, well known is Theseus' injustice: too quick to believe, he cursed his own son. Dutiful and punished for it, the
740 young man was making for Troezen. A bull divides with its chest the waters in its path. Alarmed, his horses are thrown into panic, and held back in vain they drag their master through the rocks and hard boulders.
Hippolytus had fallen out of the chariot and been swept along with
745 the reins impeding his limbs, his body mangled. He had given up his life, much to Diana's outrage.

'There's no reason for grief,' says the son of Coronis, 'for I shall give back life without wound to the dutiful young man, and the grim fates will yield to my skill.'

At once he brings out herbs from ivory boxes; they had been of use 750 before to the *manes* of Glaucus, at the time when the augur resorted to herbs he had observed, and a snake used help given by a snake.* Three times he touched his chest, three times he said healing words. The young man lifted his head from the ground where it lay. A grove, 755 and Dictynna in the recess of her wood, conceals him: he is Virbius at the Arician lake.

But Clymenus and Clotho are resentful, she that the threads of life are kept intact, he that the rights of his realm are diminished. Jupiter, fearing the precedent, aimed his thunderbolts down at the very man 760 who had moved the power of too much skill.

Phoebus, you were complaining. He's a god, be reconciled with your father. For your sake he himself does what he forbids to be done.*

[22 June] Although you are in haste to conquer, Caesar, I would not wish you to move your standards if the auspice were to forbid it. Let Flaminius and the shores of Trasimene be your witnesses that the just 765 gods give many warnings by means of birds. If you ask the rash date of the ancient loss, it was the twice-fifth day from the end of the month.

[23 June] The next day is better. Masinissa overcomes Syphax, and Hasdrubal himself has fallen by his own weapons.* 770

[24 June] Times slip away, and we grow old in the silent years, and the days flee without a bridle restraining them. How quickly the honours of Fors Fortuna have come! Seven days from now, June will be done.

Go, Quirites, joyfully celebrate the goddess Fors. On the bank of 775 Tiber she has her gift from the king. Hurry down, some of you on foot, some even by swift skiff, and don't be ashamed to come back home drunk from there. Be garlanded, boats, and carry the parties of young men, and may quantities of wine be drunk in the midst of the 780 waters.

The common people worship her, because it's said that he who established her was one of the common people, and took the sceptre from a lowly rank.* She's appropriate for slaves as well, because a slave-girl's son, Tullius, built the neighbouring temple to the fickle goddess.

785 [25–6 June] See, someone far from sober, on his way back from the shrine near the city, throws words like these at the stars: 'Your belt is hiding now, and perhaps it'll be hiding tomorrow. After that, Orion, I'll be able to see it.'

But if he hadn't been drunk, he'd have said that the time of the
790 solstice would come the same day.

[27 June] As the next Light-bringer comes along, the Lares got a shrine at the place where many a garland is made by skilful hand.*

The Stayer has the same date for his temple. Romulus founded it long ago before the face of the Palatine ridge.

795 [29 June] The same number of days of the month remain as the number of names of the Parcae, on the date when a temple was given to your *trabea*, Quirinus.*

[30 June] Tomorrow is the birth-time of the Kalends of Iulus. Pierides, add the conclusion to what I began.

'Say who it was, Pierides, who attached you to the one his con-
800 quered stepmother reluctantly offered her hands to.'* So I said. So Clio said:

'You're looking at the monument of renowned Philippus, from whom chaste Marcia takes her birth—Marcia, a name derived from priestly Ancus—in whom beauty is equal to her noble descent. Her
805 figure, too, matches her mind; in her is breeding and beauty and intelligence all at once. And don't think it's disgraceful that we praise her figure: we praise great goddesses in this respect as well.

810   'Caesar's aunt was once married to that man.* Oh glory! O woman worthy of the sacred house!'

So sang Clio, and her learned sisters agreed. Alcides nodded assent and struck a note on his lyre.*

EXPLANATORY NOTES

Notes are keyed to book and line numbers of the Latin text, as shown at the top of the left-hand page and in the margins of the translation.

BOOK 1

1.25 *bard...a bard's reins*: Ovid uses the same appeal when addressing Germanicus in AD 15 (*Ex Ponto* 4.8.67).

1.41–2 *marked off by number*: i.e. March and April (for Mars and Venus) were followed by May and June, and then by the 'fifth to tenth' months Quintilis (later 'July' after Julius Caesar), Sextilis (later 'August' after Augustus), September, October, November, December.

1.47 *three words*: the legal formula '*do, dico, addico*', 'I give, I announce, I assign'.

1.53 *in the enclosures*: the *dies comitiales* were days when it was permitted to hold voting assemblies of the Roman People (*com-itia*, literally 'coming together'); the enclosures were where the citizens were divided up into their voting units.

1.54 *ninth rotation*: *nundinae* were market days. They occurred every eight days, which was every nine days by the Romans' inclusive counting.

1.76 *Cilician spike*: saffron.

1.82 *on the bright ivory*: the magistrate's official chair (*sella curulis*) was made of ivory.

1.93 *in my mind*: Ovid alludes to the preface of Callimachus' *Aetia* (1.21–2): 'For when first I had placed a writing-tablet on my knees, Lycian Apollo said to me...'

1.103 *Chaos*: i.e. *Ianus*, because Greek *chaskein* and Latin *hiare* both mean 'to gape'.

1.125 *the gentle Seasons*: the *Hōrae*, who hold the gates of heaven in Homer (*Iliad* 5.749, 8.393).

1.127 *Hence I'm called Janus*: the Latin for 'door' is *ianua*, whence *Ianus*. See also 1.257, 2.51.

1.209 *the Fortune of this place*: the goddess Fortuna was worshipped at Rome as 'the Fortune of the Roman People, the Quirites', or 'Fortuna Publica'.

1.217 *your census rating*: periodically, at the census, the Roman citizen had to make a sworn declaration of his financial situation before the censors; those with property of over 400,000 sesterces were qualified for selection as Roman Knights (*equites*), those with over 1,000,000 were qualified to stand for senatorial office; those are the 'honours' Ovid refers to.

1.234 *sickle-bearing god*: Saturn, whose cult-statue showed him carrying a sickle: either because he used it to castrate his father Uranus (Hesiod, *Theogony* 160–82), or because he was the inventor of agriculture (Plutarch, *Roman Questions* 42).

1.238 *the god in hiding*: the Latin for 'to hide, lurk, be unobserved' is *latere*, whence Latium.

1.250 *to leave the earth*: as in Virgil, *Georgics* 2.473–4; at *Metamorphoses* 1.149–50 Ovid follows Aratus (*Phaenomena* 96–136) in making the maiden Astraea the last to leave.

1.260 *Oebalian Tatius*: i.e. Sabine Tatius, since the Sabines were supposedly descended from the Spartans (Plutarch, *Romulus* 16.1), and Oebalus was a legendary Spartan king.

1.261 *top of the Citadel*: after the abduction of the Sabine women by Romulus, Titus Tatius led a Sabine army to Rome to recover them. They captured the Citadel by treachery: Tarpeia (daughter of the commander in one version of the story) promised to open the gates to them if they gave her what they had on their arms. She meant their bracelets, but they crushed her with their shields.

1.294 *his mighty grandfather*: Aesculapius, as the son of Apollo, was grandson of Jupiter. Ovid does not need to spell out that Germanicus, as the son of Tiberius, is grandson of Augustus.

1.307 *Pelion's summit*: when the Giants made war on Jupiter (3.439–42, 5.35–42), 'they longed to place Ossa on Olympus, and Pelion with its quivering leaves on Ossa' (Homer, *Odyssey* 11.315–16).

1.322 *unless he's told*: he says '*Agone?*', 'do I go on?', whence *Agonalia*. The rival derivations that follow are from *agere*, 'to drive' (1.323–4); from *agnus*, 'lamb' (1.325–6); from the Greek *agōnia*, 'anguish' (1.327–8); and from the Greek *agōn*, 'competition' (1.329–30).

1.336 *from conquered enemies*: besides the play on 'victim' and 'victorious', Ovid also derives *hostia* (sacrificial beast) from *hostis* (enemy).

1.365 *his sea-blue mother*: the nymph Cyrene: Ovid retells Virgil, *Georgics* 4.315–558.

1.387 *instead of a virgin*: Iphigeneia, daughter of Agamemnon, was offered by him as a sacrifice to Artemis (Diana), in order to get fair winds for his fleet to Troy.

1.391 *guardian of the countryside*: the phallic god Priapus was thought of as the protector of fields, especially orchards, and also of gardens.

1.412 *bound with pine*: i.e. Pan.

1.436 *rousing the whole grove*: at *Metamorphoses* 9.347–8 Lotis escapes Priapus' obscene attentions by being turned into a lotus flower.

1.453 *daughter of Inachus*: i.e. Isis, who had a cult site on the Capitol (Suetonius, *Domitian* 1.2); when the besieging Gauls climbed the cliff of the Capitol in 390 BC, the alarm was raised by the sacred geese of Juno.

1.461 *leaving him behind*: the formula is borrowed from Homer (*Iliad* 11.1, *Odyssey* 5.1).

1.464 *Virgin water*: the aqueduct called *Aqua Virgo*, built by Agrippa in 19 BC to feed his new baths in the Campus Martius. It was so named because when the soldiers were prospecting for a good water supply eight miles east of Rome, a young girl pointed out the springs to them (Frontinus, *Aqueducts* 10.3).

1.467 *derived from song*: the Latin for 'song, chant, prophecy' is *carmen*, whence the name of the prophetic goddess Carmentis.

1.520 *cause of a new Mars*: Lavinia, the cause of the war between Aeneas and Turnus in Italy, just as Helen had been of the Trojan war.

1.531 *in Augustan hands*: the *pontifex maximus* had the ultimate responsibility for Roman religious ritual, and thus for the cult of Vesta; Augustus was elected to the position in 12 BC.

1.533 *his father's burden*: Tiberius (never named in the poem) was by adoption the son of Augustus and grandson of Julius Caesar; after Augustus' death in AD 14 he succeeded to the powers of the principate, with a display of reluctance that may well have been genuine.

1.535 *consecrated at eternal altars*: 'I have discovered that annual public sacrifices are carried out for Evander and for Carmentis, just as for the other heroes and divinities, and I have seen the altars set up for them—that for Carmentis below what is called the Capitolium, near the Porta Carmentalis, and that for Evander by a different hill, called Aventine, not far from the Porta Trigemina' (Dionysius of Halicarnassus, *Roman Antiquities* 1.32.2).

1.544 *the length of the world*: Hercules' tenth labour was to capture the cattle of Geryoneus in the far west and bring them back to Greece; on his way south through Italy he stopped at Evander's settlement. Ovid retells Virgil, *Aeneid* 8.184–279.

1.582 *takes its name from the ox*: the Latin for ox is *bos*, whence *Forum Boarium* (see 6.478).

1.589 *restored to our People*: on 13 January 27 BC, the young Caesar 'Octavian' handed back authority to the Roman People after the civil wars, and was granted the honorific name 'Augustus'.

1.593 *names her conqueror after herself*: Publius Scipio *Africanus*, who defeated the Carthaginians at the battle of Zama in 202 BC. The following references are to Quintus Metellus *Creticus* in 69–67 BC; Publius Servilius *Isauricus* in 76–74 BC; Quintus Metellus *Numidicus* in 109–107 BC;

Marcus Valerius *Messalla* in 263 BC; and Publius Scipio *Numantinus* in 134–133 BC.

1.598 *how short-lived that valour was*: Nero Claudius Drusus, brother of Tiberius and father of Ovid's addressee in book 1, conquered Germany for Augustus from 12 BC and died there in 9 BC; he was posthumously granted the honorific name *Germanicus*, which was inherited by his son.

1.601–2 *derive their titles...battle*: Titus Manlius *Torquatus* got his name from stripping the torque from a Gaul he killed in single combat (361 BC); Marcus Valerius *Coruinus* got his from a raven sent by the gods to help him kill a Gaul in single combat (349 BC). The following lines refer to Gnaeus Pompeius *Magnus* ('Pompey the Great') and the Fabii *Maximi*, whose name meant 'greatest'.

1.614 *protect your doors*: the 'civic crown' of oak-leaves (*corona ciuica*), granted for saving the lives of Roman citizens, was bestowed on Augustus in 27 BC and hung above the door of his house on the Palatine.

1.620 *took their name...mother*: the Latin for carriage is *carpentum*, supposedly derived from Carmentis.

1.635 *further back*: although *porro* means 'ahead', Ovid's derivation of Porrima implies that here, uniquely, it means the opposite.

1.646 *offers her hair unbound*: Tiberius had triumphed over Germany in 7 BC, and used the spoils to rebuild the temple of Concordia.

1.649 *both in deeds and with an altar*: as wife of Augustus, Livia set an example of marital concord, and she also dedicated an altar to Concordia in the 'Portico of Livia' in 7 BC (referred to at 6.637–8).

1.670 *the parish's hearths*: 'parish', despite the anachronism, is the nearest equivalent of *pagus*, a rural district.

1.707 *brothers from the race of gods*: in AD 6 the ancient temple of the brothers Castor and Pollux was rebuilt and rededicated by Tiberius in the name of himself and his brother Drusus, who had died in 9 BC.

BOOK 2

2.23 *particular houses*: probably the houses of the *rex sacrorum* and the *flamen Dialis* are meant; these senior priests were attended by lictors.

2.51–2 *is first...was last*: see note on 1.127 above for Janus and *ianua*; February is sacred to the shades below because of the Feralia on the 21st (2.533–70). There is an untranslatable play on two senses of *imus*, 'below' and 'last'.

2.54 *the twice-five men*: the ten commissioners (*decemuiri*) who were entrusted with the composition of Rome's first written code of laws (traditional date 451–450 BC).

2.81–2 *Either...or*: first explanation: the sea-nymph Amphitrite was hiding from the amorous Poseidon when the dolphin found her and persuaded her to become Poseidon's consort. Second explanation: Ovid retells Herodotus 1.23–4, the story of the Lesbian poet Arion.

2.89 *bird of Pallas*: the wise owl.

2.120 *a thousand voices*: Homer had wished for ten tongues (*Iliad* 2.489), Virgil for a hundred (*Georgics* 2.43).

2.128 *have given this name*: the formal title *pater patriae* ('father of the home-land'), granted to Augustus in 2 BC.

2.140 *guilt in your grove*: at Romulus' *asylum* in the grove of Veiovis (3.129–34) all comers were welcome, whatever their history.

2.144 *he made his father one*: Mars took Romulus to heaven (2.481–96); the future Augustus and his triumviral colleagues consecrated the mur-dered Caesar as Divus Iulius in January 42 BC.

2.145 *the Idaean boy*: the Trojan Ganymede, identified as Aquarius.

2.195 *This was the famous day*: all other sources (e.g. Livy 6.1.11) put the fall of the Fabii at the river Cremera on 18 July, which was also the date of the disastrous defeat at the river Allia in 390 BC; Ovid's version no doubt reflects the preference of the Fabii themselves, detaching the death of their ancestors from the shameful 'day of the Allia' (*dies Alliensis*).

2.208 *Tyrrhenian column*: the Etruscans of Veii are called Tyrrhenian after Tyrrhenus, leader of the Lydian colonists of Etruria (Herodotus 1.94.5–7).

2.226 *Guileless nobility*: guilelessness (*simplicitas*) is one of the virtues attri-buted by Ovid to his patron Paullus Fabius Maximus in AD 13 (*Ex Ponto* 3.3.100).

2.242 *save the state by delaying*: like Virgil (*Aeneid* 6.846), Ovid half-quotes Ennius' famous line on Fabius Maximus (*Annales* fr. 363): 'One man alone saved the state for us by delaying.' Fabius was given the name Cunctator ('the Delayer') because of his tactics of attrition in the war against Hannibal.

2.286 *sudden flight*: panic (Greek *panikon*) is named after Pan.

2.305 *in attendance on his mistress*: by order of the Delphic oracle, Hercules (the 'Tyrinthian youth') paid for his killing of Iphitus by being sold into slavery for three years. He was bought by Omphale, queen of Lydia.

2.325 *the lion spoil*: Hercules normally wore the skin of the Nemean lion, killed as the first of his Labours.

2.331 *shameless passion*: Ovid uses a Virgilian phrase (*Aeneid* 4.412, on Dido).

2.360 *its own dusty track*: the reference may be to the Circus Maximus (2.392), which occupied the valley where this episode is placed.

2.375 *so do the Fabii*: the Luperci were divided into two groups, *Fabiani* and
       Quinctiales, evidently named after two patrician families, the Fabii and
       the Quinctii. Why Ovid calls the latter Quintilii (2.378) is not known.

2.384 *whose uncle*: Amulius, brother of Numitor, was king of Alba (4.53).

2.421 *a name for the place … Luperci*: the Latin for 'she-wolf' is *lupa*, whence
       Lupercal.

2.422–3 *Lycaean Faunus*: the Arcadian mountain is Lukaios (Greek *lukos*,
       a wolf); the local deity Pan Lukaios (*Lycaeus* in Latin) is assumed to be
       identical with Faunus.

2.449 *gave you this name*: the Latin for 'grove' is *lucus*, for 'light' is *lux*;
       whence Lucina.

2.458 *receive the heavenly horses*: the sun's chariot will enter Pisces.

2.487 *'There will be one … heaven'*: Mars quotes Jupiter's words from Ennius'
       Annales (fr. 54).

2.534 *bringing small gifts*: the Latin for 'bring' (here and at lines 545 and 569)
       is *ferre*, whence Feralia, the name of the festival on 21 February.

2.548 *the Parental days*: the period 13–21 February was marked out for hon-
       ouring the dead; the Latin word for making the appropriate sacrifices
       was *parentare*, and the days were sometimes called Parentalia.

2.558 *pine torch*: as used at weddings, where the choir might invite Hymen,
       the god of marriage, to 'join in the wedding chorus, beat the ground
       with dancing feet and in your hand shake the torch of pinewood'
       (Catullus 61.12–15, trans. Guy Lee).

2.560 *comb your virgin hair*: in the traditional Roman marriage ceremony the
       bride's hair was parted with the point of a spear.

2.567–8 *feet in my song*: hexameter plus pentameter = 6 + 5 = 11. But on the
       usual inclusive reckoning that would end the Parentalia at 18 February,
       three days too early. The inconsistency is unexplained.

2.601 *because of her failing*: the Greek for 'to chatter' is *lalein*, whence Lala,
       the nymph's original name.

2.628 *the woman who gave toasted seeds*: Ino (3.853–4, 6.556).

2.665 *read on the piled-up weapons*: the battle of the 300 Spartans and 300
       Argives over Thyrea in the mid-sixth century BC ended when only two
       Argives and one Spartan were left alive. The Argives went home, but
       Othryades put up a trophy, and the Spartans therefore claimed victory
       (Herodotus 1.82.1–6).

2.685 *flight of the king*: *regis fuga* = Regifugium, the name of the festival on 24
       February; so too at the end of the episode (2.851) *Tarquinius* (i.e. *rex*) *fugit*.

2.713 *Phoebus is consulted*: according to Livy (1.56.7–12) Tarquinius sent his
       sons Titus and Arruns to Delphi, with Brutus to accompany them 'as
       an object of mockery rather than a companion'.

2.722 *a long-protracted siege*: Ovid retells Livy 1.57.4–11; in the other version of the Tarquin–Lucretia story (Dionysius of Halicarnassus, *Roman Antiquities* 4.64.2–4), Sextus comes to Collatia from his barony at Gabii.

2.734 *No need for words*: the phrase is taken from Livy 1.57.7.

2.787 *enemy as a guest*: the play on *hostis* (enemy) and *hospes* (guest) is taken from Livy 1.58.8.

2.790 *her own enemies*: the plural is unexplained, unless it means Tarquinius and his servants.

2.859 *truthfully given name*: the Latin for 'horse' is *equus*, whence Equirria, the horse races held on the Campus Martius, 'the plain of Mars'.

BOOK 3

3.29 *the Ilian fires*: on the altar in the temple of Vesta. Ilian = Trojan; and Silvia the Vestal is also called Ilia, 'the Trojan woman' (e.g. 3.602 below).

3.35 *my uncle*: Amulius, king of Alba, brother of Silvia's father Numitor.

3.107–8 (*one of them... to observe*): the parenthesis is an abbreviated translation of Aratus, *Phaenomena* 37–43.

3.109–10 *the brother... the sister's horses*: the sun and moon are identified as the siblings Apollo and Diana.

3.114 *signs of their own*: *signum* (star sign) could also mean a military standard.

3.118 *gets his name*: *manipulus* (bundle) could also mean an infantry unit.

3.150 *name from a number*: see note on 1.41–2 above.

3.153 *the man of Samos... born again*: it was believed, despite chronology, that King Numa had been a pupil of Pythagoras, associated with the doctrine of reincarnation.

3.184 *the house of reed and straw*: the hut, preserved and constantly rebuilt, which was revered as that of Romulus. Evidently on the Palatine (Dionysius of Halicarnassus, *Roman Antiquities* 1.79.11; Varro, *De lingua Latina* 5.54), though there was also a 'hut of Romulus' on the Capitol (Vitruvius 2.1.5; Seneca, *Controuersiae* 2.1.4; Martial 8.80.6; *Corpus inscriptionum Latinarum* 16.23).

3.200 *Consus... on that day*: the reference is to book 8 (lost, or never written), and the festival of Consus on 21 August. Romulus invited the Sabines of Cures and the Latins of Caenina, Crustumerium, and Antemnae (Livy 1.9.8–9, alluded to by Ovid in the next line) to the Consualia games, and abducted their daughters.

3.202 *made war on sons-in-law*: an allusion (like that of Virgil in *Aeneid* 6.826–31) to the civil war between Caesar and Pompey in 49–8 BC; Caesar's daughter had been married to Pompey.

3.206 *my daughter-in-law*: Hersilia, whom Romulus had taken as his own wife. Ovid tells the story of her deification at *Metamorphoses* 14.829–51.

3.245 *where the Roman king kept watch*: the Latin for 'watch' in the military sense is *excubiae*, whence *Esquiliae*, the Esquiline hill on the eastern side of the city. The king is Servius Tullius, whose house on the Esquiline is referred to at 6.601.

3.251 *my mother's crowd*: Mars' mother is Juno, here Juno Lucina, goddess of childbirth.

3.271–2 *Royal power...each one perishes*: the priest of Diana's temple at Aricia was called King of the Wood (*rex nemorensis*). 'A barbaric custom prevails in the sacred rites, for the man installed as priest is a runaway slave who has killed the previous incumbent with his own hand; so he is always armed with a sword, looking around for attacks and ready to defend himself' (Strabo, *Geography* 5.3.12).

3.328 *calls you Elicius*: the Latin for 'draw out' is *elicere*, whence Jupiter Elicius, the name by which the god was worshipped at his altar beneath the Aventine.

3.364 *lifted his hands*: the attitude of prayer (except to the gods of the under-world) was to hold the palms of the hands facing upwards.

3.370 *but they happened*: see note on 6.612 below.

3.377 *cut away on every side*: the word *ancile* was derived from *ambecisus*, 'cut on both sides' (Varro, *De lingua Latina* 7.43), since the shields the *salii* bore were figure-eight shaped.

3.387 *derived from dancing*: the Latin for 'to dance' is *salire*, whence *salii*.

3.412 *from the name of the boy*: the Greek for 'vine' is *ampelos*.

3.422 *pledges of empire*: like the shield that fell from heaven (3.345, 354), and the Palladium and other sacred items kept in the Vesta temple (1.527–8), Augustus is thought of as a divine talisman guaranteeing Rome's prosperity.

3.447 *the force of the word*: the force of the prefix 've-', supposedly meaning 'small'. Other authorities interpreted it as 'harmful' (Aulus Gellius 5.12.8–12).

3.456 *the Aonian waters*: Hippocrene (*Hippokrēnē*, 'Horse-spring'), a water source on Mount Helicon in Boeotia, was said to be the result of a blow from Pegasus' hoof.

3.460 *through Theseus' wrongdoing*: Ariadne, daughter of Minos (whose palace was at Cnossos), gave Theseus the thread to find his way out of the labyrinth, and ran away with him; he abandoned her, but she was rescued by Dionysus (Roman Liber) and became the god's consort.

3.462 *threads to be gathered up*: the Latin could also mean 'threads to be read'; it was a famous story.

3.473–5 *I used to say ... now too I shall cry*: Ariadne quotes from her speech in Catullus' poem 64, lines 132–5 and 143.

3.499 *my mother*: Pasiphae, who fell in love with a bull and gave birth to the Minotaur.

3.503–4 *born in fire, and snatched from fire*: Semele, pregnant with Dionysus (Liber), was burned up by Jupiter, who rescued the unborn child (6.485).

3.540 *the blessed ones*: a phrase normally used of the gods, or the virtuous dead (5.198, *Ex Ponto* 3.5.54).

3.549 *left as she died*: Ovid quotes his *Heroides* (7.195–6), where Dido, writing to Aeneas, drafts her own epitaph.

3.566 *looking back at the walls*: as Aeneas had done too (Virgil, *Aeneid* 5.3).

3.602 *the two peoples*: Trojans and Latins: see Virgil, *Aeneid* 12.819–40.

3.614 *a more favourable destiny*: see Virgil, *Aeneid* 4.340–61; and 4.219–78 for the divine reproaches referred to at line 616.

3.620 *the dwellings of Tartarus*: see Virgil, *Aeneid* 6.450–76.

3.654 *I am called Anna Perenna*: the Latin for 'perennial river' is *amnis perennis*, whence Anna Perenna.

3.658 *the Inachian cow*: Io, daughter of Inachus (the river-god of Argos), was loved by Jupiter and turned into a heifer (*Metamorphoses* 1.583–621).

3.664 *the Sacred Mount*: scene of the first secession of the *plebs*, traditional date 494 BC.

3.708 *those whose scattered bones*: the murderers of Julius Caesar, and in particular Brutus and Cassius, the leaders of the conspiracy, who committed suicide when their armies were defeated at Philippi in 42 BC.

3.716 *small and unarmed*: text corrupt, meaning uncertain.

3.721 *prey of your Theban mother*: Pentheus, torn to pieces by his mother Agave in a Bacchic frenzy.

3.723 *Tyrrhenian miracles*: Dionysus (Liber) was seized for ransom by Tyrrhenian pirates, but caused them to hurl themselves into the sea, where they were turned into dolphins (*Metamorphoses* 3.597–691).

3.733 *take their name from their inventor*: *liba*, 'cakes', as if from Liber.

3.745 *the smooth-headed old man*: bald Silenus, father of the satyrs.

3.763 *a woman presides*: 'The Liberalia are so called because on that day throughout the town old women crowned with ivy as priestesses of Liber sit with cakes and a brazier and sacrifice on behalf of the buyer' (Varro, *De lingua Latina* 6.14).

3.769 *his stepmother*: Juno, hostile to all the offspring of Jupiter's love affairs.

3.771 *the free toga*: the adult toga (*toga uirilis*) symbolized the status of a free citizen; the Latin for 'free' is *liber*, and the presentation was usually made at the Liberalia.

3.784 *popular enthusiasm*: Ovid probably alludes to the violence of the fans at the theatre games of his own time (Tacitus, *Annals* 1.16.3, who uses the same word, *studium*).

3.786 *the torch-carrying goddess*: Ceres (4.493–4), with whom Liber and Libera shared their temple below the Aventine. The games of Ceres were on 12–19 April (4.393, 680).

3.794 *the Kite*: unidentified, but not Ovid's invention: the Kite featured in Julius Caesar's commentary on his new calendar (quoted in Pliny, *Natural History* 18.237).

3.810 *five days joined*: Quinquatrus, 19–23 March.

3.814 *when swords are drawn*: gladiatorial contests were held on spread sand (*harena*, whence 'arena').

3.831 *burn the panel with colours*: i.e. use heated wax pigment in encaustic painting.

3.842 *her father's head*: the first two explanations, like the fourth, derive *capta* (literally 'taken, captured') as if from *caput*, 'head'; Minerva sprang fully armed from the head of Jupiter.

3.849 *the valiant god*: the day is marked in the calendars '*Tubilustrium*, festival of Mars'; the purified trumpets were those used in rituals (Varro, *De lingua Latina* 6.14).

3.853 *the wicked stepmother*: Ino (2.627–8, 6.556).

3.863 *floated in the air*: their mother is Nephelē (Greek for 'cloud'), deceased first wife of Ino's husband Athamas.

3.865 *dragon-born city*: Thebes, founded by Cadmus after sowing the dragon's teeth (*Metamorphoses* 3.1–137).

3.870 *made the name of the water from herself*: she fell off into the Hellespont (*Hellēs pontos*, Greek for 'Helle's sea').

3.882 *the altar of Peace*: in 11 BC, when the Senate and People collected money to pay for statues of Augustus, he used it instead on statues of Public Safety, Concord and Peace (Dio Cassius 54.35.2).

BOOK 4

4.1 *the twin Loves*: otherwise unknown to mythology; however, on the coins of Lucius Julius Caesar, minted about 103 BC, Venus is portrayed in a chariot drawn by two cupids, which may suggest a particular version of Venus' offspring current among her descendants, the Julii. 'Loves' (*Amores*) is the title of Ovid's first poetry collection, but since it was in five books, later re-edited as three, 'twin Loves' is not an obvious allusion to it.

4.10 *trodden by my horses*: Ovid quotes from his own farewell to love poetry, *Amores* 3.15.18. In the following line he repeats 1.1–2 and 1.7.

4.15 *touched my brow*: the text could also mean 'touched my *Times*', with the opening word of the poem used as a quasi-title.

4.21 *from a great image*: if the text is sound, the reference may be to ancestral images in the *atrium*, or to the cult statue of Venus Genetrix in Julius Caesar's *forum*; either way, what matters is Augustus' descent (by adoption) from the Julii, and therefore from Venus.

4.42 *was called Silvius*: the Latin for 'wood' is *silua*. According to Livy (1.3.7) all the Alban royal house bore the name Silvius, which is why the Vestal who gave birth to Romulus and Remus is sometimes called Ilia, sometimes Silvia.

4.48 *the Tuscan water*: so the Albula was renamed the Tiber (2.389–90).

4.50 *thunderbolts were hurled at Remulus*: Ovid explains why at *Metamorphoses* 14.617–18: Remulus imitated Jupiter and was blasted by him, like Salmoneus at Virgil, *Aeneid* 6.585–94.

4.62 *named from the foam of the sea*: the Greek for foam is *aphros*, whence Aphrodite (Venus) and April.

4.64 *greater Greece*: the Greek cities on the south coast of Italy, from Lokroi under the toe to Taras (Taranto) under the heel, were known as 'great Greece'—*megalē Hellas* (Polybius 2.29.1) or *magna Graecia* (Cicero, *Tusculan Disputations* 4.2).

4.74 *thinks it was named*: because the Greek aspirate was sometimes transliterated in Latin with *f*.

4.89 *from the open time*: the Latin for 'to open' is *aperire*, whence April.

4.120 *her tender hand*: Aphrodite intervened in the duel between her son Aeneas and Diomedes, and was wounded in the hand by the latter (Homer, *Iliad* 5.311–430).

4.133–4 *matrons...the long robe*: i.e. all women, those formally married and those not.

4.146 *wet with cold water*: presumably the public swimming-pool (*piscina publica*); some manuscripts read *calida* for *gelida*, which would give 'wet with warm water', no doubt in the baths.

4.154 *she was a wife*: the reference may be to Aphrodite's marriage to the lame smith-god Hephaestus, i.e. Vulcan (Homer, *Odyssey* 8.266–71).

4.160 *a name from the turning of the heart*: Venus Verticordia, to whom a temple was dedicated in 114 BC.

4.165 *When the night has passed*: Ovid's error: in early April the Pleiades set in the evening, not the morning (Julius Caesar, in Pliny, *Natural History* 18.246).

4.191 *her learned granddaughters*: the Muses, as daughters of Jupiter, who is a son of the Mother of the Gods.

4.236 *goddesses of Palestine*: the text is probably corrupt. The goddesses who wield whips and torches are the Furies, but they have no attested connection with Palestine.

4.245 *the Aonian Camena*: Erato is characterized both as a Greek Muse (Aonian) and a Latin quasi-Muse (Camena).

4.274 *made use of as he fled*: the ships that took 'dutiful' Aeneas and his followers from Troy were built of wood from the Mother's sacred grove on Ida (Virgil, *Aeneid* 9.80–92).

4.287 *dip the white-hot iron*: the forge of the Cyclopes was under either Etna or the volcanic island of Lipara (Virgil, *Aeneid* 8.416–22).

4.347 *who founded her temple*: according to Livy (36.36.3–4) the temple was dedicated in 191 BC by Marcus Junius Brutus. It was rebuilt twice, after fires in 111 BC and AD 3; Metellus was no doubt responsible for the first rebuilding, Augustus certainly for the second. Evidently Augustus' inscription did not record the name of the original dedicator, an ancestor of the assassin of Julius Caesar.

4.360 *the honour bestowed*: the stage and circus games were thought of as an honour to the gods (3.748).

4.383–4 *the twice-five men*: Ovid and his neighbour were in the first fourteen rows of the theatre, reserved for Knights; Ovid's service as a junior magistrate, one of the 'board of ten for judging lawsuits' (*decemuiri stlitibus iudicandis*), qualified him in the same way as the other man's commission as a military tribune.

4.445 *Her uncle*: the Latin specifies 'paternal uncle'—i.e. Dis (Hades or Pluto in Greek), brother of Jupiter.

4.474 *the name of the curved sickle*: the Greek for 'sickle' is *drepanon*, whence the city of Drepanon; however, according to Thucydides (6.4.5) the Sicilian for 'sickle' was *zanklon*, whence the city of Zancle.

4.480 *horns of her land*: the three capes of triangular Sicily (3.419, *Metamorphoses* 13.724–7), respectively to the south, west, and north-east.

4.482 *the bird bewails the loss of Itys*: Philomela, mother of Itys, was metamorphosed into a nightingale (*Metamorphoses* 6.424–674).

4.500 *dogs of Nisus*: Scylla, who consisted of rabid dogs from the waist down, was the daughter of Nisus in one version of the myth (Virgil, *Eclogues* 6.74–7).

4.504 *the sons of Cecrops call it sad*: according to Apollodorus (*Library* 1.5.1), on her arrival at Eleusis Demeter sat down on 'the Laughterless Rock' (*agelastos petra*).

4.577 *Parrhasian stars*: i.e. Arcadian Callisto, as the Bear.

4.632 *has its name from this*: the Latin for 'to carry' is *ferre*, whence 'fertile' and 'foetus' (*fecunda, fetus*).

4.669 *most dear to the grove*: the grove of Diana at Aricia (3.261–76).

4.675 *the title of command*: on 16 April 43 BC, two days after the victory at Mutina (4.627), the future Augustus, at nineteen years of age, was for the first time hailed by the soldiers as 'commander' (*imperator*).

4.709 *the naming of a specific fox*: text corrupt, meaning uncertain.

4.716 *a larger sacrificial victim is there for him*: i.e. the sun goes from Aries (3.851–75) into Taurus.

4.720 *against the will of Juno*: whether it is Io as a heifer (5.619–20, *Metamorphoses* 1.583–667) or the bull that carried Europa (5.603–18), it reminds Juno of Jupiter's infidelity.

4.733 *the blood of a horse and the ash of a calf*: perhaps blood from the 'October horse', sacrificed after the annual chariot race on 15 October (Festus 190L), as well as the ash from the burned calf embryo (4.639–40).

4.791–2 *these are what... becomes a wife*: the exile was formally forbidden fire and water; the bride was escorted with torches to the bridegroom's house, and sprinkled with water at the threshold.

4.809 *Numitor's brother*: Amulius (3.67).

4.813 *no need for any contest*: according to Livy (1.6.4) there was indeed a contest, and a disgraceful one at that (*foedum certamen*).

4.872 *its name from a Sicilian hill*: it was the temple of Venus Erucina, a copy (Strabo, *Geography* 6.2.6) of the ancient temple of Aphrodite at Eryx in western Sicily.

4.875 *the song of the long-lived Sibyl*: Syracuse was captured by Marcus Claudius Marcellus ('Claudius' in line 874) in 211 BC; however, the Sibyl had been consulted in 217 BC, and as a result a temple to Venus Erucina was dedicated on the Capitol (Livy 22.9.8–10, 23.31.9). The temple by the Porta Collina was a later creation (181 BC).

4.904 *the Dog rises too*: in fact, the 'dog-star' Sirius *set* at the end of April (Pliny, *Natural History* 18.285; Columella 11.2.37), and rose in July; notoriously, it was the height of summer when 'the heat-bringing Dog cracks the fields' (Virgil, *Georgics* 2.353).

4.943 *Phrygian Assaracus*: according to Homer (*Iliad* 20.231–9) Assaracus was Tithonus' uncle, not his brother.

4.946 *the custom of freer fun*: it is the beginning of the games of Flora (5.183–90).

4.949 *her kinsman's threshold*: as daughter of Saturn (Hesiod, *Theogony* 453–4, Hestia daughter of Kronos), Vesta is the aunt of Augustus' ancestor Venus.

4.953 *wreathed with oak*: see note on 1.614 above. The laurels at Augustus' door were granted on the same occasion in 27 BC.

BOOK 5

5.21 *walk alongside*: literally 'join his side to'; it was a sign of respect to support an old person while walking (see also 5.57–8).

5.31 *respect for honours*: 'honours'—i.e. magistracies held—were the criterion of seniority and authority in the Roman Senate.

5.34 *fell from his citadel*: Saturn was overthrown by Jupiter (1.236, 3.796); since Saturn's temple was below the Capitol, and Jupiter's on the summit, there may be an allusion to the Citadel at Rome.

5.37 *A thousand hands*: a hundred hands according to Hesiod (*Theogony* 150). See on 2.120 above.

5.51 *chair of office*: see note on 1.82 above.

5.64 *the mellow name of age*: the Latin for 'old man' is *senex*, whence *senatus*.

5.70 *conferred the right to rebuke*: the Latin could mean 'conferred the censorship'. The prime concern of the office of censor was the moral health of the citizen body; only senior senators were elected to it.

5.73 *gave their name to May*: the Latin for 'elders' is *maiores*, whence *Maius*. So too June from *iuniores* (5.78).

5.116 *hidden Jupiter in the woods*: to save the baby from Saturn (4.197–209).

5.128 *its mistress's name*: reference unknown: Capricorn is derived from *caprae cornu*, 'the she-goat's horn'.

5.133–6 *the reason... bring help*: they were the *Lares Praestites*, and the derivations are all from *prae* and/or *stare*: 'stand by' (*praestant*, line 134), 'stand up for' (*stant pro*, 135), 'protect' (*praesunt*, 135), 'on hand' (*praesentes*, 136).

5.146 *three divinities each*: in 8 BC Augustus divided the city of Rome into 14 regions and 265 *uici* (streets, blocks, neighbourhoods), each of which had an altar of the Lares at the principal crossroads. Some at least of these altars were shared with the cult of Augustus' *genius*.

5.150 *the good part of the hill*: perhaps a reference to the idea that the Aventine was ill-omened (Messalla the augur, quoted in Aulus Gellius 13.14.6).

5.156 *has known no man*: the Vestal Virgin Licinia, in 123 BC (Cicero *De domo* 136). The Licinii used the *cognomen* Crassus.

5.157 *imitate her husband*: for Augustus' restoration of temples, see 2.59–64 and Livy 4.20.7.

5.163 *brings in the night*: the Hyades rose in the morning of 2 May, not the evening (Julius Caesar, in Pliny, *Natural History* 18.248).

5.166 *from the rain*: the Greek for 'to rain' is *huein*, whence *Huades*, Hyades in Latin.

5.184 *postponed your role*: see 4.945–8.

5.197–8 *fortunate men had business*: the reference is to the Elysian Fields; Flora is euphemistically discreet about the nature of the pleasures the fortunate dead enjoyed.

5.204 *a prize from the house of Erechtheus*: Orithyia, daughter of the king of Athens (*Metamorphoses* 6.675–713).

5.224 *written on its petal*: the reference is to the story of Hyacinthus (*Metamorphoses* 10.209–16). See *Metamorphoses* 3.505–10 for Narcissus; 4.283 for Crocus; 10.728–39 for Adonis. The story of violets being generated from the blood of Attis is in Arnobius, *Aduersus nationes* 5.7.

5.251 *from the fields of Olenus*: where the healing god Aesculapius had a temple (Strabo, *Geography* 8.7.4).

5.257 *the left of Propontis*: she was going from the Aegean into the Black Sea. For Thrace as the origin of Ares (Mars), see Homer, *Iliad* 13.301; *Odyssey* 8.361.

5.281 *hence ... money itself*: the Latin for 'wealthy' is *locuples*, 'rich in land'; the Latin for 'money' is *pecunia*, derived from *pecus*, 'livestock'.

5.305 *he was on fire*: Meleager's life depended on the continued existence of a particular piece of wood; his mother Althaea, daughter of Thestius, burned it (*Metamorphoses* 8.445–532).

5.307 *held back his sails* : Agamemnon had to sacrifice his daughter to persuade Artemis (Diana) to send favourable winds for his fleet to sail to Troy.

5.329–30 *Consul Laenas with consul Postumius*: Marcus Popilius Laenas and Lucius Postumius Albinus were the consuls of 173 BC.

5.361 *The lights*: the Floralia games went on until after dark. In AD 32 the magistrate responsible 'made sure that up to nightfall all the performers were bald, in mockery of Tiberius, and then had 5,000 boys with shaven heads carrying torches to light the audience as they left the theatre' (Dio Cassius 58.19.2).

5.389 *the two fates of Troy*: Laomedon, king of Troy, asked Hercules to deal with a sea-monster, promising him horses in return; when he failed to honour the agreement, Hercules sacked the city (Homer, *Iliad* 5.640–51, 20.144–8). The Trojan war took place in the next generation (Priam was Laomedon's son), but in Ovid's scene Hercules is still a young man when Achilles is a boy.

5.400 *the Haemonian boy*: Achilles, whose father Peleus was king of Thessaly.

5.427 *the ancestors*: i.e. *maiores* in a different sense from 5.73 above.

5.481 *into a smooth one*: *L* is a smooth letter; *R* is rough like the growling of a dog (*littera canina*, Persius 1.109).

5.486 *at the time of Feralia*: see 2.563–4 (and 2.559–62 on no marriages).

5.492 *on any intervening day*: the syntax is obscure, but the meaning is established by surviving calendars: the three Lemuria days were 9, 11, and 13 May.

5.542 *goddess mother of twins*: the twins are Diana and Apollo, children of Latona.

5.555 *trophies won from Giants*: the rebellion of the Giants against the gods was sometimes used as a metaphor of Roman civil wars (e.g. Horace, *Odes* 3.4.37–80; Lucan 1.33–45).

5.560 *occupy the highest part*: there were evidently two Victoria statues on the pediment; already in the late republic (attested in the *fasti* of Antium) sacrifices to 'the two Victoriae' were offered on 1 August, which Augustus chose as the dedication day of his Mars Ultor temple.

5.563 *the dear weight*: his father (4.38).

5.565 *a leader's arms*: those of Acron of Caenina, killed by Romulus in single combat; the spoil from such a duel between commanders was called *spolia opima* (Propertius 4.10; Plutarch, *Romulus* 16.5–7).

5.566 *inscribed beneath*: the wording of the title under the Romulus statue was probably the same as the surviving equivalent from the *forum* of Pompeii (*Corpus inscriptionum Latinarum* 10.809): 'Romulus, son of Mars. He founded the city of Rome and reigned for 38 years. He was the first, having killed Acron king of the Caeninenses, to consecrate to Jupiter Feretrius the *spolia opima* taken from an enemy leader. He was received among the gods and called Quirinus.'

5.569 *took up dutiful arms*: for a campaign of vengeance on the assassins of his adoptive father Julius Caesar (3.705–10).

5.584 *were lost together*: in 53 BC, when Marcus Crassus and his son were killed in a catastrophic defeat by the Parthians at Carrhae in Syria.

5.590 *recaptured*: in 20 BC, as Augustus himself reports in the account of his achievements (*Res gestae* 29.2): 'I compelled the Parthians to return to me the spoils and standards of three Roman armies, and to request as suppliants the friendship of the Roman People.' The other two occasions were probably lesser Parthian victories in 40 and 36 BC.

5.591 *the usual way*: the Parthian tactic of shooting behind them as they withdrew is first mentioned by Virgil (*Georgics* 3.31).

5.618 *has your name*: Europa. 'The whole circle of the earth is divided into three parts: Europe, Asia, and Africa' (Pliny, *Natural History* 3.3).

5.620 *goddess from cow*: Io, who was transformed into a heifer and roamed the world; when she reached Egypt she became the goddess Isis (*Metamorphoses* 1.583–746).

5.621 *effigies of men of old*: the effigies were called *Argei*, 'Argives', and the Vestal Virgins were accompanied by the *pontifices* and senior magistrates in the rite of throwing them from the old wooden bridge, the *pons Sublicius* (Dionysius of Halicarnassus, *Roman Antiquities* 1.38.3). Ovid rejects the tradition that men of sixty years of age were thrown from the bridge as an offering to Father Dis, the god of the underworld (Festus 450L).

5.627 *the old sickle-bearer*: Saturn (see note on 1.234).

5.630 *in the Leucadian manner*: at Leucas there was an annual sacrifice to Apollo in which a malefactor was thrown off a steep cliff into the sea (Strabo, *Geography* 10.2.9).

5.634 *from the bridges*: here the 'bridges' are the gangways that led from each voting-group's enclosure to the urn where their ballots were deposited (Festus 452L).

5.693 *Ortygian cattle*: Apollo's cattle on Delos; the theft is narrated in the Homeric *Hymn to Hermes*.

5.719 *alternating their positions*: since Leda's twin sons had different fathers—Jupiter in the case of Pollux (Polydeukēs) and her mortal husband Tyndareus in the case of Castor—only Pollux would have been immortal if he had not begged for his brother to share the privilege; so they spend alternate days in Hades and on Olympus (Pindar, *Nemean* 10.55–91).

5.724 *in another place*: see 4.939.

5.727 *the place with four marks*: this day's place in the calendar is marked *QRCF*, either for *quando rex comitiauit fas* or for *quando rex comitio fugerat*: the day became a *dies fastus* after the *rex sacrorum* had either (a) carried out a sacrifice at the Comitium or (b) fled from the Comitium in imitation of Tarquin's flight (2.686, 851).

5.729 *public Fortune*: see note on 1.209 above: the goddess's full name was *Fortuna Publica Populi Romani Quiritium*.

5.732 *pleasing to Jupiter*: because it is part of the Eagle constellation.

BOOK 6

6.6 *a sacred mind*: bards (*uates*) were thought of as sacred: *Amores* 3.9.17 and 41; Tibullus 2.5.114; Horace, *Odes* 4.9.28; *Ars poetica* 400.

6.13 *the instructor of ploughing*: Hesiod, who claimed to have met the Muses (*Theogony* 22–34).

6.16 *one of those*: Juno (Hera); the other two goddesses at the judgement of Paris were Venus (Aphrodite) and Minerva (Pallas Athene).

6.18 *on Jupiter's Citadel*: the temple of Juno Moneta was on the Capitoline *arx* (6.183).

6.32   *next after heaven*: see 1.235–8 for Saturn in Latium after his expulsion from Olympus.

6.34   *that of Tarpeian Jupiter*: the temple of Jupiter Optimus Maximus on the Capitol consisted of three separate shrines: Jupiter's in the middle, flanked by those of Juno and Minerva.

6.39–40   *called Lucina after them*: see note on 2.449 above.

6.43–4   *the abduction... the judge on Ida*: Virgil gives the same two reasons for Juno's hostility to the Trojans (*Aeneid* 1.26–8).

6.46   *chariot and weapons are at that place*: another Virgilian reminiscence (*Aeneid* 1.16–17).

6.59   *the grove*: Diana's sacred wood at Lake Nemi (3.261–6, 6.755).

6.62   *the goddess of Praeneste*: Fortuna, who had an oracular cult there (Cicero, *De diuinatione* 2.85–7).

6.66   *signs of vigour*: appropriate to the goddess of youth, Juno's daughter Iuventas; the Greek Hēbē, she was given to Hercules as a reward for completing his Labours (Hesiod, *Theogony* 950–5).

6.81   *his father's gift*: Cacus was a son of Vulcan (1.554 and 571–4).

6.127   *the right of the hinge*: at 1.120 he told Ovid that that right was entirely his own. The Latin for 'hinge' is *cardo*, whence Carna—but we have been led to believe that the goddess's name is a Latinization of the Greek Cranaē (compare Flora from Chlōris, 5.195–6), and the story of the *striges* presupposes a derivation from *caro* (genitive *carnis*), 'flesh, soft tissue'.

6.140   *the reason for this name*: the Latin for 'to screech' is *stridere*, whence *striges*.

6.160   *a little victim falls*: in place of Proca, a *porca* (piglet, female).

6.175–6   *Neither... nor... blood*: respectively, the francolin (*Attagen ionicus*, Pliny, *Natural History* 10.133) and the crane (Homer, *Iliad* 3.3–60).

6.189   *condemned on a charge of tyranny*: in 384 BC (Livy 6.18–20).

6.192   *next to the road on the right*: the temple of Mars was between the first and second milestones on the Via Appia; the fork of the Appia (right) and the Via Latina (left) was half-a-mile outside the Porta Capena.

6.194   *the waters of Corsica*: the temple was dedicated by Lucius Scipio, consul in 259 BC, after his naval campaign around Sardinia and Corsica in the first Punic war.

6.201   *consecrated in a Tuscan war*: by Appius Claudius, consul of 296 BC, in his campaign against the Etruscans (Livy 10.19.17 for his vow to the goddess).

6.203   *by denying peace to Pyrrhus*: in 279 BC (Plutarch, *Pyrrhus* 18–19).

6.210   *Euboean song*: the Sibylline books (compare 4.257) ordered the erection of the temple. The *cognomen* of the Cornelii Sullae was corrupted from 'Sibylla' (Macrobius, *Saturnalia* 1.17.27).

6.243   *a consul's death*: when Gaius Flaminius, consul in 217 BC, was defeated and killed at the battle of Lake Trasimene in Umbria, the way seemed to be open for Hannibal to march on Rome.

6.259   *the peaceful king*: Numa; however, the innovation was also attributed to Romulus (Dionysius of Halicarnassus, *Roman Antiquities* 2.65–7).

6.278   *image of the boundless sky*: 'Archimedes fastened on a globe the move-ments of the moon, the sun and the five planets' (Cicero, *Tusculan Disputations* 1.63). This celestial globe was taken by the Romans (and Archimedes was killed) at the capture of Syracuse in 212 BC.

6.287   *are said to have given birth*: Juno to Mars (5.255–8), Iuventas (6.67–8), and Vulcan (Homer, *Iliad* 1.577, Hephaistos); Ceres to Persephone (4.425).

6.299–300 *Vesta is named... her Greek name*: the Latin for 'to stand by force' is *ui stare*, whence Vesta; the Greek for 'to stand' is *hestanai*, whence Hestia.

6.301   *because it warms everything*: the Latin for 'to warm' is *fouere*, whence *focus*, 'hearth'.

6.303–4 *who occupies the first place*: in Cicero's time (*De natura deorum* 2.67), Vesta always came at the *end* of Roman prayers; and no house ever had its hearth in the *uestibulum*. However, in 12 BC a shrine of Vesta was set up in the *uestibulum* of Augustus' house on the Palatine (4.949–50); per-haps there was also a change in the liturgical order of address at that time.

6.330   *rapid triple step*: the triple-stamp dance (*tripudium*) was particularly associated with the *salii* (Horace, *Odes* 4.1.28).

6.345   *sacrificing this animal to Priapus*: see 1.439–40.

6.359   *world power had been promised*: Mars reminds Jupiter of what he said about the Romans in Virgil, *Aeneid* 1.278–9: 'On them I put no limits of space or time; I have given them empire without end.'

6.362   *driven from her own home*: the temple of Spes (Hope), in the Forum Holitorium below the Capitol, was in the Gauls' control.

6.363–5 *We have seen... we have seen... abode*: see Livy 5.40.7–10 (Vesta) and 5.41 (the old men); for the 'pledges', see note on 3.422 above.

6.402   *flooded by the river*: the stream that ran through the valley between the Palatine and the Capitol to the river was culverted as the *cloaca maxima*. Still in Ovid's time, when the river was in flood the valley could be under water as far back as the Roman Forum and the temple of Vesta (Horace, *Odes* 1.2.13–16).

6.409 *that fits his various shapes*: the Latin for 'turn away the river' is *uertere amnem*, whence Vertumnus, a shape-shifting god whose statue stood on the Vicus Tuscus within sight of the Roman Forum (Propertius 4.2, esp. lines 5–10, 49–50).

6.419 *descendant of Dardanus*: the phrase *Ilus Dardanides* is borrowed from Homer (*Iliad* 11.166, 372); as the brother of Assaracus, Ilus was Dardanus' great-grandson (4.30–4, from *Iliad* 20.215–32).

6.432 *vanquished in the contest*: see note on 6.16 above.

6.433 *Adrastus' son-in-law*: more accurately grandson-in-law; Diomedes was the son of Tydeus and Deipyle, daughter of Adrastus, king of Argos.

6.438 *overwhelmed by her own roof*: in 241 BC, when Lucius Caecilius Metellus was *pontifex maximus*.

6.478 *from the ox placed there*: 'A bronze ox taken from Aegina is in the *Forum Boarium* in Rome' (Pliny, *Natural History* 34.10); the Latin for 'ox' is *bos*.

6.485 *Jupiter's compliance*: 'Zeus slept with Semele because of her beauty, but since he was gentle in his intercourse she thought he despised her; so she requested him to come to her embrace with the same attitude as he would to Hera. Accordingly Zeus came to her like a god, manifesting himself with thunder and lightning as he embraced her. But Semele, who was pregnant, could not endure the magnitude of the event and died in the fire, having given birth prematurely' (Diodorus Siculus 4.2.2). The baby was of course Dionysus (Liber, Bacchus).

6.489 *a false vision*: 'Through madness, Athamas killed his son with arrows while hunting' (Hyginus, *Fabulae* 5), so perhaps the Furies made him see Learchus as a deer.

6.496 *pounded by two waters*: the Isthmus of Corinth; however, according to Pausanias (1.44.7), Ino jumped from the Molourian Rock on the road west of Megara, and Melicertes was taken to the Isthmus on a dolphin.

6.499 *Panope and her hundred sisters*: Hesiod (*Theogony* 240–64) says there were fifty Nereids, and names them all; Homer (*Iliad* 18.39–49) names thirty-three. Panope is no. 27 in Hesiod's list, no. 22 in Homer's.

6.556 *given to the farmers*: see 2.627 and 3.853 above for Ino's plot to destroy her stepchildren Phrixus and Helle.

6.586 *to the inside track*: i.e. the shortest way round the Circus Maximus for a charioteer.

6.612 *but yet it happened*: like the similar phrase at 3.370, *sed tamen acta* here could mean 'but yet it was performed on stage'. See 4.326 for Ovid's use of stage plays; Fortuna was a familiar character in drama (Diodorus Siculus 32.10.5).

6.624 *he who was seventh king*: in the usual sequence of Roman kings Servius Tullius is sixth; perhaps Ovid was including Titus Tatius (6.93–4) in the list.

6.625 *burned down*: in 213 BC (Livy 24.47.15).

6.627–8 *Ocresia...was his mother*: enslaved after Tarquinius Priscus' capture of Corniculum (Livy 1.39.5).

6.636 *there burned a cap of flame*: while Servius was growing up as a slave-boy in Tarquinius Priscus' palace (Livy 1.39.1–4).

6.638 *which she herself has bestowed*: ambiguous: the relative pronoun could refer back either to the shrine of the goddess or to 'concord' in the sense of marital harmony between Livia and Augustus.

6.640 *a vast house*: it belonged to Vedius Pollio and was bequeathed to Augustus in 15 BC; the Portico of Livia was dedicated on the site in 7 BC (Dio Cassius 54.23.1–6, 55.8.2).

6.647 *a censor's duty is fulfilled*: Augustus was never elected to the censorship, but held the census three times 'with consular power' (Augustus, *Res gestae* 8.2–4), in 28 BC, 8 BC, and AD 14.

6.653 *parade all over the city*: on the Ides of June 'the pipe-players are on holiday, and roam through the city and assemble at the temple of Minerva' (Varro, *De lingua Latina* 6.17).

6.664 *only ten performers*: according to Cicero (*De legibus* 2.59) this limit was fixed in the Twelve Tables law-code. It is possible that some text has been lost before 'In addition...'.

6.676 *the man who freed you*: a freedman continued to have a duty of obedience (*obsequium*) to his ex-master.

6.685 *Claudius*: probably Appius Claudius, censor in 312–311 BC. Livy (9.30.5–10) gives a version of the story under 311 BC, but without naming the censor concerned.

6.690 *his colleague's instructions*: Claudius' colleague was Gaius Plautius Venox. According to Livy (9.29.7–8) Plautius had already resigned, and the anonymous author of *De uiris illustribus* (34.1) says it was Claudius who had banned the pipers in the first place. But there were various versions of the story: Plutarch (*Roman Questions* 55) tells the same tale as Ovid, but attributes it to the Decemvirate in 450 BC.

6.695 *by that name*: see 3.809–50, on 19–23 March.

6.703 *A satyr found it*: Marsyas (*Metamorphoses* 6.382–400).

6.731 *whoever he is*: 'Etruscan writings take the view that there are nine gods who send thunderbolts...The Romans have kept just two of these, attributing daytime thunderbolts to Jupiter and nocturnal ones to Summanus' (Pliny, *Natural History* 2.138); his temple was next to the Circus Maximus.

6.735 *young man blasted by his grandfather's weapons*: Aesculapius, son of Coronis by Apollo and therefore grandson of Jupiter, identified as the constellation Anguitenens (Greek Ophiouchos), 'the snake-holder'.

6.752 *help given by a snake*: the seer Polyidus, ordered by Minos to bring his young son Glaucus back to life, killed a snake and then saw another snake bring a herb and apply it to the first, which revived; Polyidus used the same herb on the boy (Apollodorus, *Library* 3.3.1).

6.762 *what he forbids to be done*: Jupiter forbids Aesculapius to reverse death, but does so himself with Aesculapius, killing him and then making him a god (and a constellation).

6.769–70 *overcomes...fallen by his own weapons*: Massinissa defeated Syphax in 203 BC (Livy 30.8.6–9). Hasdrubal was killed at the battle of the Metaurus in 207 BC (Livy 27.49.3–4); it is not clear why Ovid suggests a death by suicide.

6.782 *from a lowly rank*: a plebeian spokesman in Livy (4.3.12) says of Servius Tullius that 'his father was no one, his mother was a slave' (see note on 6.627–8 above).

6.792 *where many a garland is made by skilful hand*: not the medieval (and modern) Via de' Coronari: the Lares' temple was at the top of the Sacra Via (Augustus, *Res gestae* 19).

6.796 *a temple was given...Quirinus*: the temple of Quirinus on the hill named after him was dedicated in 293 BC (Livy 10.46.7).

6.800 *attached you...her hands to*: the temple of Hercules and the Muses, dedicated in or about 187 BC, was rebuilt by Lucius Marcius Philippus after his triumph in 33 BC (Suetonius, *Augustus* 29.5). Hercules' hostile stepmother was Juno.

6.809 *married to that man*: i.e. to Marcia's father Philippus. The sister of his wife Atia had been married to Gaius Octavius, Augustus' natural father.

6.812 *a note on his lyre*: the temple of Hercules and the Muses contained statues of the nine Muses looted from Ambracia in north-west Greece (Pliny, *Natural History* 35.66), evidently with Hercules—and not, as usual, Apollo—playing the music for their dance.

GLOSSARY

aediles (sing. *aedilis*) magistrates responsible for looking after public property and putting on public games, 5.287, 6.663

aegis the goatskin shield carried by Minerva (and Jupiter), 3.848

ancilia (sing. *ancile*) the shields borne by the *salii* in their ritual dance, 3.377

ara maxima 'the greatest altar', centre of the Roman cult of the deified Hercules. It was between the Palatine and the Tiber, not far from the present-day church of S. Maria in Cosmedin, 1.581

caduceus the staff carried by a herald (Greek *kērukeion*), and by Mercury as the messenger of the gods, 4.605, 5.449

cognomen the third of the Roman citizen's three names, after his personal name and his family name: e.g. Marcus Tullius *Cicero*, Gaius Julius *Caesar*; also used metaphorically of the added names of gods, 1.605, 4.621, 5.133, 5.579, 6.461

curia the thirty *curiae* were the archaic districts into which the Roman People was divided, 2.530–1, 3.140, 4.635

curio priest in charge of sacrifices in each of the *curiae*; the chief of the college was called *curio maximus*, 2.527

Dialis see *flamen*.

fasces the bound-up rods and axes carried by the magistrates' lictors, symbolizing the power to administer corporal and capital punishment, 1.81, 3.781, 5.51

fastus a *dies fastus*, derived from *fari*, 'to speak', was a day on which legal business was allowed, 1.48, 1.50

februa 'Means of purification, expiatory offerings' (*Oxford Latin Dictionary*); the main evidence for the meaning of the word is Ovid's own text, 2.19, 2.22, 2.27–8, 4.726, 5.423

flamen (plu. *flamines*) priests associated with a particular god; the major *flamines* were the *Dialis*, *Martialis*, and *Quirinalis* (named after Jupiter, Mars, and Quirinus respectively); the minor *flamines* were the *Carmentalis*, *Cerialis*, *Falacer*, *Floralis*, *Furinalis*, *Palatualis*, *Pomonalis*, *Portunalis*, *Virbialis*, *Volcanalis*, *Volturnalis*, and one other unknown (there were fifteen altogether), 2.21, 2.27 (*flaminica*, wife of the *flamen Dialis*), 2.282, 3.137, 3.397, 4.907, 4. 910, 4.938, 6.226

forda technical term for a pregnant sacrificial victim, 4.630–1

forum (plu. *fora*) marketplace, public square; unless otherwise stated, the Roman Forum, 1.258 (the Roman Forum and the Julian Forum created by Julius Caesar), 1.264 (the same), 1.302, 2.391 (the Roman Forum and the *Forum Boarium*), 2.529, 3.704, 5.552 (the Augustan Forum), 6.396, 6.401 (the Roman Forum and the *Forum Boarium*), 6.684

genius the immortal part of any (male) individual; the power of generation, 2.545, 3.58, 5.145

hastati infantry in the first line of the legion, 3.128

lustrum a five-year period, named after the censors' quinquennial act of purifying (*lustrare*) the citizen body, 3.120, 3.165

manes spirits of the dead, thought of as analogous to gods (*di manes* was the normal formula), 2.535, 2.570, 2.609, 2.842, 5.422, 5.443, 6.750

nefastus a *dies nefastus*, derived from *fari*, 'to speak', with a negative prefix, was a day on which legal business was not allowed, 1.47, 1.50

pilani infantry in the third line of the legion, usually called *triarii*, 3.129

pontifices (sing. *pontifex*) college of priests responsible for the religious behaviour of the citizens, presided over by the *pontifex maximus*, 2.21, 3.420, 3.706, 6.106, 6.454

praetor the second-most senior elective office in the Roman Republic, responsible for legal judgements; literally 'he who goes in front (*prae-itor*)', 1.52, 1.207

princeps 'first citizen', informal description of Augustus' position, 2.142, 3.697 (retrospectively of Julius Caesar), 5.570, 6.37 (metaphorically of Juno)

principes infantry in the second line of the legion, 3.129

rex sacrorum the senior priest who took over the sacrificial duties of the king (*rex*) when the Roman monarchy was abolished, 1.333, 2.21, 3.139

salii priests entrusted with the ritual dance in armour, carrying the *ancilia*, on 1 March, 19 March, and 19 October, 3.260, 3.387

strix (plu. *striges*) blood-sucking bird of ill omen. 'It is agreed that the *strix* appears in ancient curses, but I do not think it is known what sort of bird it is' (Pliny, *Natural History* 11.232), 6.139

thyrsus the pine- or ivy-tipped Bacchic wand, associated particularly with the frenzied maenads, 3.764

trabea a particular form of short cloak associated with the Roman Knights (*equites*), its use attributed to Romulus, 1.37, 2.503, 6.375, 6.796

vestibulum the broad forecourt, open to the street, in front of grand houses in Rome; it was where the clients gathered in the morning to wait for admittance to pay their respects to the master of the house, 6.303

INDEX OF NAMES

Aegeus father of Theseus, receives Medea at Athens, 2.41–2

Aeneas Trojan prince, son of Venus and Anchises, 4.35–7

Escapes the fall of Troy because of his piety, 1.527, 4.799–800

Takes the Palladium from Troy?, 6.434

Loves and leaves Dido, 3.545–50, 3.612

Brings the gods of Troy to Italy, 1.527–8, 3.423–6, 4.37–8, 4.76–8, 4.250–1, 4.273–6

His kingdom in the Laurentine land, 2.680, 3.599–606

His war against Mezentius, 4.881–96

Marries Lavinia, 3.601, 4.879

Host to shipwrecked Anna, 3.606–32

Ancestor of the Romans, 1.717, 4.161

Institutes the Parentalia, 2.543–4

His statue in Augustus' *forum*, 5.563

Aeolus the god who keeps the winds, 2.456

Aequi people of central Italy, eastern neighbours of the Latins, 6.721

Aequiculi people of the central Appenines; their month named after Mars, 3.93

Aesculapius son of Apollo and Coronis, 1.291, 6.746, 6.761–2

Restores Hippolytus to life, 6.746–54

Killed and deified by Jupiter, 6.759–61

Becomes a constellation, 6.735–6

Temple on the Tiber island, 1.290–4

Aethra 'Clear Sky', daughter of Oceanus and Tethys, wife of Atlas, mother of Hyas and the Hyades, 5.167–72

Africa Roman province, roughly corresponding to modern Tunisia; gives honorary *cognomen* to Publius Scipio, 1.593, 4.289

Agamemnon son of Atreus, grandson of Pelops, great-grandson of Tantalus; king of Mycenae; offends Diana at Aulis, 5.307–8

Father of Halaesus, 4.73

Aganippe spring on Mount Helicon; source of the river Permessus, to which Latin poets attributed the inspiration of elegiac poetry, 5.7

Agave mother of Pentheus, tears him to pieces, 3.721

Agenor king of Tyre, father of Europa, 6.712

Agon(al)ia festival on 9 January; meaning of name disputed, 1.317–32, 5.721

Agrippa Alban king; son of Tiberinus, father of Remulus, 4.48–9

Alba king and eponym of Alba Longa; son of Latinus (2), father of Epytus, 4.43–4

Alba Longa legendary Latin city about 20 miles south-east of Rome, 2.499

Has month named after Mars, 3.89–91

Albula original name of Tiber, 2.389, 4.68, 5.646

Alcides i.e. Hercules: the quasi-patronymic name may be because his mortal father Amphitryon was the son of Alcaeus, or because *alkē* means 'strength' in Greek, 1.575, 2.318, 2.355, 4.66, 5.387, 5.400, 5.645, 6.812

Alcmaeon son of Amphiaraus, purified by Achelous after killing his mother Eriphyle, 2.43

Alcyone one of the Pleiades, loved by Neptune, 4.173

Alernus deity, otherwise unknown, whose sacred grove was near the mouth of the Tiber, 2.67, 6.105

Algidus range of hills in Latium, scene of Roman victory over the Aequi and Volsci in 431 BC, 6.721–4

Almo river-god, father of Lara; the Almo was a tributary of the Tiber just downstream from Rome, 2.601, 4.337–40

Alps home of Gauls, 6.358

Amalthea Naiad of Crete whose goat fed the infant Jupiter, 5.111–28

Amata wife of Latinus (1), mother of Lavinia, 4.879

Amenanus river in eastern Sicily, 4.467

Amores, *see* Loves

Ampelos 'Grape-vine', youth loved by Liber; becomes constellation, 3.407–14

Amphiaraus Argive prophet, participant in the war of the 'seven against Thebes'; father of Alcmaeon, 2.43

Amphitrite goddess of the sea, wife of Neptune, 5.731

Amulius king of Alba, son of Proca, brother of Numitor, 2.384, 4.53
Orders Romulus and Remus drowned, 3.49–51
Killed by Romulus, 3.67, 4.809

Anapus river in eastern Sicily, 4.469

Anchises Trojan prince, son of Capys (or Assaracus), lover of Venus, who bears him Aeneas, 4.35–8, 4.123
Rescued by Aeneas from the fall of Troy, 4.38, 5.563

Ancus Marcius king of Rome, founder of the Marcian family (*see* Marcia, Philippus), 6.803

Anio river-god, husband of Ilia, 2.598

Anna sister of Dido and Pygmalion, identified as Anna Perenna, 3.545–654

Anna Perenna year-goddess, her festival on 15 March, 3.145–6, 3.523–42
Identified as Anna, sister of Dido, 3.654
Identified as Luna, Themis, Io, or an Arcadian nymph, 3.657–60
Old woman of Bovillae, deified, 3.661–74
Acts as procuress for Mars, 3.675–94

Antenor Trojan senior statesman, founder of Padua, 4.75

Aonia district of Boeotia in central Greece, site of Mount Helicon and the spring Hippocrene, 1.490, 3.456, 4.245

Aphidna town in Attica, scene of Castor and Pollux' battle with Idas and Lynceus, 5.708

Apollo (*see also* Cynthius, Paean, Phoebus, Smintheus), 6.91

Appius, *see* Claudius

April named from Aphrodite (Venus), 4.61
Named from 'opening', 4.85–9

Apulia region of south-east Italy, 4.76

Aquarius (*see also* Ganymede) constellation, 2.457

Aquilones north winds, 3.401, 4.643

Arabia source of incense, flown over by Ceres, 4.569

Arcadia (*see also* Azan, Lycaeus, Maenalus, Nonacris, Pallantium, Parrhasia) mountainous interior of the Peloponnese in southern Greece, reputedly older than the moon, 1.469–70, 2.290, 5.90

    Home of Callisto, 2.167, 2.192

    Home of Carmentis, 1.462, 6.531

    Home of Evander, 1.471, 1.478, 1.542, 2.279, 5.91, 5.643, 6.505–6

    Home of Mercury, 5.89–90, 5.664

    Home of Pan, 2.272–80, 2.424

Arcas son of Callisto, eponym of Arcadia, 1.470, 2.183–8

    Also called Lycaon after his grandfather?, 6.235

Arctophylax, *see* Guardian of the Bear

Arctos, *see* Bear

Ardea Latin town about 24 miles south of Rome, besieged by Tarquin, 2.721, 2.727, 2.749

Arethusa nymph of a spring at Syracuse, 4.423, 4.873

Argei 'Argives', straw effigies thrown into the Tiber on 17 March and 14 May 3.791, 5.621–2

    Identified as companions of Hercules, 5.650–60

Argestes 'Cleanser', the north-west wind, 5.161

Argos Greek city in the northern Peloponnese, favoured by Juno, 6.47

    Argives follow Hercules (*see* Argei), 5.651

    Argives found Tibur, 4.72

Ariadne daughter of Minos and Pasiphae, abandoned by Theseus, rescued by Liber, 3.459–64

    Jealous of Indian princess, 3.465–506

    Reconciled with Liber, deified as Libera, 3.507–16

Aricia Latin city close to the lake and grove of Diana, 3.263, 6.756

    Local calendar cited, 3.91, 6.59

Arion famous musician of Lesbos, late seventh century BC, 2.83–116

Aristaeus Thessalian shepherd, son of the nymph Cyrene and Apollo, 1.363–80

Ascra town in Boeotia, home of Hesiod, 6.14

Asia region of Lydia, 4.567

    Used of Asia Minor in general, 6.420

Assaracus Trojan, son of Tros, father of Capys, 4.34

    Grandfather of Anchises, 4.123

    'Brother' of Tithonus, 4.943

Athamas king of Boeotia, husband first of Nephele, then of Ino; tricked by Ino into sacrificing his children Phrixus and Helle, 3.852–76, 4.903

    Sleeps with slave-girl, discovers Ino's trick, 6.553–6

    Driven mad by Juno, kills his son Learchus, 6.489–92

Atia aunt of Augustus, wife of Philippus, mother of Marcia, 6.809

Atlas the giant who supports the sky, 2.490, 5.180

Husband of Pleione, father of the Pleiades, 3.105, 4.31, 5.83–4, 5.663–4
Husband of Aethra, father of the Hyades, 5.167–72
Atreus Greek hero, father of Agamemnon, 4.73
Attalus I king of Pergamum, 241–197 BC, 4.265–72
Attica territory of Athens, visited by Ceres, 4.502
Attis Phrygian boy, devoted to Magna Mater; driven mad, castrates himself, 4.223–44
Violets grow from the blood of his wound, 5.227
Augustus (63 BC–AD 14) born Gaius Octavius, adopted by Julius Caesar in 44 BC, given the honorific name Imperator Caesar Augustus in 27 BC (*see also* Caesar)
Descendant of Aeneas, 3.425
Related to Vesta, 3.426, 4.949
His aunt Atia married to Philippus, 6.809–10
Wins the battle of Mutina, 14 April 43 BC, 4.627–8
Hailed as *imperator*, 16 April 43 BC, 4.673–6
Avenges Julius Caesar, 3.705–10, 5.569–78
Restores temples, 28 BC, 2.59–66
Receives the name Augustus, 13 January 27 BC, 1.589–616
Recaptures lost standards from Parthia, 20 BC, 5.579–94
Elected *pontifex maximus*, 6 March 12 BC, 3.419–28
Shares house with Apollo and Vesta, 4.949–54
His new *forum* and temple of Mars Ultor, 5.552–68, 5.595–6
Destroys Vedius Pollio's luxurious house, 8 BC, 6.637–48
Creates new cult of Lares, 8 BC, 5.146–7
Rebuilds temple of the Mother of the Gods, AD 3, 4.348
Grandfather (adoptive) of Germanicus, AD 4, 1.10
Equated with Jupiter, 1.650
As divine talisman, 3.422
Imperial descendants, 1.531–2
Aurora (*see also* Eōs) goddess of the dawn, 4.721
Wife of Tithonus, 1.461, 3.403, 4.943, 6.473, 6.729
Daughter of Hyperion, 5.159
Daughter of Pallas (2), 4.373, 6.567
Mother of Memnon, 4.714
Ausonia Italy, from the Greek term *Ausones* for those who lived in the south and south-west of the peninsula, 1.55, 1.542, 1.619, 2.94, 4.266, 4.290, 5.588, 5.658, 6.504
Austri south winds, 3.401, 5.323, 5.381
Avenger (*Ultor*) title of Mars in Augustus' *forum*, 5.551, 5.577, 5.595–6
Aventine hill on the south side of Rome, 3.884, 4.52, 4.816, 6.728
Scene of Hercules' fight with Cacus, 1.551, 4.67, 6.82, 6.518
Scene of capture of Picus and Faunus, 3.295
Scene of Numa's bargain with Jupiter, 3.329
Aventinus king of Alba, father of Proca, eponym of Aventine, 4.51–2
Azan eponym of Azania, a region of northern Arcadia, 3.659–60

Bacchus one of the names of Liber, 1.360, 1.393, 2.313, 3.713–14, 3.736, 3.767, 3.772, 5.345
  Infancy of, 5.167, 6.483–4, 6.523
  Lover of Ampelus, 3.410
  Lover of Ariadne, 3.460–506, 5.345–6
  Name used as metonymy for wine, 3.301, 5.264
Baker (*Pistor*) epithet of Jupiter at an altar on the Capitol, 6.350, 6.394
Battus king of Melita, 3.570
Bear (*Arctos, Ursa*) Callisto transformed into a constellation, 2.153, 2.189–92, 3.107–8, 3.793, 6.236
Bellona war goddess, her temple at the Circus Flaminius, 6.201–8
Berecyntus mountain in Phrygia, sacred to the Mother of the Gods, 4.181, 4.355
Boeotia home of Orion, 5.493
Bona Dea, *see* Good Goddess
Boōtes 'Herdsman', name of the Guardian of the Bear, 3.405, 5.733
Boreas the north wind, brother of Zephyrus, 2.147, 5.203–4
Bovillae town in Latium, home of Anna Perenna, 3.667
Bowl (*Crater*) constellation, 2.244, 2.266
Briareus one of the Titans, 3.805
Brontes 'Thunder', one of the Cyclopes, 4.288
Brutus, Decimus Junius consul in 138 BC, conqueror of the Callaici, 6.461–2
Brutus, Lucius Junius feigns stupidity, overthrows Tarquin, 2.717–18, 2.837–52

Cacus son of Vulcan, fire-breathing cattle-thief, 1.549–78, 5.648, 6.81–2
Cadmus exile from Tyre, founder of Thebes, son of Agenor, brother of Europa, father of Semele and Ino, 1.489–90, 6.553
Caelian hill at Rome, alternative venue for Equirria, site of Minerva Capta temple, 3.522, 3.835
Caenina Latin town about 9 miles north-east of Rome, conquered by Romulus, 2.135
Caesar *cognomen* of the patrician Julii, used as a quasi-title under the principate:
  Referring to Julius Caesar, 3.156, 3.702, 4.379, 4.381
  Referring to Augustus, 2.15, 2.138, 2.141, 2.637, 3.419, 3.422, 3.710, 4.20, 4.124, 4.627, 4.859, 5.568, 5.588, 6.455, 6.763, 6.809
  Referring to Augustus or Tiberius, 1.13, 1.282, 1.599
  Referring to Germanicus, 1.3, 1.31
Calabria the 'heel' of Italy, 5.162
Callaici people of north-western Spain, defeated by Decimus Brutus, 6.461
Calliopea 'Fair-faced', one of the Muses, explains the name of May, 5.79–107
Callisto Arcadian nymph, daughter of Lycaon, metamorphosed as constellation (*see* Bear), 2.155–92

Calpetus Alban king, son of Capys (2), father of Tiberinus, 4.46–7

Camenae water-nymphs, identified with the Muses, 3.276, 4.245

Camere region in south-west Italy, 3.582

Camerina city in south-east Sicily, 4.477

Camillus, Marcus Furius dictator in 390 and 367 BC, vows temples to Juno Moneta and Concordia, 1.641, 6.184

Campus Martius 'Field of Mars', the open area north-west of the city, enclosed in the great bend of the Tiber, 1.463–4, 2.858–60, 3.519, 6.237–40

Cancer, *see* Crab

Capitol (*Capitolium*) hill in Rome, site of the temple of Jupiter Optimus Maximus, 1.203, 2.69, 2.667, 6.73

Besieged by Gauls, saved by geese, 1.453, 6.351

Capricorn constellation, 1.651

Capta 'Captured', title of Minerva at her Caelian temple, 3.835–48

Capys (1) Trojan, son of Assaracus, father of Anchises, 4.34

Capys (2) Alban king, son of Epytus, father of Capetus, 4.45

Caristia, *see* Karistia

Carmentis Arcadian prophetic goddess, mother of Evander, 1.467–538, 1.634, 5.95

Protectress of childbirth, 1.627–30

Foretells Evander's exile, 1.475–6

Foretells greatness of Rome, 1.515–36, 5.96

Foretells apotheosis of Hercules, 1.583–4

Receives Ino and Melicertes, foretells their apotheosis, 6.529–50

Carriages (*carpenta*) named after her?, 1.620

Her gate at Rome, right-hand arch unlucky, 2.201–4

Carna goddess of hinges, originally Cranaē, loved by Janus, 6.101–28

Saves Proca from *striges*, 6.129–68

Prefers old-fashioned food, 6.169–72

Carseoli town of the Aequiculi, 42 miles east of Rome on the Via Valeria, 4.683–4, 4.710

Carthage city in north Africa, colony of Phoenician Tyre, 3.551–6, 6.45–6

Carthaginians (*Poeni*), 3.148, 6.242–3

Carystus town on the southernmost point of Euboea, 4.282

Castor son of Tyndareus, twin of Pollux, horseman, killed by Lynceus, 6.699–710

He and Pollux share immortality, become the constellation Gemini, 6.711–20

Cecrops son of Erechtheus, king of Attica, whence Cecropidae (sons of Cecrops) = Athenians, 3.81, 4.504

Celaenae town in Phrygia, 4.363

Celaeno 'Black', one of the Pleiades, loved by Neptune, 4.173

Celer 'Quick', Romulus' foreman for wall-building, kills Remus, 4.835–44, 5.467–70

Celeus humble farmer at Eleusis, 4.507–28

Cynosura 'Dog's tail', the Little Bear constellation, 3.107
Cynthia one of the names of Diana, from Mount Cynthus on Delos where she and Apollo were born, 2.91, 2.159
Cynthius one of the names of Apollo, 3.346, 3.353
Cythera island off the south of Greece, sacred to Venus, 4.15, 4.286
Cytherea one of the names of Venus, 4.195, 4.673
Applied to her son Aeneas, 3.611

Dardanus son of Jupiter and Electra, founder of Troy, 4.31–2, 6.42, 6.419
hence 'Dardanian' meaning 'Trojan', 1.519, 2.680
Daunus king of Apulia, father-in-law of Diomedes, 4.76
Delia Diana, born on the Aegean island of Delos, 5.537
Delphi oracular cult site of Apollo in central Greece, 3.586
Deucalion survivor of the flood with which Jupiter wiped out mankind, 4.794
Diana (*see also* Cynthia, Dictynna, Phoebe) huntress goddess (Greek Artemis), 1.387–8, 2.155, 4.761, 5.141, 6.111–12, 6.745
Twin of Phoebus Apollo, 1.387, 6.112
Worshipped in Crete, 3.81
Punishes neglect, 5.305–8
Her grove at Aricia, 3.261–72
Dicte mountain in Crete, 5.118
Dictynna one of the names of Diana, 6.755
Didius, Titus consul in 98 BC, fought against Rome's rebellious allies in Campania in 89 BC, 6.567–8
Dido (*see also* Elissa) queen of Carthage abandoned by Aeneas; sister of Anna, 3.545–50, 3.597, 3.639–41
Didyme one of the Liparian islands, north of Sicily, 4.475
Dindymus mountain in Mysia, sacred to Magna Mater, 4.234, 4.249
Diomedes Argive hero, survivor of Trojan war, 4.76, 6.433
Wounds Venus, 4.120
Dione one of the names of Venus, 2.461, 5.309
Dis (*see also* Clymenus) king of the Underworld (Greek Hades), brother of Jupiter, 4.445–50, 4.584, 4.597–600, 5.448
Keeps Persephone half the year, 4.604–14
Dodona town in north-west Greece, home of the Hyades, 6.711
Dog (star) constellation, 4.909, 4.939–41
Dolphin constellation, 1.457, 2.79, 6.471, 6.720
Dōris consort of Nereus, the Old Man of the Sea, hence metonymic for the sea itself, 4.678
Drusus, Nero Claudius (38–9 BC) brother of Tiberius, father of Germanicus, 1.597
Drusus Caesar (14 BC–AD 23) son of Tiberius, adoptive brother of Germanicus, 1.12
Dryads wood-nymphs, 4.761
Duo Luci, *see* Two Groves

Earth (*Tellus, Terra*) the Romans worshipped two goddesses of the Earth, but Ovid uses the names interchangeably, 1.671, 1.673, 2.719, 3.799, 4.634, 4.665, 5.35, 5.541, 6.460

Eëtion king of Mysia, 4.280

Egeria nymph or goddess, consort and adviser of Numa, 3.154, 3.261–2, 3.275–6, 3.289–94, 4.669–70

Electra one of the Pleiades, bears Dardanus to Jupiter, 4.31–2, 4.174, 4.177–8, 6.42

Eleusis town in Attica, centre of the worship of Ceres, 4.507

Elicius epithet of Jupiter at his Aventine altar, 3.327–8

Elissa original Phoenician name of Dido, 3.553, 3.612, 3.623

Eōs Greek name of Aurora, the dawn, 3.877, 4.389

    Eōan, 'of the dawn', eastern, 1.140, 3.466, 5.557, 6.474

Epeus master-carpenter who made the Trojan Horse, 3.825

Epytus Alban king, son of Alba, father of Capys (2), 4.45

Equirria horse-races on 27 February and 14 March, 2.859, 3.519

Erato one of the Muses, named after love, 4.195–6, 4.349

Erechtheus king of Athens, his daughter abducted by Boreas, 5.204

Erichthonius Trojan, son of Dardanus, father of Tros, 4.33

Erigone daughter of Icarius, brought to his body by the dog Maera, later the Dog-Star, 5.723

Erythea land in the far west, from where Hercules took the cattle of Geryon, 1.543, 5.649

Eryx city in western Sicily, 4.478, 4.872–4

Esquiline (*Esquiliae*) hill on the east side of Rome, 2.435, 3.246, 6.601, 6.683

Etna volcano in western Sicily, reputed prison of Typhoeus, 1.574, 4.491

Etruscan (*see also* Tuscan, Tyrrhenian) of Etruria, the territory north-east of the Tiber, 1.641, 2.444, 4.880, 6.361, 6.714

Euboea island off eastern Greece, origin of Cumae and the Sibyl, 4.257, 6.210

Euphrates river in Mesopotamia, 1.341, 2.453, 6.465

Europa Phoenician princess, daughter of Agenor, abducted by Jupiter, 4.719–20, 5.605–18

Evander Arcadian exile, son of Carmentis, 1.469–96, 1.583, 1.620

    Settles at the site of Rome, 1.497–508, 1.580, 4.65, 5.91–8, 5.643–4, 6.505–6

    Brings Arcadian deities, 2.279–80, 5.92, 5.99–102

    Receives Hercules, 1.545, 5.647

Fabii patrician family descended from Hercules, 2.237–42, 2.375–7

    Use *cognomen* 'Maximus', 1.605–6

    Defeated at the Cremera, 2.195–36

Fabius Maximus, Quintus consul in 233, 228, 215, 214, and 209 BC, used defensive strategy against Hannibal, 2.241–2

Falisci people of Falerii, about 40 miles north of Rome, 1.84, 4.74

Father i.e. Father Liber (*Liber pater*), 3.775, 3.789

Fathers (*patres*) Roman senators; their formal title was *patres conscripti*,
'conscript fathers', 1.69, 1.290, 1.625, 1.643, 2.497, 3.127, 4.261,
4.950, 5.71, 5.153, 5.312, 5.327, 5.669, 6.437

Faunus rustic deity worshipped at Lupercalia, 2.193, 2.268, 2.361, 4.762,
5.101
    Identified as Arcadian Pan, 2.271–82, 2.424, 3.84, 4.650–3, 5.99
    Half-goat, horned and hoofed, 2.268, 2.346, 3.312, 4.663, 5.101
    His grove and oracle, 4.649–66
    Captured by Numa, 3.291–328
    Fails to ravish Omphale, 2.303–58

Faustulus rescuer and guardian of Romulus and Remus, 3.56
    Mourns dead Remus, 4.854, 5.451–78

Fear (*Metus*) personified as deity, 5.29

Feralia festival in honour of the dead, 21 February, 2.34, 2.569, 5.486

Fidius one of the names of Sancus, 6.213

Fish (*Pisces*) constellation, 2.458, 3.400

Flaminius, Gaius consul in 217 BC, defied the auspices and was defeated by
Hannibal at Lake Trasimene, 6.765–8

Flora goddess of flowers, her games in April and May, 4.945–7, 5.183–378
    Originally Chlōris, nymph of the Elysian Fields, 5.195–260
    Wife of Zephyrus, 2.205–12, 2.319–20
    Her magic herb makes Juno pregnant, 2.231–58
    Punishes the Senate for their neglect of her, 2.311–30
    Licentiousness of her games, 4.946, 5.331–54

Fornax, *see* Oven

Fors 'Chance', epithet of Fortuna, 6.773–5

Fortuna goddess of chance, cult centre at Praeneste, 6.62
    Temples at Rome founded by Servius Tullius, 6.569, 6.611, 6.781–4
    Her love affair with Servius Tullius, 6.573–80
    Orders his statue to be muffled, 6.570–80, 6.617–24

Fortuna Publica goddess of the Roman People, 1.209, 4.375–6, 5.729–30

Fortuna Virilis 'Fortune of men', worshipped on 1 April, 4.145–50

Forum, *see the Glossary*

Forum Boarium 'cattle market', the area between the Palatine and the river
harbour, 1.582, 6.478

Furies goddesses of madness, 3.722, 6.489, 6.526

Furius, *see* Camillus

Gabii Latin town about 15 miles east of Rome, 2.689–710, 2.783

Gaetulia area in north-west Africa, 2.319

Galatea sea-nymph, one of the hundred daughters of Nereus, 6.733

Galli eunuch priests of Magna Mater, 4.361

Gallus river in Phrygia, 4.363–6

Ganges river in India, 3.729

Ganymede Trojan boy abducted by Jupiter, 6.43
  Identified as Aquarius, 2.145–6
Gaul 4.362, 6.378
Gauls besiege the Capitol in 390 BC, 6.185–6, 6.351–94
Gela river in southern Sicily, 4.470
Gemini twins, i.e. Castor and Pollux metamorphosed as constellation, 5.693–720
Germanicus Caesar (15 BC–AD 19) son of Drusus (1), adopted son and heir of Tiberius, addressee of Ovid's revised text, 1.3–26, 1.31, 1.58, 1.63, 1.590–1, 1.614, 1.649, 1.701–2, 4.81
  Campaign in Germany AD 14–16, 1.285
Giants sons of Earth, rebels against Jupiter, 3.439, 5.35–42, 5.555
Glaucus son of Minos brought back from the dead, 6.750–2
Good Goddess (*Bona dea*) temple for women only, 5.148–58
Gorgon, *see* Medusa
Graces (*Charites*) Aglaia ('Brightness'), Euphrosynē ('Cheerfulness'), and Thaleia ('Abundance'), daughters of Jupiter and Eurynomē, 5.219
Gradivus ('Marcher'), one of the names of Mars, 2.861, 3.169, 3.677, 5.556
Grape-gatherer (*Vindemitor*) Ampelos, transformed as a constellation, 3.407
Great Circus, *see* Circus Maximus
Guardian (*Custos*) epithet of Hercules, 6.209
Guardian of the Bear (*Arctophylax*) Arcas, transformed as a constellation (*see also* Boōtes), 2.153, 2.190, 3.405
Gyges one of the Titans, 4.593

Haemonia alternative name for Thessaly, 2.40, 5.381, 5.400
Haemus mountain in Thrace, 1.390
Halaesus son of Agamemnon, eponym of the Falisci, 4.73–4
Hamadryads tree-nymphs, 2.155
Harpies monstrous birds that snatched Phineus' food, 6.131–2
Hasdrubal Carthaginian general defeated by the Romans in 207 BC, 6.770
Hebrus river in Thrace, 3.737
Hecate witch-goddess, worshipped at road junctions, 1.141–2
Hector prince of Troy, killed by Achilles, 5.385
Heliades daughters of the Sun, 6.717
Helice 'Spiral', the Great Bear constellation (*see* Callisto), 3.108, 4.580
Helicon mountain in Boeotia sacred to the Muses, 4.193
Helle daughter of Athamas, sister of Phrixus, rescued from death by her mother Nephelē ('Cloud'), 3.852–76
  Falls off ram into the Hellespont, 3.869–70, 4.278, 4.715, 4.903
Hellespont 'Helle's sea', strait between Asia and Europe, 1.440, 3.870, 4.278, 4.567, 6.341
Helorus river in south-east Sicily, 4.477

Pergamum (2) kingdom in north-west Asia Minor, including Phrygia, 4.265–6

Persephone daughter of Jupiter and Ceres, abducted by Dis, 4.417–54, 4.483–5, 4.579, 4.587–92

Must stay in the underworld half the year, 4.607–14

Persia where horses are sacrificed to Hyperion, 1.385

Phaedra wife of Theseus, falsely accuses Hippolytus, 6.737–8

Phaethon son of the Sun; borrowed the chariot and crashed it, 4.793

Pharos island off Alexandria, hence Pharian = Egyptian, 5.619

Phasis river in Colchis, home of Medea, 2.42

Philippi scene of the defeat and death of Caesar's assassins, 3.707

Philippus, Lucius Marcius consul in 38 BC, restored the temple of Hercules and the Muses 6.801–2

Philomela sister of Procne; raped and mutilated by Tereus, metamorphosed as nightingale, 2.629

Phil(l)yra daughter of Oceanus, loved by Saturn in the form of a stallion; mother of Chiron, 5.383, 5.391

Phineus Thracian hero plagued by Harpies, 6.131

Phocus son of Aeacus, killed by Peleus, 2.39–40

Phoebe (1) one of the names of Diana, 2.163, 5.306, 6.235

Phoebe (2) daughter of Leucippus; she and her sister were betrothed to Idas and Lynceus, abducted by Castor and Pollux, 5.699–702

Phoebus one of the names of Apollo, 2.106, 6.707

Son of Jupiter, brother of Diana, 6.111–12, 6.761

Identified as the sun, 1.164, 1.651, 3.361, 3.416, 3.416, 4.390, 4.688, 5.17, 5.420, 5.694, 6.199

God of healing, 3.827

God of prophecy, 2.262, 2.713, 4.263

His laurel, 3.139, 6.91

His raven, 2.247–50, 2.261–5

Father of Aesculapius, 1.291, 6.761–2

His temple part of Augustus' house, 4.951–4

Phoenicia motherland of Carthage, 3.595

Pholoe mountain in north-west Arcadia, 2.273

Phrixus son of Athamas, brother of Helle, rescued from death by his mother, 3.853–74, 4.278

Phrygia region of north-west Asia Minor, home of Magna Mater, 2.55, 4.214, 4.223, 4.265, 4.362

Alternative name for Troy, 4.79, 4.272–4, 4.943, 6.473

Picus 'Woodpecker', rustic deity, 3.292, 3.309, 3.315

He and Faunus captured by Numa, 3.291–328

Pierides one of the names of the Muses; Pieria was an area north of Mount Olympus, 2.269, 4.222, 5.109, 6.798–9

Piraeus harbour of Athens, 4.563

Pisces, *see* Fish

The Oxford World's Classics Website

www.worldsclassics.co.uk

- Browse the full range of Oxford World's Classics online

- Sign up for our monthly e-alert to receive information on new titles

- Read extracts from the Introductions

- Listen to our editors and translators talk about the world's greatest literature with our Oxford World's Classics audio guides

- Join the conversation, follow us on Twitter at OWC_Oxford

- Teachers and lecturers can order inspection copies quickly and simply via our website

www.worldsclassics.co.uk